Flower of China Mountain

Intercultural, Interracial Love Affair in the Idaho Mountains

Jess T. Ellis, DDS, MS
Dentist Turned Romance Fiction Author

PUBLICATION CONSULTANTS
We Believe In The Power Of Authors

8370 Eleusis Drive, Anchorage, Alaska 99502-4630
books@publicationconsultants.com—www.publicationconsultants.com

ISBN Number: 978-1-59433-588-4
eBook ISBN Number: 978-1-59433-589-1

Library of Congress Number: 2025931647

Manufactured in the United States of America

DEDICATION

*Flower of China Mountain is
dedicated to all the Flowers that
have bloomed in my life.*

PROLOGUE

West of the little gambling outpost of Jackpot, Nevada, a little south of the Idaho border on US Highway 93, sits the prominent geologic feature known as China Mountain.

Jackpot offers convenience to Idahoans who wish to gamble but are unwilling to go to Reno or Las Vegas. Few people live in Jackpot or anywhere near it. A few ranchers and farmers are all the inhabitants you are likely to find.

Because the area is so sparsely populated, finding help is difficult. It was even harder in 1863 to 1869 when the transcontinental railroad was being built. The builders had trouble finding help, so they imported workers from China.

Afterward, one enterprising rancher hired some unemployed coolies to help him. Rather than pay them, when the job was done, he killed them. As a result of the dastardly deed, the locals named the scene of the crime, China Mountain, in honor of the murdered Chinese. It was a nice but rather hollow gesture of community penance.

Spiny prickly pear, Opuntia polyacantha, is a spiny cactus favoring desert-like surroundings but also grows in fairly high elevations. Its flat stem joints are covered with many spines, meaning polyacantha. Attractive flowers adorn it briefly in some seasons, ranging from light yellow to bright red. Opuntia polyacantha is found throughout the US and Canada.

One might guess the name opuntia was derived from a Native American word. Not so. It was the name of a now-unknown plant that grew near Opus in ancient Greece.

Some species of cacti don't flower till they are fifty years old, and even then, it depends on the weather. China Mountain usually had the right conditions for the prickly pear to bloom, but their beautiful blossoms don't last long. You are lucky to see one bloom!

The Duck Valley Indian Reservation is located in southwestern Idaho. Ben Walkingbull was a Native American, specifically a Bruneau Shoshone Indian. Recognizing that reservation life was a dead end, he changed his name to Ben Walker, left the reservation, and applied for an agriculture bank loan to buy an old ranch located about fifty miles to the east of the reservation.

Ben and his wife, Abby, wanted to raise Appaloosa horses in the white man's world. Their ranch was in the Jarbidge Mountains near the hamlets of Jarbidge and Mountain City, a few miles from China Mountain.

The biggest obstacle to self-sufficiency on the reservation was crooked agents from the Bureau of Indian Affairs (BIA). Even the honest ones were so arrogant that they were impossible to work with.

It was a widely held opinion President Reagan was spot on when he said, "The most terrifying words in the English language are, I am from the Government, and I am here to help." Off the reservation, things weren't much different; now he had to deal with the Bureau of Land Management, the BLM.

Recently, their agents had taken to wearing guns and had adopted a more adversarial posture. The BLM already owns 81% of Nevada and 61% of Idaho. The feds not only don't want to transfer promised land to the western states but also act as though they want back what they don't own. Ben didn't trust any representative of the U.S. government. U.S. history didn't provide many examples of why he should.

When Ben married Abby, she was the prettiest girl on the reservation. They had a daughter, Chenoa, Shoshone for white dove or peace, who was even prettier than her mother, if possible. Ben became a widower when Abby died during a botched surgery in a reservation hospital.

Ben and Abby had sought to be self-sufficient to succeed as ranchers. With Abby gone, Ben was left with little choice but to utilize Chenoa's child labor potential to do what needed to be done. Children are the labor pool from which nearly all rural families must draw.

Ben and Chenoa discussed the tasks they would need to complete to survive. Chenoa was most capable of riding the range to check on the well-being of their far-flung herd of horses.

Ben recognized this posed a risk to Chenoa's well-being. What would protect her from the dangers a young girl might face in the wilds of the Jarbidge mountains? The answer seemed to Ben she would need to be a ghost; people wouldn't bother her if they never saw her.

At first, Ben went with Chenoa as often as possible to teach her the job. He taught her as many survival skills as he could remember, but mainly how to not be seen and be a phantom of the forest. He taught her always to be alert, to watch for the dust columns which would alert her to the presence of strangers, and to watch the behavior of Sky Walker and other animals in the area for clues of danger.

Ben told her stories to emphasize the importance of avoiding contact with people while looking after their horses. The Walker Ranch, as people had started calling it, was relatively isolated. Ben was trying to grow his stock numbers, so he only sold the few animals he needed to sell to make his modest loan payments. Thus, few buyers visited the ranch. Rarely did family or friends come around due to the distance to Duck Valley.

Few people had seen Chenoa in recent years for these and other reasons. Those who had claimed she was drop-dead gorgeous. Hoping to protect his daughter, Ben had filled her head with so many horror stories Chenoa had developed a case of near paranoia.

Chenoa was proud of her heritage. She loved dressing up in her white buckskins, braiding her long black hair in traditional fashion, then using Sky Walker, her dad's magnificent Appaloosa Stallion, to ride the range to check on their growing herd of Appaloosa mares. If anyone tried to approach her, she would take off as fast as the stallion could run.

A couple of sneaky BLM range examiners had watched her for 15 or 20 minutes one day using a spotting scope. When they tried to move closer to her, she saw them and bolted into some nearby tree, never to be seen by them again. Try as they might, they had yet to manage that feat since. They didn't need to embellish the truth about Chenoa's beauty. Still, when they got through bragging about what they had

seen, everyone who visited the area after that carried the highest power and best quality spotting scope they could find, just in case they were fortunate enough to see her.

Another area town on U.S. Highway 93, eighteen miles north of Jackpot, was Rogerson, Idaho. Before the railroad between Twin Falls, Idaho, and Wells, Nevada, was decommissioned, it boasted a railroad stockyard; otherwise, it consisted of little more than a service station, cafe, and post office where the locals could gather and get their mail. Interest in the mysterious girl got really serious as the stories grew, and the bar owner posted a reward offer for the best picture of Chenoa. Someone, nobody remembers precisely who dubbed Chenoa the Flower of China Mountain cause, like the cactus flower, she was beautiful, rarely seen, and lived in the area of China Mountain.

CHAPTER 1—WELCOME TO IDAHO

Glenn Briggs was pioneer stock. He had built the largest ranch in Twin Falls County. A big chunk of his grazing land was privately owned, 'deeded land' which qualified him for grazing rights on even more government land, administered by the Bureau of Land Management, or BLM.

When Glenn started out as a young rancher, most of Southern Idaho was open range. Under this policy, the grass belonged to whoever got to it first. This caused range wars in some areas and severe overgrazing generally.

The Taylor Grazing Act of 1936 closed the open range and the free-for-all for grass. Grazing rights were created called AUMs or animal unit months. AUMs were bought and sold between ranchers. The more AUM accumulated, the more cattle you were allowed to feed on BLM rangeland. Glenn had more AUMs than anyone in the county.

Glenn's headquarters were near Hollister. When his friends wanted to tease him, they called him Sir Briggs or Lord Briggs because he had built a walled home on top of a small hill previously nicknamed Molly's knob. It had a unique design, reminiscent of an Old English manor house. It's not quite a castle, but it's as close as you were likely to find in Idaho. Sitting on top of the four-walled base was a seemingly single-story ranch-style house, typical for southern Idaho. Looking from a distance, what was not obvious were all the rooms/stories concealed within the four walls of the base, such as an underground garage, a shop, an indoor shooting range, a hanger, a four horse stable, and a small riding arena. The house was beautiful, well landscaped, and had a swimming pool in the rear. The large front room picture window had a grand view of the mountains to the south, including China Mountain.

The Greyhound bus slowed, then stopped at Henstock's gas and grocery store, also known as Dude's, nicknamed for its owner Elwood Henstock. Had the passenger arrived in Hollister on a Trailways bus, it would have stopped across the street at Monte's. You could fill your gas tank at either establishment.

Jerry Briggs, Glenn's grandnephew, stepped off the bus and collected his one bag from the driver. He spotted the phone booth at the side of the Henstock's. He had the phone number for Uncle Glenn and was reaching for a dime when he heard his name being called. His Aunt Martha was just stepping out of Henstock's front door.

"Aunt Martha, I was just going to call you!" replied Jerry. "How are you? It is so great to see you." Jerry walked up and gave his Aunt the biggest hug he could without hurting her. Being 6-foot 4-inches and 200 pounds, Jerry was capable doing damage.

Aunt Martha chimed in, "It's such a beautiful sunny day, I thought it would be fun to come and get you with our taxi."

"Taxi?" Jerry looked puzzled.

"Yes, Babe is hitched around the corner," continued Martha. "Bring your bags, and let's go."

Jerry grabbed his one bag and followed Aunt Martha to an antique looking carriage.

"One bag? Man, you do travel light!"

"Lot easier to keep track of just one bag," said Jerry, smiling sheepishly.

"Granted," conceded Aunt Martha. "Me, I don't think I have ever gone anywhere with just one suitcase."

Jerry was hoping he would get to drive the carriage, but no such luck. Sitting atop the carriage driver's seat was Ole George, reins in hand ready to start for the ranch. Ole George snapped the buggy whip over Babe's back, and they were off at a brisk trot.

A trot was a good sustainable speed for Babe. She could literally keep up the pace for hours, and barely break a sweat. This was nice, if you wanted to treat a guest to a leisurely carriage ride.

The road to the ranch passed several old buildings suggesting Hollister had enjoyed a more prosperous era. If not for the travelers on highway 93, plus trade with the local farmers and ranchers, Hollister would likely have faded into history years ago. A local irrigation project had failed due to insufficient water.

The road cut through the banks an abandoned irrigation canal, a remnant of the failed system. Had there been enough water, several thousand acres could have been cultivated which now were used as winter pasture for Glenn's cattle.

Jerry had been promised he could participate in the spring cattle drive, taking a herd of cows and calves to their summer range in the nearby mountains. On the other side of a barbed wire fences which lined the road to the ranch headquarters, Jerry saw a dozen or so cows grazing with young calves at their sides. Jerry broke out laughing when he saw how vigorously the cute little calves wiggled their tails as they sucked down their lunch.

This was such a beautiful time of year on Uncle Glenn's ranch. The winter snow was gone. The mud holes had dried up. The grass was lush and green. With few exceptions the cows had given birth. Adult animals had shed their shaggy winter coats. Their new coats shown with a beautiful high gloss. Soon the heat of summer would dry everything out, but for now things were just beautiful. Aunt Martha said as much as they neared the ranch headquarters.

"Well, Jerry, welcome to our little part of paradise!"

Ole George drove Babe up the tree lined lane leading from the main road to the headquarters, and into the underground garage. There Babe would be unhitched, and the carriage parked in its own special reserved parking spot.

George invited Jerry to accompany him and Babe to the stable so he could show him how to unharness a horse properly. George continued, "There are only about five buckles you need to undo to take a harness off a horse. Had a green horn here once. Sent him to the barn to unharness a horse. The nitwit didn't do anything but undo every buckle on the harness. Took me dang near a week to figure out how to put it all back together. Of course, it was my own stupid mistake. Should have never assumed a city slicker would know anything about horses or ranching. They are as lost here as Crocodile Dundee in Manhattan!"

With Ole George's help, Jerry was able to remove Babe's harness and stow it on the stable wall in just a couple minutes. George had Jerry turn Babe out into the pasture, where much to Jerry's surprise, Babe lay down and roll in the dust.

"What's with that?" Jerry ask Ole George.

"Taking a dust bath," responded George. "Horses love it after a strenuous day. Sort of a self-rub down."

Ole George invited Jerry to grab his bag and follow him upstairs. "I'll show you to your room, young man! Follow me."

CHAPTER 2—CULTURE SHOCK

Jerry was stowing his one bag of clothing when he heard a rap on his bedroom door. It was Old George inviting him to supper. Jerry was a bit of a fitness buff. He had spent a couple hours swimming laps to stay in shape after sitting on a bus for three days. Jerry had worked up a good appetite, ready for whatever was being served.

"Be right there!"

Jerry had been impressed by the western architecture and decor of Uncle Glenn's home. He had noticed in particular its consolidation of facilities within 4 walls reminiscent of castles and fortified chateaus he had seen on a visit to Europe. Jerry didn't know if Uncle Glenn was worried about some entity storming his home, but he couldn't recall seeing any place in the USA more prepared. Jerry estimated the compound walls had to be at least 16 feet high. He had seen Ole George trimming a hedge, so apparently, he doubled as the gardener, too. The whole place was beautiful.

Supper was barbecued ribs and baked potatoes. Uncle Glenn had welcomed Jerry to Idaho with a graciousness and an enthusiasm he had never before experienced. Jerry found himself thinking, Hey, I'm just your nephew; not the latest European Royalty to visit America. Ole George showed his utility once again by manning the BBQ grill. It was a big one, large enough to cook the food for a church picnic.

Uncle Glenn gave a bit of a welcome to Idaho speech, then announced that as the guest of honor, Jerry was to receive the Potato of Honor. Just at that moment Old George appeared at the dining room door with a potato that could only be described as "Huge." Jerry's eyes

betrayed his astonishment. He had no idea a potato could grow that big. Everyone burst out laughing as Jerry exclaimed, "Wow! I'm supposed to eat all of it? Has anyone ever been able to eat the whole thing?"

With a wry smile Uncle Glenn quipped, "We don't want you going away hungry"!

When the fun was had and the laughter died down, Old George appeared with a bowl of normal size Idaho #1 baking potatoes for everyone. He served Jerry the first of the best barbecued ribs he had ever tasted. Old George took 'Gargantua' away to the kitchen with a comment about turning him into breakfast hash browns.

Jerry fielded a number of questions about his home and background from Uncle Glenn, Aunt Martha, and the other dinner guests. Uncle Glenn's questions turned to ones which would help him understand Jerry's skill-set applicable to being a ranch hand.

Yes, he could ride a horse. No, he had never roped a steer. No, he had never driven a team of draft horses or a farm tractor. Yes, he had experience driving a two-ton truck. No, to driving an 18-wheeler. No, he didn't know the difference between netting and barbed wire. No, he had never branded a calf or harvested Rocky Mountain oysters. His major in school? Civil Engineering. Minor? Girls until he was told to get his grades up or loose his scholarship, Jerry confessed. A ripple of laughter went around the room.

Aunt Martha was not surprised at Jerry's answer. She could see how Jerry would have no trouble with the girls. He was ruggedly handsome, athletic, and built like a football cornerback. She had seen him swimming lapses that afternoon and appreciated how any red-blooded coed would likely do more than the double take she let herself enjoy. Reminded her of another hunk from years past, the one who had put his brand on her 51 years ago come June 7th.

Jerry slept well. He awoke early, excited to get started doing the things Uncle Glenn had outlined last evening. First on the agenda after breakfast was meeting Fleet, a 5-year-old Arabian gelding who was to be his horse for the summer. When Old George heard Uncle Glenn tell Jerry he would be allowed to ride Fleet during his summer stay, Old George had commented there was not a nicer horse on the ranch.

"Yah, he has just enough Thoroughbred in him to outrun any other horse in the county, and enough Arabian to have unbeatable stamina. Not another horse on the ranch can keep up with him," claimed Old George.

Breakfast was eggs, beacon, hash browns, milk, and crack wheat mush.

"Eat up! This food will stick to your ribs, not your hips. No one who works for Glenn's brand worries about gaining weight; he works it off," Old George told Jerry.

Uncle Glenn escorted Jerry to the stable which was located on the east side of the headquarters compound. The horses were saddled and tied to a hitching rail outside the wall. Fleet and the other horses were waiting patiently, sensing the hard day's work about to start.

Uncle Glenn introduced Jerry to Fleet saying, "I think you two should get along fine. Fleet reins easily, so don't be too rough on him." With a bit of a playful smirk Uncle Glenn ask, "Do you need any help getting on?"

Jerry took the ribbing congenially and countered, "Perhaps. Could you lift me on, please?"

"Sure, if you want to wait here while I go get the front-end loader!" quipped Glenn.

Glenn and Jerry saddled up and headed to the sorting corrals. They had a lot of work to do before sunset.

By the time they reached the sorting corrals, the regular cowhands had gathered the herd into the corrals. Before the herd could be turned out on the mountain summer range near the Idaho/Nevada border, the calves needed to be vaccinated, branded, the bull calves castrated, the dry cows pregnancy tested, and old cows culled.

It was a lot to do in one day, so the work started early with all hands on deck. The sorting corrals had numerous individual pens allowing the herd to be sorted any way Uncle Glenn wished. His main goal today was to get the cows with new calves ready to go to the summer range.

Jerry found the whole spring roundup a fascinating process. His city slicker background caused him to question the appropriateness of brutalizing young calves by branding them with a red hot branding iron, and cutting off their 'family jewels', especially sans sterile instruments and anesthesia.

Jerry quickly learned that a calf has a lightning quick ability to kick. He was nailed by the first calf he went after, when the branding started. At first, he was angry, but later found himself thinking he deserved his bruised shin for helping in this cruel, archaic process. Two more whacks to the same leg removed all sense of sympathy from Jerry.

The crew worked nonstop till lunch time when Old George arrived with the grub. After the 4-star food served last evening, Jerry was expecting more awesome vittles. He was quite surprised when George set a rather large wooden lunch box on the tailgate his pickup truck, opened it up, took out a large bottle of peanut butter, a bucket of strawberry jam, two large loaves of sandwich bread, and three cans of meat.

Jerry had seen Spam before but never tasted it. Old George started slapping peanut butter sandwiches together as fast as the crew came to get them. Jerry noticed Uncle Glenn had washed up at the stock water trough, then joined Old George making sandwiches.

There was a line of cowboys washing up at the trough, doing their best to scrub off the dirt, blood, smoke, and grime from the morning's work. The cow dogs hovered close to the grub box in anticipation of be given a few scraps. When Jerry had advanced to the head of the line, and it was his turn, Old George handed him a sandwich open face.

Uncle Glenn asked, "Spam"?

Jerry was shocked! Spam on a strawberry and peanut butter sandwich! At any other time, the thought of that combination would probably have caused him to throw up. But the thought was suddenly overcome with the realization he was tired and so hungry Old George could have served him a piece of old shoe leather, and he would probably have taken a bite. Uncle Glenn carved off a big slab of greasy looking ham and added it to Jerry's sandwich. Jerry slapped the top piece of bread on his sandwich and took a bite. Much to his surprise, it actually tasted great!

As Jerry hurried off to sit with the other cow hands, he couldn't believe how a little hard work improved one's appetite.

He said as much to one of his co-workers who fired back, "You think this is good, wait till we start trailing cattle up to North Fork. First day is always homemade sandwiches, but the second day is usually the

Boss's special: Pork 'n Beans and Sardine sandwiches! Oh, yummmm. Helps to be real hungry for one of those treats!"

Jerry thought about this strange cow hand cuisine for a time as everyone resumed work, and finally settled on the thought, maybe Philly cheese stakes might seem strange to these cowpokes.

Jerry turned in early that evening. He couldn't remember ever being as tired, even after two-a-day workouts. Jerry was asked about swimming a few laps before bed. Normally he would have accepted the invitation.

Jerry politely declined, saying "Maybe tomorrow night."

He took a nice soothing shower, then fell asleep the instance his eyes closed. Jerry was normally a restless sleeper. Not this night. Only a corpse could have slept more sound.

Uncle Glenn was gone by the time Jerry dragged himself down to breakfast. It was late because Old George had been told to let him sleep in. He would have slept even longer but his shins were aching where he had been kicked repeatedly yesterday. Jerry now knew why cowboys wore high top boots. He was going shopping for his own pair ASAP.

Nikes were great on an athletic court, not so on a ranch. Cowboy boots might look out of place in a big city, but they had obviously stood the test on time working cattle. Jerry was not repeating yesterday by having improper footwear.

Tomorrow was supposed to be the start of the cow drive to the summer pasture. It would involve a lot of hard riding; another job for which Uncle Glenn counseled boots were better.

Jerry recalled seeing a plaque for sale at Henstock's with a quote from John Wayne, "Life is hard; it is harder, if you are stupid." Jerry might fit the definition of a city slicker, but he didn't want to be stupid.

After breakfast, Jerry would ask to go to town with Old George. Time to get some supplies.

Chapter 3—Chenoa

Chenoa was very young when, Abby, her mother died. She barely remembered anything about her. Her father had raised her. No wonder she had quite a few tomboy traits. Her female qualities were either inherent, or the product of her spending time with Little Feather, her mom's sister. Little Feather wasn't as pretty, according her father, as Abby had been, but she was a better cook and seamstress. Her skills had earned her a job with the Diamond Bar Ranch owned by one Orrie LaVal.

Little Feather's husband, Jake, had been a bossman for Orrie on his Three Rivers ranch until he was thrown and killed by a mustang stallion known locally as WM, "Widow Maker."

The common law of the range regarding mustangs was: If you can catch a Mustang, it is yours. WM was therefore a tempting prize. More than one cowboy had met his end daydreaming about how grand he would look riding through Jarbidge or Mountain City astride such a magnificent steed. After all, all you had to do was catch him, then break him to ride.

Little Feather had begged Jake to not get anywhere near WM. She knew his reputation. Jake, however, had never gotten over being called a half-breed. He had earned his way to the foremanship of the Diamond Bar ranch, but he nevertheless coveted the respect he would have, were he the one to tame this magnificent stallion with the killer reputation. In spite of his, or maybe because of his love, for Little Feather, Jake attempted to ride WM.

For a while it appeared Jake might succeed where everyone else had failed. WM was not a horse you could trust. He would catch his captors off guard by appearing to submit, then literally kill them. He earned his Widow-Maker name as often as he was captured. There never seemed to be an end to the tough-guy cowboys who thought they were better than the last fellow who died trying.

Orrie LaVal was a sharp operator, but not without compassion. He had liked Jake a lot. Jake had been a good hand, a hard worker, and the best half-breed Orrie had ever known.

Orrie offered to keep Little Feather on to cook, sew, and help around the ranch house for the same money he had been paying Jake. It wasn't all that much, but employment opportunities were scarce in this area, so she accepted.

Wagging tongues speculated about what other duties came with the job. Orrie punched out a couple hands who were foolish enough to say out loud what dirty minds were thinking. People with nothing better to do could be so cruel.

Chenoa, as a young girl had thus been a frequent guest on Orrie's Diamond Bar ranch. Little Feather appreciated the female companionship. Chenoa was able to help with more and more chores as she got older, but she was reluctant to help Little Feather with anything that brought her into contact with men.

White strangers were strictly avoided. Little Feather had to provide lunch once when Orrie brought in a big crew to help with the round up. Chenoa disappeared. Little Feather found her cowering in the hayloft of the barn. She never again allowed Chenoa to visit when a lot of strangers were expected.

Indian braves to whom she had been properly introduced weren't as frightening because everyone knew from Ben's threats what would happen if one of them mistreated her. Only the buzzards would know their fate. More importantly, no one would care. No one wanted to find out how serious Ben was.

Chenoa became ever more beautiful and increasingly recluse. To make matters even more difficult for would be suitors, Ben bought Chenoa a 308-sniper rifle, taught her how to use it, then spread rumors about how good she was. Ben figured a reputation for being a sharpshooter probably protected his daughter as much as being one. He played mind games with folks by leaving dead ground hogs and other small varmints hanging on fence posts with little notes bragging about the incredible distances at which they had been shot.

It was mostly B.S., but very effective. Unwritten but equally as threatening were the rumors Ben spread about Chenoa's preparedness to defend herself. She might ride all alone out in the wilderness, but Ben claimed she was anything but defenseless against a would be attacker.

Asked by one curious young man how close he might be allowed to approach, Ben casually responded, "I suppose you are safe if you are out of range. Look it up, she carries a Tikka T3x Superlite 308 Winchester Magnum with a 22.4-inch stainless steel barrel. If you are within 400 yards, you are dead. If you are at 600 yards, you have a chance if you travel with a level one trauma physician. If you really want to be safe, I wouldn't let her see you anywhere within 1000 yards. Of course that's just my opinion!"

Ben then tossed a couple pictures of her varmint kills on the table with the quip, "This could be you! Since you are a mite bigger, I'd add a few more yards."

That conversation so rattled the young man that he went out and bought a Nikon 1000-yard Rangefinder. He never regained his composure until he could recognize an object at 1000 yards without the rangefinder. He was overheard complaining to a slightly drunk, but sympathetic ear, "It just don't seem fair; at home you might get slapped if you go over the line with a girl. Here I have to stay 1000 yards from the line if I don't want to be buzzard bait."

Ben was developing a great reputation for raising premium Appaloosa horses. His horses won Best In Show more often than not. Much of his success could be traced to having Sky Walker, the best stallion money could buy. He not only had good genes, he passed them on. The trick was to make sure Sky Walker was the sire breeding his mares. Other stallions were roaming the range who were ready and willing to be of service. Problem was they weren't Appaloosa. Most were mongrels. Their progeny didn't bring premium prices.

Keeping the gene pool clean required constant vigilance. Playing dorm mother to a couple hundred mares was Chenoa's job. She rode constantly. If Chenoa encountered a mare in heat, she was to make sure Sky Walker earned his oats before any mongrel happened along. It really didn't require a lot of expertise for her to know which mares were ready. Get Sky Walker anywhere near a mare, and all doubt disappeared.

Ben's horses roamed over a rather large area. Occasionally, Ben and Chenoa would hear about some politician or celebrity who was spending a weekend at their 40-acre ranch in California, Montana, Texas, or some other cool-sounding place. If they knew how to ride a horse, maybe their "spread" might be as big as 80, 100, or even 200 acres. It was a source of great amusement to Ben.

Ben would tell Chenoa, "I could drop their "ranch" into ours, and it would take you a week to find it!"

It was no exaggeration. Ben's deeded land was only a few thousand acres, but along with his government land, for which his base land and AUMs qualified him, he could run his horses on literally thousands of BLM and Forest Service acres. Because his was not an exclusive allotment, a little unusual in today's world, Ben's stock were legal in an even larger area. It took a rider days to check it all.

Ranchers such as Orrie LaVal had a bunch of cowboys to ride their range. With Ben, it was different. His success depended on keeping his expenses low. If he hired a lot of help, there would be less money to grow his operation. Ben was the only one in the area who raised Appaloosas. This proved a great benefit. If you saw an Appaloosa horse anywhere between the Duck Valley Indian Reservation and Rogerson, odds were good you were looking at one of Ben's horses.

Ben had had some long discussions about hiring help. They had decided to do without. Ben's concern for Chenoa's safety had been his primary reason for instilling in her a fear of white men. Now that he could use one, he couldn't re-knit the sweater.

Chenoa was paranoid. Whatever they decided to do, that was a stump in their field around which they would have to plow. They considered hiring someone from the reservation. The good men had jobs;

the available ones were available due to reliability problems. Ben wasn't interested in running a rehab program.

They decided the best strategy was to handle things themselves. Ben would cover the things close to home so he would be available to handle customers; Chenoa would take the eastern range as far as China Mountain. She would ride Sky Walker in case his services were needed.

Ben commented, "Hey, it might not be a great plan, but it is affordable."

Because of the distances involved, Ben realized it would require Chenoa to be gone over night. He assured her he would deploy a couple of sheep camps to strategic locations.

A sheep camp was a small four-heeled mobile home provided by sheep ranchers for their herders. As a home away from home, they worked pretty well. First, they were mobile. You could move one easily where ever the grass grew, and the band of sheep went.

Second, they provided off-the-grid living; no electricity required. Coleman lanterns provided the light and gave them along with the wood stove their unique smell.

Third, they were the perfect size for one guy; herders almost always worked solo, except for the occasional round up. But in that case the extra help came and went the same day. In an emergency it would accommodate a second or even third person, but that was rare.

Fourth, they were remarkably well insulated, given the era in which they were manufactured. Light a fire in the built-in wood camp stove; you could be toasty and warm in any weather in minutes.

Fifth, given their iconic design, they had surprising storage space. Sheepherders generally traveled light. What possessions did they have stowed away handily in the numerous little spaces of a sheep camp?

Sixth, sheep camps have a small footprint. They can be taken almost anywhere you can drive a pickup truck. Putting one deep in the woods for some splendid, maximum privacy is possible.

Chenoa could stay out indefinitely should she need to be gone that long. Ben would make sure the camps were well stocked.

CHAPTER 4—CATTLE DRIVE PREPARATION

Jerry showed off his new cowboy boots to Aunt Martha. He wanted to buy a nice pair of Lucchese boots, but they were $450.

Old George stood by, shaking his head and muttering, "Those are going to town boots. You will need a work boot that will get wet, take a beating, and not get destroyed in the process."

Jerry put the Luccheses back and held up a pair of rugged-looking Justin. Old George nodded approvingly. $199.99 for the boots, $30 for three pairs of socks, and they were out the door. Jerry came west with three pairs of Levi jeans and was already set with britches.

George further counseled, "Now, I know you youngins like your ball caps, but you spend all day out in the hot sun, your ears and neck are going to be medium rare to well done unless you are one of those dopes who wear their hats backward, in which case you are going to be Rudolph, the red-nosed cow hand."

A few shin kicks had convinced Jerry that traditional garb was well thought out and the way to go.

Jerry asked, "Well, George, is that everything I need to be a real, honest-to-goodness, rootin, tootin, shootin cowhand?"

George chuckled to himself, then responded with his signature grin, "I think they are sold out of horse sense, but a good pair of leather gloves would probably save you a few blisters on those baby soft hands!"

George recommended elk leather gloves for handling barbed wire and deer skin, a softer leather, for lighter work. Another 30 dollars, and Jerry had both.

"Put your name on them," ordered George. "Can't keep track of them otherwise. The other fellows just love not having to pay for new gloves!"

Jerry borrowed a ballpoint pen and put his initials in big block letters on the back side of his new gloves. He was surprised at how easy it was to write on leather. No one needed to wonder now to whom the gloves belonged.

In the meantime, back at the ranch, Uncle Glenn was directing final preparations for the cow drive to get the cows and calves from the Hollister winter range to the North Fork summer pasture. Come June, July, and August, the weather was typically hot in Hollister, whereas by moving the cattle up into the mountains, things would be much more pleasant there, the weather cooler, the grass greener, and cool mountain spring water to drink, and good shade for the heat of the day. By moving the herd to the mountains as early in the spring, as the snow melted and the grass started to green, it also saved the lowland grass for winter grazing. It was a grazing regimen perfected over decades to maximize the ranch's grazing capacity and make the best use of the available resources.

Some ranchers had to truck their cattle between their wintering locations and summer range. Trucking is expensive and stressful on the cattle. Properly organized and skillfully executed, trailing the herd from Hollister to the North Fork pasture would be a one or two-day "walk in the park."

The most important preparation was to make sure there were enough riders to handle the job. The job was easy when one was trailing dry cows, meaning no young calves along, especially cows who had made the trek before. The job could be handled by as few as two or three cowboys and a good dog. If the cows knew where they were going, all one had to do was open the gate and get out of their way.

Trailing cows and young calves was much more challenging. It requires more riders and those who are better cowhands. If not harangued too much, a calf will follow its mother. Like a child at a mall, a young calf can get lost. A young calf separated from its mother is a problem. If you have a herd of hundreds, you have a potential nightmare. If too many cows get separated from their calves, a good trail boss will try to stop and let them find each other, or "motherup." As the expression goes, young calves without their mothers are like herding cats.

Glenn had spent time the week before rounding up extra help for the cow drive. He had his cowhands upon whom he could count. To get extra help, Glenn called up horse-loving friends who were wanna-be cowboys but worked in town. To a person, they jumped at the invitation to spend a day living their dream, being a real-life cowboy on a cow drive. This would be better than a day at Disney Land.

Glenn had three guest riders committed to being at the sorting corrals, saddled, and ready to ride at daybreak on the day of the drive. One of the three had been on a drive before. This was good. He would need less guidance from the tail boss and be able to help the newbies know what to do.

Glenn also recruited Ron Probst, borrowing him for the day from a neighboring rancher, Jerry Pickett. Ron would bring his dog, Ripple, an amazing Australian Sheperd, possibly the best cow dog Glenn had ever seen. Together, Ron and Ripple were better than 2 or 3 typical riders.

First, the trail they would be following would go through some farmland. Keeping Glenn's cattle from trampling his neighbor's crops was important. Their crops were so green and tender, making them very tempting to a herd of cows grazing on dry grass all winter.

The trail to North Fork started from the sorting corrals, ran past the Callin and Chadwick farms, and then out into open rangeland. Open range was much easier to trail cattle through unless other ranchers' cattle were grazing there. If they were, you had to be careful not to let them mix. The trail boss needed to scout out the route to see the challenges and then be prepared for them.

It is always helpful to have older cows in the herd who have been over the trail before, preferably several times. They tended to filter to the front of the herd and become the leaders after whom the younger cows follow. The more calmly the herd moves, the more likely problems can be avoided. Hopefully, calves will not get separated from their mothers. Another problem is when young calves tire, they tend to find a cozy spot to lie down and rest. If the riders are not watching carefully, the herd will move down the trail, and the calf will become lost.

This situation will most likely occur in the afternoon when the little fellows have had enough. Riders also get tired and inattentive, so the trail boss must be especially vigilant. If he suspects a problem, one or two riders might be assigned to go back and sweep the trail to find any young stragglers. If a cowboy spots a calf who is too tired to keep going, he might pick the little guy up, put him across his saddle, and carry him. If too many calves give out, arranging for a truck or wagon to haul them might be necessary.

Trailing through someone else's land or herd is a problem that requires some degree of cowboy etiquette. Most rangeland is fenced nowadays. Before you trail through, it is courteous to get permission. Any gate you have to open, it is expected you will close. If cattle are grazing in the pasture through which you need to go, it is not nice to spook or harangue them unnecessarily.

A good neighbor policy is to dispatch a few riders ahead of one's arrival to calmly move them out of the way, then have enough cowboys riding alongside your herd to assure that none of the resident herd mixes in with yours. If any try, then is when a good cow dog earns his keep. A veteran of many drives, Glenn knew the problems; he was prepared.

Chapter 5—Cow Drive Eating Dust

Jerry woke up before his alarm sounded. He was excited. His adrenalin was pumping. He pulled on his new clothes and headed to the stable. He wanted to saddle Fleet before going to breakfast. Jerry could smell bacon cooking as he left his bedroom. What a glorious smell. Everything tasted better with bacon.

Jerry was suddenly reminded of the words of wisdom he had heard from a lecturer who asked about the difference between a pig and a chicken regarding breakfast. Jerry's first reaction at the time had been, "Well, I would rather pick up the tab for the chicken!"

Once the laughter died, the lecturer continued, "The chicken is involved; the pig is committed!" The bit of wisdom had made a lasting impression on Jerry. He could see how Uncle Glenn had given his life to ranching; he wasn't just involved.

Furthermore, he could see how Aunt Martha and Uncle Glenn were committed to each other and their family. Their struggles to survive the hard times were legendary in the family. Their success had required more than involvement. It had taken a commitment not seen in the 50% of marriages ending in divorce. Jerry hoped he would find a girl with whom he could be committed, not just involved. But he wasn't ready for that yet. Today was yet a new adventure!

Much to Jerry's surprise, when he got to the stable, Fleet was already saddled. He was wearing a feed bag with a strap which crossed over his head just behind his ears.

"Thought he would like some oats to start what is going to be a long day," explained Uncle Glenn.

27

"Good Heavens, Uncle Glenn, what time do you get up? I thought for sure I would get here before you."

"Ah, us old codgers don't need nearly as much sleep as we once did," commented Uncle Glenn. "Don't need as much food, either. Except on a day like this. Let's go fill the tank. I think George should be ready for us by now."

Glenn and Jerry climbed the stairs to the house's main floor. Old George had the breakfast bar set with eggs, hash browns, bacon, orange juice, oatmeal, milk, and several kinds of fruit. Everyone ate hardily, knowing lunch would be a sack lunch.

Aunt Martha eventually joined them, still dressed in a bathrobe and declining everything but orange juice, some scrambled eggs, and a bowl of fruit.

Old George handed Glenn and Jerry each a brown bag as they left the kitchen for the stable. He predicted, "By the time lunch rolls around, your sandwiches ought to be saddlebag tenderized really well."

Uncle Glenn added, "For sure! Jerry, you will never have a better-tasting sandwich than one that has been beaten up in your saddle bag for half a day. The honey or jelly melts into the bread, giving it a flavor which just can't be duplicated."

Old George agreed, "Amen, brother! Also, if you are lucky, your Hershey bar won't melt."

The eastern sky was turning grayish blue when Glenn and Jerry rode out of the stable and reined their mounts toward the sorting corrals. There was no moon, so Uncle Glenn advised Jerry to let Fleet have his head.

"What does that mean," asked Jerry.

"Horses can see better in the dark than humans," answered Uncle Glenn. "As long as he is going in the right general direction, let him pick his own path. He will be able to avoid hazards you can't see. Had a horse almost jump out from under me one time. He saw a ditch I had forgotten about, and I didn't. He decided to leap over it. I barely caught the saddle horn or would have rolled right off his back. Would have had a hard time living that one down, even if I were lucky enough not to break my neck."

"Makes sense to me!" said Jerry.

When Jerry and Glenn arrived at the sorting corrals, they joined the rest of Uncle Glenn's crew. They fanned out into the pasture where the cows and calves were and started gathering them. When the critters were all rounded up, Jake, Glenn's foreman, slipped in and opened the gate. He then preceded the first cow through the opening and down the trail. His objective was to go ahead of the herd and close any gates which might have been left open.

Since the first two and a half miles of the trail was down a fenced lane, all the riders needed to do was ride along and ensure no cattle broke through the fence.

Uncle Glenn held back and let the herd string out for a half mile. The herd was fresh, so without much coaxing, they set out at a fairly brisk pace. The old cows knew where they were going and seemed anxious to get there. The younger cows followed. Things were starting out well. Uncle Glenn was pleased.

Since Jake was riding point out in front, Uncle Glenn put his other good riders along either side of the herd to keep them on the trail. Everyone else rode drag behind the herd. Depending on the direction of the wind, riding drag could be dusty unless you got caught in a summer rainstorm; in that case, it could be muddy. Dusty conditions were more common.

Things went smoothly for the first few miles. Trailing the herd down a fenced lane was easy; any bunch of city slickers drafted from a sports bar could have handled things. The situation got more challenging when the herd reached the Callin farm. They had a large field of alfalfa with no fence along the road. Jake and Uncle Glenn were well aware of the problem. Their riders had been instructed to form a phalanx along any gap in fencing to keep the hungry cows off fields of hay or other crops.

Callin's hay field was a good warm-up for the real challenge. Chadwicks had a mile of fenceless farm fields. Uncle Glenn's cattle must be kept on the road and off the fields.

One factor in their favor was that the fields had only recently been planted; there was not much growing yet to entice the cows off the road. Every available rider was on hand lining this stretch of trail to keep the herd moving along and on the road. This was where experienced cowhands were essential.

It was a fine difference between riding close enough to the cattle to dissuade them from getting off the trail and getting too close, causing them to get spooked and bolt off the trail in the opposite direction. A good crew could get a herd to string out, stay on the roadway, and walk calmly through an open area like a class of properly chaperoned grammar school students on a field trip.

Uncle Glenn had advised Gerald Chadwick about the impending cow drive. He had come to check things out and lend a hand if needed. He was primarily a farmer. He had never had a big itch to deal with a bunch of ornery cows. He got his pride of ownership from the best line of John Deere equipment in the community.

Gerald's one venture into ranching was his love of horses. He especially liked palominos. A few years back, he won some beautiful silver studded tack in a card game at Jackpot. When a good opportunity came, he loved throwing it on Trigger, his prize Palomino, and imitating Roy Rogers.

Gerald knew Glenn had some good men on hand to make it through his fenceless farmland, but what amazed him, as he observed from his vantage point, were the dogs. He watched Ripple work with Ron Probst. Ripple patrolled back and forth along the left side of the herd, keeping the cattle out of the field where he had just finished planting pinto beans the night before. The dog seemed to have a sixth sense about which cow was about to attempt to leave the roadway to wander into his field. He usually stayed far enough back not to activate the protective instincts mamas had for their babies but close enough to be an effective deterrent. With a wave of his arm and a whistle, Ron could redeploy Ripple to another location where the cows were ignoring the hooting and hollering of the cowboys.

Cows are much more inclined to pay attention to a dog than a rider on a horse, even if he is popping a bullwhip. Gerald was also pleased Ripple was on the job because a dog running through his field caused less damage than a horse and rider. It really appeared to Gerald as a casual observer that the two dogs he saw working either side of the herd could have done the job themselves. They were that good.

Uncle Glenn spotted Gerald and rode over to say hello to his neighbor. "I think we ought to make it through here, ok, Gerald!" commented Glenn. "I have a great crew this year. They are handling these cows like pros, in fact, most are!"

Gerald responded, "Where did you find the Australian? He is smarter than most of the people whom I can hire. If I had one here, I would give him a T-bone steak like the one I had last night. Who needs a fence with dogs like him? Without question, he is the best I have ever seen."

"He belongs to Ron Probst. Dog's name is Ripple. Check with him; he might swop you straight across for Trigger. Of course, you might have to throw in your fancy tack," ventured Glenn with a wink and a smile.

"If the dog can drive a tractor, I'll think about it," joshed Gerald.

By 10 AM, the herd had reached a vacant open-range pasture. Uncle Glenn dispatched Jerry to the front of the herd to tell Jake to hold, let the herd rest, and the cows and calves to mother up. Within minutes, everywhere one looked, you could see cows standing dutifully still so their calves could suckle.

The telltale sign of connection was the vigorously wiggling tails. Every once in a while, a calf would thrust his face into its mom's udder to hasten the milk let down as if to say, "Hey, mom, let's get with it; I'm hungry!"

Everything was so beautiful and peaceful. These were the moments Uncle Glenn relished. Times like this had kept him in the saddle literally and figuratively for fifty years. Why retire when this is what you love to do?

Ron Probst rode up to where Jerry and Uncle Glenn were sitting cross-legged on their horses and asked, "How far out do you want to let the critters graze, Mr. Briggs?"

"We will only hold up here for about thirty minutes, Ron," answered Glenn. "Let's not let them wander far, just enough to have some elbow room." As if Ripple knew exactly what Uncle Glenn wanted, he trotted off with a wave of Ron's arm and began pushing the herd a bit closer together.

To back up the rest of the crew who were now riding along the side of the herd, Glenn had Ron with his dog Ripple and Jake with his dog Thunder.

Thunder was an old English sheep dog whom Jake rescued from their veterinarian as a six month old pup. At first he was afraid of cows, but had gradually gained confidence until he had become a first rate cow dog. He normally looked as though he would weigh 85 to 90 pounds, until he would climb into a water trough to cool off. When he would come out, it became obvious his bulk was an illusion; he was mostly hair. Wet, he was skinnier than a Greyhound. If the mid-summer weather got too hot, Jake would give him a haircut, after which he looked a bit ridiculous. Jake had been accused of not adequately feeding Thunder. In fact he ate like a horse, and never seemed to gain a pound. He ran it off. A good cow dog has to run many miles every day to do his job. They are constantly in motion when they are on the job.

Ron and Jake were working either side of the herd as they headed out across an unfenced three mile stretch of trail. Glenn only needed two men riding drag.

By early afternoon the herd had reached Twitchel Station, a fenced area through which an irrigation canal ran. The cows were able to quickly water, and do a little grazing while their calves nursed. Glenn and his crew were able to relax, too. Twitchel Station had a very good netting wire fence around it. No cattle were likely go get out of it's enclosure. There were a few shade trees under which the cowboys were soon eating lunch.

Ripple and Thunder arrived dripping wet from swimming in the irrigation canal. They got everyone's attention by doing what dogs do; in unison they shook themselves dry midst cries of cowboys getting wet. The dogs made the rounds offering to help eat any food in their lunch the cowboys didn't like.

One could almost hear them thinking, 'We are here, there is no need to waste food!" Ron and Jake did carry dog food in their saddle bags, but Thunder and Ripple obviously found it not nearly as appetizing as random gifts from sack lunches.

Ron pulled the saddle off his horse, and turned him loose to graze while they ate lunch. After finishing his lunch, Ron stretched out in the grass under a tree, lay his head on his saddle, and was snoring in two minutes. Ripple joined him immediately, curling up at his feet. As a pair, they were used to getting some rest when you had a short break, taking what city slickers called power naps. It made surviving a long day much easier.

When Uncle Glenn looked around a few minutes later, it looked like a mass murder scene; there were bodies lying every where. He would have liked to have joined them, but he was the trail boss. Time to mosey through the herd, and check for problems.

The first thing to grab his attention was a young cow who didn't have a calf at her side, but was calling loudly. His first concern was maybe her calf had been left behind. A few minutes later, though, he noticed a calf suckling eagerly at her side. It never ceased to amaze him how cows and calves could find each other in a herd of hundreds. If a calf tried to nurse on the wrong cow, one not its mother, it was certain to get kicked. In cattle world, that was a no-no.

The trick for a calf to get away with stealing milk was to latch on when the cow was distracted, make it fast, and get away before she recognized you as an intruder. Get too greedy; expect to get kicked.

Uncle Glenn would have gladly let everyone take a long siesta, but the herd needed to reach North Fork before dark. Driving cattle after dark was fraught with possible complications.

Not far from Twitchel Station, the trail would cross the Salmon Falls Creek dam. If the herd cooperated, it wasn't a big problem. If the leaders were spooked by anything unusual, they might not want to across it. In that case, they would need to be pushed across. Everyone was hoping the old cows would again lead the way.

After an hour of rest, Uncle Glenn bellowed the traditional command, "Head'm up; move'm out!" Even the cows seemed to understand. After an hour, many of the cows were lying down. They lumbered to their feet and stood ready to continue.

Jerry was really impressed when Ron got up, and let out the loudest whistle he had ever heard. The result was his horse, who had been grazing several hundred yards away, came trotting up, and stood perfectly still as Ron threw on his saddle.

Jerry asked, "How did you train him to do that?"

"Oh, it wasn't too hard," asserted Ron, "I usually reward him with some oats; today I saved the apple from my lunch. He also knows, if he doesn't come, I will have Ripple come after him. He prefers the oats to the dog."

"I can understand that" agreed Jerry.

"Head'm up; move'm out" called Uncle Glenn again.

Everyone swung into their saddle and started to regather the herd. Jake opened the gate, and they were off once more.

Jerry was fascinated by all he was experiencing. He had never done anything quite so novel. City life had its benefits; ranch life was a whole new world. Definitely low tech and unsophisticated in an urban sort of way, however, rural life was highly developed in its own sphere. He recognized, in Uncle Glenn's world, he was a novice. He could ride a horse, yes, but he didn't understand or know how to work cattle. Uncle Glenn, Jake, or Ron could look at a critter, and from nonverbal clues know what it would most likely do; whether it would go with the flow or try to break from the herd.

In the second case they knew just how to position themselves to compel the former. A crew who knew how to get a herd of hundreds of cows and calves to cooperate and go with the flow, was a crew who could have an easy day. An inept crew could find themselves chasing after what appeared to be a very unruly bunch of ornery critters.

By the time the point riders guided the lead cows onto the road across the Salmon Falls dam, the herd stretched out for over a quarter mile. As hoped the leaders were some old cows who had made the trip many times. They never hesitated. Confidently they forged ahead, and were across so quickly, Jake had to slow them down to let the drag element catch up.

No sooner had everyone made it across the dam than a new complication greeted them. An afternoon squall blew in from the west hitting them head on. The wind was strong, and cold. When next the rain hit, the driving wind made the droplets sting their faces. The old hands dawned their rain slickers, and stayed right with the herd. This was not an abnormal event; they were prepared.

Jerry noticed an interesting thing with the cows. Some lowered their heads and kept walking into the wind; others turned tail and stood still as the weather beat at their butt ends. Only one of the guest riders had come prepared for this turn of events. He graciously shared his poncho with the other two as they huddled behind their horses, letting them take the brunt of Mother Nature's fury.

Fortunately, the squall ended as suddenly as it had started. The sun came out, and things returned to normal with the exception of now everything was wet. It took several hours of afternoon sunshine for things to dry out.

Jerry was glad Uncle Glenn had told him about the emergency rain gear in his saddle bags. He had been spared the discomfort of getting soaking wet. He was just wet enough to appreciate the wisdom of being prepared for inclement weather . The squall had dampened the fun factor for the guest riders. Being a cowboy was not all sunshine and gentle breezes. To their credit, they recovered quickly and rejoined the drive.

Uncle Glenn made a point to check on them, make sure they were ok, and attempt to cheer them up. He still needed their help, and didn't want them to get discouraged, or 'fold their tent', and go home. The short powerful storm had temporarily disrupted the smooth running nature of the cow drive. It was about four miles between the dam and where the trail turned south. It would now be a long up hill climb to the North Fork pasture.

Time was fast becoming a critical factor. It was getting late in the afternoon. If Uncle Glenn were to get the herd to their North Fork destination before dark, they would have to keep moving as quickly as possible.

Glenn joined Jake for a quick huddle where they decided to reorganize. Jake and Ron would drop back with their dogs and ride drag. This would serve two purposes: speed things up, and make sure none of the calves were missed as they tired out from the long climb.

Ripple and Thunder had a way of convincing tired calves to keep going and not lie down. When an especially young calf just refused to go any further, Jake called Jerry over to where the calf was lying, boosted the calf across his saddle, and said, "Here, got a hitch-hiker for you!"

Some horses would have been spooked by a calf on their back. Not Fleet; he was a veteran. This was old hat for him. Jerry was a little concerned about the calf's mother. She had been very disturbed by the presence of dogs near her calf. Now she was still visibly upset with

Jerry carrying it. Jake suggested Jerry move up a bit and ride flank. The cow followed him like she was on a leash. This was one good mom!

The sun was getting low in the western sky as the herd climbed the hill high enough for Jerry to see back to where they had started the day. He could spot various land marks by which they had passed: the dam, Twitchel Station, and Chadwick Farms. Jerry had to use the field glasses he had received for Christmas to see Uncle Glenn's house. It was a pretty big house, but a long way off. Jerry could also make out Holister and another village nearer the dam. He would have to ask some one to identify it.

Jerry scanned the surrounding area before putting his binoculars back in his saddle bags. He didn't notice anything especially remarkable. He wondered if water skiing were allowed on the reservoir created by the dam. It didn't look like there were any good beaches around the reservoir; mainly just rocky canyon walls. He would have to remember to ask about that, too.

Jerry stroked and talked to the calf as he carried him. He was rewarded by the calf peeing on his leg. Ron happened to see what happened as he patrolled back and forth behind the herd.

"No good deed goes unpunished, my friend!" he teased.

"Thanks for the warning," called back Jerry. "Now I know why I was chosen for the honor."

"Most honorable hand on the trail," chimed in Jake. "Don't take it personal!"

"Does this honor come with a plaque or anything," questioned Jerry.

"In about a year you can be the guest of honor when we barbecue him." stated Jake. "We will let you do the butchering, if you want revenge."

"Thanks, but no thanks. I have more important fish to fry!" responded Jerry.

Passing by, Uncle Glenn heard the banter, and ask for an explanation.

Pointing at Jerry, Jake said simply, "Check the pant leg. Calf just baptized his first cowboy!"

Uncle Glenn decided not to rub it in. He just smiled, shook his head, and rode on.

Just before dark, three things happened almost simultaneously. First, the herd reached the North Fork pasture. Second, Old George and Aunt Martha arrived, each driving a dually pickup truck, pulling a large goose-neck horse trailer. Together they were large enough to haul all the horses and riders back home. Third, Jerry saw what he thought may have been a mirage.

Day light was fading fast; he couldn't see well, but what it appeared to be was a beautiful girl riding a magnificent spotted horse. After a brief moment, she was gone.

CHAPTER 6—RIDING THE NORTH FORK RANGE

Jerry slept in again. How a cow drive could be so exhausting was a mystery. Also, Jerry thought he had arrived in Idaho in pretty good physical condition, but he awoke with muscles aching he didn't even know he had.

How did an old man such as Uncle Glenn do this kind of hard, physically demanding work day in and day out? Was he Superman, some sort of genetic mutant who had developed super human endurance?

Jerry finally concluded he hadn't been in as good condition as he thought. In that case he had better step up his exercising a couple notches. He started with stretching and some calisthenics in his room. Next he swam a calculated half mile of laps in Uncle Glenns swimming pool.

Jerry had been a high school swimmer, so he could do the flip turns with ease. When he finished swimming, and began drying off, Old George invited him to breakfast. He dressed in work clothes, and reported to the kitchen. The menu looked amazingly similar to yesterday's except for a different array of fruit and no oatmeal. Today it was cracked wheat.

"I personally like cracked wheat," confessed George, "but the boss prefers oatmeal. So I alternate the two. Boss claims cracked wheat gives him the runs. I do most of the boss's laundry, so I know he ain't lying. Any time he goes out punching cows after eating cracked wheat, he's spending lots of time out in the bushes. Doesn't bother me at all; I have got pretty much a cast iron gullet. Eat anything I want, and as much as I want. Never had to buy Rolaids in my whole life, except for the boss or some pansy friend. I won the hot pepper eating contest at the

New Mexico State Fair the year before I moved up here. No sir, I am no wimp. Only thing stopping me now-a-days is my weight. Have to watch it, now."

After breakfast, Jerry went to the stable to check on Fleet. He got him out of his stall and began currying him. He was almost done when Uncle Glenn rode in.

"How are you feeling, son," inquired Glenn. "I been wanting to tell you, for as new as you are at working cattle, you did a right impressive job. Got a good attitude, too! Not just anybody will let a calf pee their pants and keep smiling. Everyone who has commented thinks you are all right!"

Jerry wasn't used to such direct praise. "Gee, thanks boss, uh I mean Uncle Glenn. Yesterday was the experience of a life time. Most people I pal with will never get a chance to do anything like that. I really feel lucky! I want to thank you from the bottom of my heart. I'll always remember it!"

"My pleasure, Jerry. Besides you pulled your weight as well as I could have wanted. Any questions, now you have had time to think about it?"

"No, not really. Everyone was kind enough to answer pretty much every question I had at the time; except the one I haven't asked. I didn't ask because I didn't think anyone would take me seriously," continued Jerry.

Jerry had such a sincere look on his face, Uncle Glenn wasn't willing to doubt him. He was curious to find out what Jerry was talking about.

"Go on, Jerry, ask me anything," coaxed Uncle Glenn.

"Well, it was just as the last of the herd had entered the North Fork pasture. I looked up, and saw someone. Or at least I think I saw someone. As you remember, the light was fading fast. It wasn't dark, yet. The light was so dim, though, it was hard to make things out. I saw, or at least I think I saw a horse and rider appear out of nowhere, watch us for a moment, then disappear. Gone! I don't think I was imagining anything. I'm telling you a rider was there, and then they weren't. They just vanished into the darkness!" explained Jerry most earnestly. If I wasn't hallucinating, do you know who it might have been?"

"What did they look like?" asked Uncle Glenn. "Can you describe anything?"

"I think it was a girl, Uncle Glenn, a pretty girl.

"What about the horse; anything noteworthy about the horse?" pressed Glenn.

"Well, like I said, the light was real dim, but I could see this was no ordinary nag . It looked, well, impressive!" recalled Jerry.

"So what do we have? As far as you could see and can remember, you saw a cute girl on a nice horse who faded into the dark on top of a mountain where my cattle are supposed to spend the summer. Does that about sum it up?" asked Uncle Glenn.

Jerry replied, "You could say so, Uncle Glenn, but I can't get her out of my head. Do you have any idea who she is? Do you know who it might have been?"

Uncle Glenn considered what he was able to tell Jerry, then ventured a bit of speculation, "Well, Jerry, most nice, ordinary girls aren't out riding any kind of horse, impressive or not, in the dark in the forest on a mountain top. But, if what you tell me is anywhere near accurate, you may have come face to face or as close as anyone has to the Flower."

"What flower?" Uncle Glenn. I didn't see a flower. I think I saw a girl riding a horse! What do you mean, Flower?"

"Sit down, son. It is a bit of a long story, but let me tell you about 'The Flower', the Flower of China Mountain!"

When Uncle Glenn finished his explanation, Jerry sat for a few minutes in stunned silence, then asked sincerely, "You really think that's who I saw in the growing darkness at North Fork?"

Uncle Glenn considered his next words carefully, then admitted in all sincerity, "Yes, fits your description, and I can think of no one else it might have been. Of course, I might be wrong."

After a few more moments of contemplation, Jerry stood up and cleared his throat, "Uncle Glenn, I gotta find out for sure; just can't sit here and not know!"

Now it was Glenn's turn to consider his options. He was sympathetic to Jerry's youthful obsession. He had chased his share of tail as a young man, but abandoned any thought of anyone else when he had met Martha. It took him awhile to convince her he was her 'one and only', but he knew it from the start. There was just something about her that lit his fire, and it had been burning ever since.

"Jerry, I need a couple of hands to ride North Fork every few days to keep track of things up there. I usually send Jake, and let him pick his side kick. If you feel strongly you need to scratch this itch you are talking about, I will talk to Jake about letting you have the job, okay?"

"I would be ever so grateful, Uncle Glenn. I like Jake. I think we would work well together. I am pretty sure his dog likes me; ought to be a good enough job reference" kidded Jerry trying to lighten the mood.

Jake had hoped to have a more seasoned hand riding North Fork with him. But as a favor to Glenn, he accepted Jerry. He thought of him as a bright young fellow with lots of potential, even if he were a green horn. He had done well on the cow drive.

If Jerry were enchanted by the young maiden of China Mountain, far be it from him to stand in his way. There had been more than one man try to pick the Flower of China Mountain. None of them had succeeded; too many thorns. Jake's willingness to cooperate with Jerry was fueled in part by his wanting to see how Jerry might fair any better. The kid didn't know much about cows. Maybe he might be a better wrangler of women.

Glenn had had to share much of what Jerry told him with Jake in order to secure his cooperation. Jake believed Jerry's report of seeing someone; he had not. However, there were just too many facets of his story, things he had no way of knowing as a new arrival, which fit Glenn's conclusion: Jerry had very likely had a close encounter with Chenoa Walker, aka, The Flower of China Mountain.

The information tidbit which Jake found most convincing was Jerry's incidental description of the person riding an "impressive spotted" horse. There were other cute girls in the area, but not ones likely to be riding a spotted horse. Ben Walker was the only rancher in the area who raised Appaloosas, or as Jerry would likely describe it, "spotted", and his stallion was by any standard "impressive."

Yes, it made sense to Jake. Jerry had experienced what many locals wished to do, namely, lay eyes, if not hands, upon the greatest local enigma. Jake had heard lots of local gossip on the subject, but never seen this local phenomena. With Jerry's apparent luck, who knew, maybe all that would soon change.

Jake and Jerry got an early start the following morning. By the time the sun had risen above the eastern mountains, they had driven across the Salmon Falls Creek dam and started the long assent of China Mountain. They had hauled their horses in a four-horse trailer in case they encountered a sick cow or calf, and needed to haul them home for treatment.

Jake parked their rig at the same gate where Jerry had seen the mystery person. They unloaded Fleet and Jakes horse Zoom, an impressive black gelding in his own right. He was a cross between Tennessee Walker and Morgan. Jake spent an awful lot of time in the saddle riding the range to check cattle and fences. With his breeding Zoom had an easy gate, and was a pleasure to ride.

Jake and Jerry spent the morning riding slowly through the herd checking, as best they could, to see if each cow had their calf with them. It was still possible some calf may have become separated from its mother. In that case they would only have a short time to find it before the coyotes did.

The cows didn't seem to mind Thunder's presence as long as he followed quietly along at Zoom's heels. There he didn't present as a threat. They spotted one calf who looked sickly, had diarrhea, and needed a shot of antibiotics. Jake asked Jerry if he wanted to try his hand at roping the calf so Jake could administer the medicine.

Jerry declined, suggesting, "Why don't I watch how you do it first."

Jake easily threw his lasso over the calf's head, and threw it to the ground. He had Jerry hold the little guy down while he retrieved his medical supplies from his saddle bag. Jake drew up 50 cc's of penicillin, and placed the shot in the calf's right hind quarter. Jake emptied a big pill out of a bottle of diarrhea medicine, and tucked it far enough down the calf's throat that he had to swallow it.

"What a massive pill," commented Jerry in surprise. "Remind me not to get Beaver Fever", a condition he had heard about which can cause severe diarrhea from drinking contaminated stream water.

"I have had it. Can ruin your whole day, not to mention your underwear," confessed Jake. "I am pretty much immune to it now, but I

am still careful where I get my drinking water. Don't care to repeat the time I drank some water from an old fashion water pump. Didn't realize it was drawing the water from a long abandoned cistern.

Water didn't taste bad, and was nice and cool on a hot day, but thirty minutes later I got as sick as I have ever been. I felt as though a grenade had gone off in my stomach. Threw up everything; and I mean everything. I had convulsions so strong! First time my sweetheart was having labor contraction, I told her empathetically, "Honey, I think I know just how you feel!"

Jerry had watched carefully everything Jake did, knowing next time he would be asked to duplicate his every move. Fortunately, all the other animals looked well. By noon they had made it through about half of the entire herd.

The North Fork pasture had a creek running through it, so the herd had a good supply of fresh water. The grass was growing well, and a steady breeze kept the flies and other insects at bay. There were plenty of trees to provide shade if the afternoon temperatures rose too high. North Fork was an ideal summer pasture.

Around 2pm they were getting hungry, so Jerry starting looking around for a place to eat lunch. When Jerry suggested a good spot to Jake, Jake said he had a better idea. "Let's go eat at the Palace,"

"The Palace?", questioned Jerry.

"Yes" chuckled Jake. "You'll see. Follow me!"

Jerry followed Jake up a heavily wooded side draw which was geographically located near the center the North Fork pasture. They followed a barely distinguishable jeep trail deep into the woods. When the trail finally opened into a small clearing, Jake pointed to a unique looking little trailer with a rounded roof, and exclaimed, "Welcome to the 'Palace.'"

Jerry thought the strange looking structure looked a bit like a small WWII era Quonset hut on wheels. "Whats this thing?" asked Jerry.

"Around this country they are referred to as 'sheep camps', even though there aren't many people raising sheep any more," answered Jake. "Now we use them mostly as hunting camps and emergency shelters. Your Uncle Glenn put this one here so we would have a place to shelter in case of bad weather. Nice place, too, for a lunch break, to

brew some coffee, or spend the night. We keep it stocked with a few basics, just in case. We have had a few deer hunters make themselves to home, too."

"You may have noticed it wasn't locked. If someone is in trouble, we don't want them to have to break in. Locks are only good for keeping out honest people, anyway. Glenn just hopes people will be respectful; sort of a code of the west policy," added Jake.

"I am really glad it is here. We get some occasional severe thunder storms in the summer, and at this elevation, sudden snow squalls in the spring and fall. When those weather conditions occur, the difference between sitting here in the palace with a nice warm cup of hot chocolate, or huddling under a tree hoping you can find enough dry wood to start a fire, can be the difference between life and death," continued Jake

"The last time I had to stay here was two years ago when my misses and I were out deer hunting. Weather report was for a nice day. Mother Nature had a change of mind. By early afternoon she was throwing every thing in the kitchen at us: snow, sleet, rain, wind, and bitter cold. It was quite a tantrum. By the time we could get here to the palace, we were wet and chilled to the bone. I built a fire in the stove, and the camp warmed up quickly. We were soon feeling better than if we had checked into a resort lodge", asserted Jake

"Since deer were likely to be hiding in this weather, we figured we were done hunting for the day. We hung our clothes up to dry, and cooked a nice meal. Although we were real disappointed our deer hunt had come to such an abrupt end, we climbed into the camp bed and did a great job of consoling each other all night", added Jake.

"By the next morning, my hunting depression was completely cured. I can't talk much about it, though. My wife would not approve. Thankfully, no-one else came along needing help. They might have had to make do with the stable, like Mary and Joseph", concluded Jake.

Jake noticed the camp needed a good cleaning after a long winter. The bedding needed to be changed. He made a mental note to bring clean sheets, took a quick inventory of the food stores on hand, and asked Jerry if he could think of anything special he wanted. It appeared varmints had spent some time in the camp during the winter.

After they finished their lunch, Jake and Jerry spent a few minutes tidying up.

Jake noted some mouse droppings and told Jerry, "Good thing my misses didn't see this, or she wouldn't have slept a wink; deathly afraid of mice!"

After lunch Jerry took a few minutes to look around. He discovered a few things he hadn't noticed earlier. About 20 yards further back in the woods, Jerry found a small three-wall wooden structure with a slanted roof. Housed under the roof was a stall large enough for two horses and a small tack room off to the side big enough to hold a few bales of hay and a couple saddles.

Yet another ten yards, Jerry found a structure which brought a smile to his face. What would a palace be without a throne? Jerry recognized the iconic look of a one-hole privy. A peek inside revealed the classic substitute for toilet paper, a Sears Roebuck catalogue.

Jerry thought it odd Uncle Glenn would have gone to the trouble of installing a privy in such a remote location until he considered the purpose of having anything here at all. If this was a foul weather retreat, who wanted to go looking for a place to relieve themselves out in the woods, when the weather might be cold enough to turn your family jewels into crystals. At such a time who wouldn't prefer the comfort of a humble 'privy to hanging your posterior over a wet or frozen log?

Asked about the wooden structure Jake explained it was what past for a stable for the horses. Nothing fancy, but Glenn told his hands they owed it to their horses to take good care of them. If the weather was bad enough to send them looking for shelter, it was bad enough to cause suffering for their animals. Any kind of protection from the wind and wet was important for their horse's comfort.

The nice thing about North Fork was the amount of woods and willows where the cows and calves could find shelter from storms. Whenever the subject came up, Uncle Glenn was likely to relate an experience when a sudden violent thunderstorm blew in. He and his crew had quickly taken shelter in a nearby truck. Not wanting to see his saddle get wet, he had pulled it off his horse, and thrown it in the truck, too.

The storm turned quickly from rain to hail. To his horror he realized his mistake as he saw his horse being pelted by large hail stones. Mercifully the squall was fast moving enough to last only a few minutes, but his memory was scared by the images of his poor horse wincing in pain from the beating he was suffering. He had silently vowed never again.

The quickest way to get in trouble with Glenn is to fail to care for his stock, especially your assigned horse. Glenn's compassion for any critter for whom he is responsible is a primary reason he is so well respected.

Jerry asked about hay for the horses. "One of Old George's many jobs; he brings it in by Jeep, a few bales at a time", explained Jake.

"Seems like a long ways to haul a few bales of hay," commented Jerry.

"You are right", agreed Jake. "So we have truckers deliver a load of hay at the beginning of the season. They stack it at the holding pen used during round up. Glenn buys the best quality hay he can find. What the horses haven't eaten by the end of the season, he feeds to the cows when we gather them in the Fall. Like giving candy to kids. Never has any trouble getting the cows to come in."

With their hunger satisfied and new shopping list in hand, Jake and Jerry filled their canteens from the spring which provided clean, fresh water to the camp, and set out to check on the rest of the stock.

Jerry got his chance to play vet when they came across another sick calf with diarrhea. Jerry was very proud of himself when he roped the calf on only the second attempt.

Fleet had considerable experience as a roping horse. He had even been part of a rodeo roping team a few years before. Uncle Glenn had loaned him to one of his cow hands who had an itch to see if he could make it as a rodeo roper.

Jerry had to chase the calf a few hundred yards before he cast his lucky throw. When the rope settled onto the calf's head, Fleet stopped as trained. He stopped so fast, Jerry was nearly thrown over his head. With his dignity barely in tack, Jerry stepped off Fleet and started following the rope to the calf as he had seen the cowboys do in the only rodeo he had ever watched. Fleet stood perfectly still as long as the rope stayed tight. When the rope went slack, Fleet backed up to keep it tight.

When Jerry reached the calf, he placed his left hand just behind the calf's right front leg and grabbed a hunk of skin. He simultaneously did the same thing with his right hand, the only difference being he grabbed a handful of skin just ahead of the right hind leg. As Jake had

demonstrated on the first calf, Jerry lifted the calf off his feet as he leaned back and lowered the calf to the ground on its left side. Jerry's full weight followed pinning the calf to the ground. Jake came immediately up, and helped hold the calf down.

Jerry took a big pill from Jake and attempted to administer it to the calf. On his first try, the calf spit it up. Jake repeated the instruction about needing to push the pill over the tongue so it couldn't be coughed up. He just about had it deep enough, when the very mad mother cow who had been bellowing her disapproval from a few yards back, suddenly bolted forward and blew snot all over Jake and Jerry. She made it very plain, enough of this messing with her calf. Jerry retreated to the safety of Fleet, and Jake looked around to see why Thunder had not been on guard. He should have intervened before the cow had gotten within snot snorting range.

Jake shouted, "Thunder, where in hell are you. Get her!" Late to the party, Thunder came growling onto the scene and chased the cow back. He returned to Jake with a sheepish, apologetic look on his face, as if to say, "Sorry, boss, I got distracted."

Jake took the pill from Jerry, shoved it not too gently down the calf's throat, then turned it loose. Still suffering the ill temper of an adrenaline-fueled fright, Jake yelled, "There, take your calf and get out of here, ya old sour puss!"

Jerry and Jake mounted up and continued their check ride, joking nervously about who came closest to peeing their pants when they felt snot being blown on their necks, and heard mama cow sounding as though she were going to eat their lunch.

My wife is going to have the last laugh tonight predicted Jake. She was helping us work some cows and calves early this spring when a cow got all agitated like the one today. The cow charged her. She was backing up, trying to get to a corral fence, when she tripped.

I tried to get to her to drive the cow away but was not quick enough. My wife rolled onto her back and was trying to fend off the mad cow with her feet. I haven't had the courage to tell her this, but when she was kicking at the cow, she looked as though she were riding some invisible bicycle. Her feet were going round and round just like she was riding our kids 10-speed.

Wouldn't have been quite so bad, but our four-year-old was sitting on the corral fence watching all this. He was crying, afraid for his mother. I think he is still having nightmares about it. When it was all over, I was apologizing but started to laugh when I remembered how she looked riding her invisible bicycle. She got mad and demanded to know what was so funny. I told her she was doing such a good job dealing with the mad cow with her feet, maybe I should hire her to show the other cow hands her technique.

She quoted that famous line from Star Wars where Harrison Ford tells Chewbacca, "Laugh it up fuzz ball!" Said she couldn't wait till some old cow had her way with me; let me see how it feels. This will really make her day.

By around 5pm they had inspected every cow and calf in the pasture; at least the ones they could find. They were ready to call it a day and go home. The standard working hours on Uncle Glenn ranch were 8 to 6. Extended hours were common to finish jobs which just had to get done. Otherwise, the standard hours were honored. If Jake and Jerry left North Fork at 5:00, they should arrive home before 6:00. They would have time to report to Uncle Glenn, they had ridden North Fork, and everything was in apparent good order.

Jake and Jerry returned to their truck and horse trailer at an easy trot. When you were in too much of a hurry to walk your horse, but didn't want to tire it out rapidly, trotting was the way to go. Glenn's hands occasionally needed to go for miles by horse back. His horses weren't as fast as racing trotters for sure, nor were they much slower.

It was about 20 miles as the crow flies from North Fork back to their Hollister headquarters. If by chance their truck broke down, good cow horses could trot fast enough to still make it home in under three hours and hardly break a sweat. The alternative to such a long ride would be to hold up in the Palace and wait for rescue.

Jake and Jerry were loading their horses when they heard a whinny. Their horses answered the call. Odd; they weren't aware of any other horses being in the area. They paused for a few moments to look and listen.

Jerry was intrigued and reminded of his first visit to this place. The girl on the horse. Might that be the source of the whinny. Suddenly, he was no longer tired. He was hit with a jolt of adrenaline such as when you fall asleep at the wheel driving and wake up just in time to avoid a head on collision. Jerry was ready to unload Fleet and go find the girl. If she weren't a figment of his imagination, he wanted to find her. He had to find her. Something deep inside would not rest till he found her. He said so to Jake.

Jake patiently acknowledged his wishes, but counseled, "Let's call it a day, son. Something tells me this won't be your last chance. I'm tired, hungry, and feeling my own hormones, but my woman and my supper are back home, not off somewhere in the woods. At ease, my boy! If she is hanging out around here, we got all summer; there is time to find her."

With Jake at the wheel, they headed for home. As the dust rose from the departing truck and trailer, the girl emerged from the cover of a small patch of trees. She didn't understand her own attraction, or to what?

Chapter 7—Jarbidge

Chenoa had been riding all day. Sky Walker had finally started sweating. He was in such good condition; he rarely broke a sweat. They stopped on the rim rock overlooking the headquarters of the ranch her father had worked so hard to establish for their home. Smoke curling from the chimney signaled her dad had a fire in the kitchen stove. Undoubtedly, he was cooking supper. She didn't much care what he was cooking; she was hungry and ready for most anything. Her dad had become a surprisingly good cook. His menu items were all pretty basic.

On her visits to Little Feather, Chenoa had learned there were such dishes as dessert, and they tasted scrumptious, but her dad didn't think they were good for you. He had seen how people on the Indian reservation who ate lots of sugary foods, ended up loosing their teeth. People who ate the Indian's traditional food rarely had cavities, let alone lost their teeth. Ben trusted his daughter would have beautiful teeth if he fed her basic foods. So far his strategy appeared to be working.

Home! It was a humble place, but her physical and spiritual refuge. She had come to love it! She loved every old board, and rusty nail in the place. It was here that she felt safe. She dared to venture out from this sanctuary, because she had to if their ranch were going to be successful. Also, she trusted Sky Walker to help her avoid danger or out run it.

Sky Walker had the senses of a guard dog and would alert whenever he saw or sensed anything troubling. When Sky Walker alerted to a danger, it was Chenoa's option how to deal with it. From most

problems, she could hide or slip quietly away. If flight were not a safe option, she had her rifle and an ample supply of ammunition.

Ben had spent time in the military. He taught Chenoa the basics of being a sniper, how to find and use concealment when needed, when to ditch concealment to make an appearance when intimidation was a more effective weapon.

When it came to shooting, in most situations, a near miss had a better outcome than a direct hit. It seemed to cure an over production of testosterone or an overactive libido. It seemed to cure a lack of good manners and self-control, too. It also saved one from the necessity of doing lots of paperwork or having to choose the shoot-shovel-and-shutup option."

Chenoa spent a few more minutes reflecting on how blessed she felt to live where she did, then walked her magnificent stallion off the rim rock and down the well-worn trail to the barn below.

Sky Walker must have caught a whiff of some mare who was ready for what he had to offer because he suddenly stopped and let loose with a loud whinny, characteristic of a stallion ready to be of service.

What she didn't understand was her own inner feeling of discontent; an appetite for something more. In spite of the love she felt for what she had, there was a growing feeling something was missing.

Chenoa loosened her cinch, unbuckled it, and pulled her saddle off the stallion. She placed the saddle in the tack room before returning to feed Sky Walker his ration of oats. He needed them. He had covered over 40 miles today and more than 200 in the past week. It was only an estimate. Her path had not been in an easily measured straight line. She had deviated from a general direction to investigate the status of Ben's horses who were scattered far and wide over the Jarbidge range.

The wide distribution of his herd was intended to reduce their impact on the habitat. This made it harder on her. Checking on the well-being of all their brood mares and colts scattered over hundreds of square miles, required a lot of hard riding. Even she was a bit saddle sore after riding hundreds of miles.

Sky Walker was the right horse for the job. He was in superb condition. He was sure-footed, having lived almost his entire life in the mountainous rocky terrain.

A pasture raised, flatland horse would likely have sprained an ankle, if not broken a leg, trying to keep up with them today.

Chenoa had been out for a week patrolling her assigned area. Fortunately, she had not come across any serious problems. The importance, though, of being on constant guard were the two problems she did find. She found one mare who had become entangled in some discarded wire. If not removed, it would have cut through her ankle within a day or two.

Another problem was caused by someone who had brought their trash to the mountains to discard it. A curious colt got his head stuck in a bucket. Chenoa was able to easily remove it, but only finding it promptly had averted a potential tragedy. The thoughts of what could have happened brought shudders to Chenoa. She was very soft hearted when it came to animal suffering.

Chenoa made sure there was hay in the manger for Sky Walker. The big fellow was sure to have a good appetite. When Chenoa turned Sky Walker out into the corral next to the barn, she watched as he lay down, rolled on to his back, and wriggled back and forth taking a dust bath. When he had satisfied himself, Sky Walker stood up and shook off the dust like a wet dog shaking himself dry. He walked over to the water trough, drank for a long time, then walked to the manger. After only a few bites, though, he again let loose with a "come to daddy whinny" and went looking for the mare emitting the attractive pheromone.

Satisfied that Sky Walker was properly cared for and would soon be forgetting any of his own aches and sore muscles, Chenoa headed for the house. Ben met her at the door, greeted her with a kiss on her forehead and a fatherly embrace.

"I made us some beef stew," Ben said. "I dished some up for you when I heard Sky Walker calling from the hillside."

"Thanks, Dad!" replied Chenoa appreciatively. "I am famished. Been in the saddle since daybreak. Wanted to sleep in my own bed tonight, so I only stopped for a couple of short breathers and bites of jerky. The food smells wonderful!"

It was nice to have his daughter home. Ben missed her when she was gone for long rides. He offered to help pull her boots off, knowing how tired she must be. She sat in her over-stuffed chair, Ben straddled her ankles, grabbed her boot heels, and easily pulled the boots off. Well-fitting boots were one thing Ben made sure Chenoa had. They sat down at the kitchen table, and Chenoa took her first spoonful of Ben's Shepherd's Stew. It was just the right cure for a tired, hungry girl, the first home-cooking she had enjoyed since riding away from the house Monday morning.

Ben and Chenoa made a number of dried foods to carry with them when they were away from home. They were made from traditional Indian recipes. The few white men with whom they had shared their dried foods weren't very impressed. Ben and Chenoa, however, enjoyed it; it was very much an acquired taste. It's convenience, though, was undeniable. Fill your saddle bags with their dried food, and a rider could survive for a week. In fact Chenoa just had.

Ben and Chenoa chatted about her week while they ate. They sopped up the last of Ben's stew with chunks of bread. Neither Ben nor Chenoa enjoyed store bought bread, nor did they have time to bake their own. Their solution to these factors was to buy bread from Little Feather. She would have cooked for them free, but Ben told her he didn't want to feel like a poor beggar or take advantage of Mr. LaVall's hospitality.

They compromised by having Little Feather come to Ben's ranch on her day off and bake enough bread to last for two or three weeks. For Ben and Chenoa, Little Feather declined to use a typical white man's stove. Instead, she had Ben construct a traditional earthen oven, only a big one. With Ben's oven, Little Feather could bake a whole month's supply of bread at one time.

This worked out well for her, too. All she had to do was make a second or third batch, and she had her bread supply for Mr. LaVall's crew as well.

Since the cow hands liked her bread better than any bakery bread Mr. LaVall could find, he readily agreed to buy the ingredients, if Little Feather would use Ben's oven to supply the bread for him and his ranch, too. It was a classic win/win deal. Everybody was happy and supplied with Little Feather's wonderful bread. Even the Jarbide General Store had asked to get in on the deal. The owner had asked for a hundred loaves per week.

Mr. LaVall nixed the deal with a curt response, "We are raising cattle; not bread!"

Ben's job in the whole process as it evolved was to fire the oven. He had to start a fire in the big oven the night before, and let the fire burn all night. By noon the next day the temperature in the oven was just right to bake the bread. It took a lot of firewood, but everyone who loved Little Feather's bread pitched in to make sure there was always a good supply of wood. With his chain saw, Ben didn't have any back breaking work to cut enough firewood to keep the oven supplied.

Ben and Chenoa didn't have electricity on their ranch. They lived "off the grid" as survivalists describe it. They used candles if needed to, but usually camp lanterns. When they wanted to wash up with warm water, they had to heat it on their cook stove. When they wanted to take a bath, they had to heat even more water.

Ben had predicted Chenoa would want to clean up after being out all week, so he had heated lots of water for her. With her hunger satisfied Chenoa slipped out of her clothes and into her bath. It felt so relaxing. Store bought soap including shampoo was one of the few luxuries Chenoa enjoyed. She soon had a week's worth of trail dust washed off and started shampooing her hair. When it, too, was washed clean, Ben used the last of the warm water to help her rinse the shampoo from her hair as he had been doing since her mother died. Wrapped in her prized Terry cloth bath robe, Chenoa sat in her chair and brushed her hair until it glistened in the flickering lantern light.

Little Feather had taught her the way to care for her hair as a young girl. Now her jet-black hair was long enough to reach her waist. When it was dry and braided, Chenoa retired to the bed she had been thinking about all day and was fast asleep in minutes.

Ben left the house, and made his nightly patrol around the place to make sure all was okay. From the corral Ben could hear the distinctive sounds of Sky Walker attending to his duties. Ben had no doubt Sky Walker had found the mare who had attracted his attention.

Finding nothing amiss, Ben paused to enjoy the sounds and smells of the evening for a few minutes before going to bed, also. He didn't immediately fall asleep, but rather spent a few minutes thinking about his life and the many things for which he was thankful.

Ben missed Abby, his long-departed wife, but had to admit he was very fortunate. He was in good health, he had escaped the social ills of the reservation, he had a successful ranching operation, he had a beautiful daughter, good neighbors, fine stock, plenty to eat, and a comfortable home.

Yes, in his opinion, God, or the Great White Spirit, or whatever name you chose to call the ruler of the universe, he or she if you wanted to think like the feminist radicals of the day, had been generous to him. What more could he want? As he resisted falling asleep to contemplate the answer to his question, he was startled by a sudden unusual noise. He listened attentively for a few moments to tell if he would hear it again. Yes, there it was again, and louder this time. Ben laughed silently. He now realized he had the answer to two questions. First, what more could he want? Grandkids! Second, what was the strange noise? The most beautiful women in his world, his grandchildren's mother, was snoring.

Chenoa slept well. It was the contented sleep of someone who has a clear conscience and faith that her life was near perfect.

Then suddenly she was awake. She was left wondering what had awakened her. She listened. She couldn't hear anything wrong; there was no disturbance outside. Her father wasn't calling her. She had not been dreaming or having a nightmare.

There was just silence, until it appeared—an apparition. There was a glow about it. At first Chenoa noticed it in the furthest corner of her room. It descended through the ceiling as though it weren't there. It kept coming closer and closer until it was standing in the air at the foot of her bed.

Chenoa wasn't frightened, on the contrary, she was filled with the most peaceful feeling. As the apparition looked down on her, Chenoa was filled with a feeling of love as strong as though she were feeling the warmth from standing close to a campfire. The feeling of love radiated to her very core. She suddenly realized the apparition was female, and more than that, she knew with certainty it was her mother.

Since her mother had died before Chenoa was old enough to really remember her, she had not recognized her at first appearance. Her mother remained in her position at the foot of her bed for several minutes, as though waiting to let the warmth of her love to soak in. Chenoa had read about Christ-like love. This had to be similar. Her mother

finally delivered a special message to her, then departed. The room was left dark, but the feeling she was loved lingered till first light.

Chenoa had always had an empty feeling when she thought about what her mother was like. Even conversations with her father had not succeeded in measurably filling the void. She no longer felt that way. Now she felt she knew her mother as well as if they were bosom buddies for years. Most importantly, she knew her mother loved and adored her.

Chenoa had always felt as though she had some unseen entity watching over her. Now she would find comfort in the thought it was her mother. Never again would she silently curse God for leaving her to wander through life without the love of a mother. If anything, she was now comforted by the thought and feeling her mother loved her more than was possible were she still alive.

At breakfast the next morning, Ben was about to tease Chenoa about her snoring until he saw her. She was different. Ben wasn't sure how, but Chenoa had changed overnight. As he dished up her breakfast, he simply ask her, "Sweetheart, are you okay?"

"Oh, yes, daddy! I met mama last night." Ben dropped the frying pan from which he had been about to dish up some perfectly cooked eggs, sunny side up. Now they were sunny side down on the kitchen floor.

"You met your mother, really?" Well, that would explain a lot, thought Ben. He wanted to know more, but was sure he should not press for more information till Chenoa volunteered it. She had frequently ask about her mother as she grew up, but this was extraordinary.

Ben knew he had never been able to adequately answer Chenoa's questions. He had never had the communication skills to convey the essence of who his wife was or describe her personality. He was not sure he knew himself. From Chenoa's simple comment, she "met mama last night", Ben came away with the impression she now knew her mother intimately and understood her so completely there would be no more questions. If anything, he could now ask her.

Chenoa continued, "I know you said she was beautiful, but I never understood just how beautiful, inside and out!"

"Yes, she was," agreed Ben. "I am sorry I didn't know how to explain any better. The best way I can describe her is to say she was a lot like you."

"Oh, thank you daddy. You really think so?" responded Chenoa.

"I sure do!" assured Ben as he cleaned up the mess on the floor and cracked two more eggs to feed Chenoa.

"Now that you are old enough to understand, there is one other thing I should tell you about your mother. She didn't exactly accept me with open arms when we first met. She had plenty of other men, young and old, who would have liked to have her. But she took her time, and carefully considered her options. It was a shared goal of what we wanted out of life which eventually sparked our love for each other."

Abby didn't want to be just one more reservation squaw, knocked up at fifteen, and every two years thereafter until she had gone to seed so badly that her drunk of a husband had no desire to come home to her.

She was determined to do more with her life than tan old hides by chewing them with her few remaining teeth. She wanted to get an education, and marry someone with a burning desire be someone, too.

She despised the welfare system which dominated reservation life. She saw it with a wisdom beyond her years. She recognized it as a social trap which ensnared too many from her once proud tribe.

"Sweet heart, what can you tell me about last night?" asked Ben cautiously.

"I don't want to talk about it, yet, daddy. But I can tell you I am a different girl than rode in here last night. I have been thinking about a lot of things lately. There has been an emptiness. I didn't really understand myself. I have been wondering about life; do I have a purpose. The hills are so beautiful. Daddy, you have always told me, I am beautiful, like my mother. Daddy, I am not blind. I see things," confided Chenoa

"This week I saw a cactus flower on China Mountain. It was so beautiful, the first one I have seen in a in a long time, and the only one this season. I found it on Tuesday. I thought about picking it. After admiring it for a long while, I decided to let it be. I came back two days later to admire it some more, and it was gone. The blossom had closed and shriveled up."

"I was sad. I turned Sky Walker towards the North Fork camp and cried. My eyes were so full of tears, I had to let him find the camp. Daddy, I wasn't crying about the flower; here today, gone tomorrow. I was crying because I couldn't escape the feeling, I was like the flower; young and beautiful today, but what about tomorrow. Soon I will be old and gone, too. I am happy now; I love the hills, the horses, our home, our life, and you. I felt love for the mother I've never met. It's been perfect and beautiful, like the flower on China Mountain. But I was racked with the question, how long can it last? Will our happiness shrivel and fade away like the flower. Will the emptiness, the feeling of something missing continue to grow till it consumes me?"

"Daddy, I don't want to be gone tomorrow; I am not ready to die or fade away. I want to be like a sagebrush; hardy, resilient, hard to kill, but rebounding when it is crushed. I want to give shelter to the small and weak things in life. I want to make the world more fragrant. The cactus flower is beautiful, but it makes little lasting impression on the world."

"Daddy, I prayed that night when I found the cactus flower was gone. I have prayed every night since. I need to know what is to be my fate. Last night a loving God answered me, not he himself, but he sent the one angel in whom I could trust. He sent my mother. Strange, she didn't actually say a lot, but she communicated volumes. I'll tell you more when I'm ready. For now I need to ride and think. I love you; mom loves you. She is proud of you. She ask me to tell you so!"

Ben was dumfounded. He had spent years trying to reconcile his feelings over the loss of his wife. He missed her. He thought about what they could have done together. In her absence, he had transferred his feelings for her to his daughter. She had become the object of his devotion. To minimize the threat of losing her, Ben had deliberately fostered a fear of white men in Chenoa. He knew how little respect such men had for Indian women; for squaws. To most white men, Indian women were little more than dogs in skirts.

When most men took an Indian woman to be their wife, they treated them poorly and with little, if any respect. Ben was an exception. His wife had been a beauty. To him she was an Indian princess; the queen of his world. In his mind, he kept her on a pedestal. He had heard a wise person make a statement which he had taken for his own personal motto, "Treat your wife like a thoroughbred, and she will never become a nag!"

Chenoa had become so beautiful; he wanted to protect her. He didn't want to share her. Through her he vicariously still had his lovely, cherished wife.

However, he now knew he needed to look beyond the moment. Ben was impressed he must consider Chenoa's future. He could not treat her like a flower preserved by pressing it between the pages of an encyclopedia. Such treatment was for dead flowers. You could preserve their memory in this manner, but not their vitality or beauty.

The time had come to repot her. She needed to live, she needed to blossom. Out there somewhere was the person who by the Grace of the Great Spirit could ride the trail of life with her. Out there somewhere was the other half of a more perfect union than a widower and his daughter living on a ranch in the mountains of Southern Idaho.

The life they both loved needed to change in a way neither yet understood, but sensed was inevitable; part of God's plan for their happiness.

As Ben cleaned up the breakfast dishes, and prepared to meet the wealthy Physician from Boise, who was coming to the ranch today to buy a two-year-old gelding for his horse-crazed daughter, Chenoa saddled Sky Walker. She rode him up the trail to the rim rock and paused to survey the place that had been her home since she was born.

How she could want more than this, she didn't really understand. Yet from what her angel mother had told her, she knew there was more. Her mother had instructed her to follow the whisperings of the Spirit and trust that God would lead her down the right trails in life.

Much like Sky Walker taking her safely back to camp when her eyes were filled with tears, Chenoa now trusted God would show her the path which would lead her to fulfillment and happiness. She had no doubt the emptiness she had been feeling would soon be a thing of the past.

Chenoa felt a need to engage in some girl talk. She headed Sky Walker toward Orrie LaVall's ranch so she could visit with Little Feather.

The day had dawned clear and bright with the exception of a few scattered low hanging fluffy clouds. They were the kind Chenoa loved to watch float by while lying in some high mountain meadow. She would try to analyze each cloud to see if its shape reminded her of anything. One day she had seen clouds which were just like the Disney characters Pluto and Micky Mouse. Most clouds required a little more imagination to recognize anything.

Chenoa had been riding for most of an hour, when Sky Walker alerted. She heard it, too, then she saw it. Two men in an open Jeep were barreling toward her at breakneck speed. She was caught out in the open. She wheeled Sky Walker toward a rock out-cropping roughly a quarter mile to her right and set him off on a full gallop. The jeep changed direction and moved to cut her off.

Chenoa preferred flight to fight, but she could see she had no chose. She brought Sky Walker to an abrupt halt, stepped down, and drew her rifle from its scabbard. Chenoa placed her first shot through the jeeps radiator. With the next two she took out both front tires. She was confident the jeep would only carry one spare. The jeep abruptly changed course, but had to stop when both tires went flat and the engine started to blow steam.

Chenoa waited a few moments for her pulse to return to normal, placed her rifle back in its scabbard, swung back into the saddle, and rode on to talk to Little Feather.

Happy now to just be alive, two humbled young men started their long walk to Jarbidge, the nearest civilization with a service station where they hoped to get help.

Little Feather had just finished preparing sack lunches so Orrie could send them off to the crew when Chenoa arrived at the ranch. She tied Sky Walker to the hitching rail and walked into the cook shack still smelling of the eggs and bacon cooked for breakfast. Little Feather was pleased to see her "favorite" niece. They embraced for a long moment before she asked Chenoa if there were any special reason for this unexpected visit.

"Do you have a few minutes we could visit?" inquired Chenoa.

"Most certainly!" answered Little Feather sensing this was no idle request. "Let's go set under the tree in Mr. LaVall's flower garden.

When they were settled in the shade of the tree, Little Feather was somewhat taken back by Chenoa's first question.

"I know you miss John. Do you ever think about getting remarried, of having children, and starting a new family? I mean you are still young enough."

"In all honesty, Chenoa, yes. I do miss John. I love children. I wanted to have a family with him. But that dream was stolen away

from me by a rogue horse and a husband with too much pride. Now the problem is with whom. There are lots of guys who like my cooking. Almost any old cowhand would gladly punch my ticket, as bunk house talk goes. But I'm not willing to sell myself cheap.

I would like a good man and a real family, a house of our own, and a good job; not a roll in the hay and a beating when ever my man drinks too much. Too many women think so little of themselves, they are willing to settle for such mistreatment. There is no free milk here. Not me. I'd rather have self-esteem, live alone, and be known as a proud widow than be the cow no one wanted buy, the whore of the Jarbidge Range."

"Oh, Little Feather, you are a wonderful person. You have been my surrogate mother for years. You ought to get married again and have your own family." said Chenoa.

"Where am I going to find a good man in these mountains," asked Little Feather with a nervous laugh. "There are only so many berries on a bush. Besides, what has you thinking on this subject, anyway?"

"Mama!" said Chenoa to Little Feather's complete surprise.

"What's your mama got to do with this?" asked a bewildered Little Feather.

"Everything", replied Chenoa. "I have been feeling an emptiness of late. As you know, I love my dad, I love you, I love myself, I love our ranch and way of life. But I keep feeling there is something else, something I'm missing. I feel fate has something more in store for me, I just haven't known what. I have been praying for guidance.

Last night God answered my prayer, at least in part. He sent a messenger. He sent my mama! She helped me answer a few questions and told me how to find answers to the rest.

Mama told me there is someone out there for me, and to be patient. We would find each other. I ask her about papa; what he would do without me? She did not answer me directly, but simply said God would provide. Little Feather, into my mind came the clear, unmistakable answer; she was referring to you. If my life with my father is about to fork into separate trails, there is no one else mama would rather have fill the resulting void than you."

Chapter 8—Little Feather

Little Feather was in shock as she bade farewell to Chenoa. As she watched Sky Walker trot off into the distance, her head was spinning. Little Feather wasn't opposed to the idea remarrying. She just hadn't given any serious consideration to its ever happening. She had the utmost respect for Ben Walker. He was a fine man. But he belonged to her sister. She couldn't shake the notion, having any kind of designs on him would be cheating on her sister, her own flesh and blood. It really didn't make any difference in her old way of thinking whether her sister was dead or alive. It just had to be wrong.

Now she was trying to get her head around the idea her own sister approved of the idea and wanted her to join her life with Ben's. She knew Ben was devoted to Chenoa. She knew Chenoa wasn't just an important part of his life; she was his life since her sister's unfortunate demise. Oh, there was the ranch and the horses and the pride of achieving success in the white man's world. These had been and would be important to Ben for as long as he lived. But none of these things were or ever would be nearly as important to him as his one beautiful daughter, especially since he had lost her mom. It only added to the depth of his devotion, having her be so incredibly beautiful. Little Feather had pondered more than once how being the father of such a beautiful freak of nature must affect his feelings.

How would he take losing her to another man? Would he look kindly on her marrying and giving him a brood of little Chenoas. Would he transition seamlessly into grandpa mode, or would such a change affect him poorly? Would he see Chenoa having a male friend or suitor

as a plus or a negative. These were all thoughts which crashed around in Little Feather's mind like bowling pins reacting to a perfect strike.

As utter shock settled into more normal confusion, Little Feather allowed her mind short moments of consideration about the basic premise of her sister's proposal. It certainly came from the most credible messenger she could think of in her world. It seemed couched in the most compelling argument of which she might accept, namely, how to fill the void created should Chenoa leave Ben's cloistered world for a time?

Setting this all aside for a bit, Little Feather was her own woman. She had her pride. She wasn't just some cheap cut of meat, like rump roast, for sale at the Market price in the Jarbidge general store. She was a woman with talent and ability. In her world, she would consider herself at the least sirloin, if not prime rib. She didn't know if she considered herself for sale at any price. She didn't dislike her life as is. Why should she consent to change anything.

Then there were other considerations. Was she too young? Was Ben too old? Could Orrie find another cook for his crew? Ha! Who cared whether the dusty, smelly, ungrateful bunch of cow pokes ended up having to order and eat Twinkies by the case. She wasn't going to let her future depend on them!

However, did she love Ben? Now there was a good question, and one she was not sure how to answer. Sure she loved him as her brother-in-law. She loved him as Chenoa's father. But, what about as a potential husband? Could she share a bed with him? Dared she have a child with him? Was she still young enough to bear a child? These and other questions brought a calm over Little Feather as she seriously considered them.

These and other questions finally consumed so much of Little Feather's attention, she was late getting supper started. Fortunately, she knew many shortcuts to preparing a meal. The dinner bell rang on time. No one went hungry. No one had reason to suspect what Little Feather had had on her mind all afternoon.

Before Little Feather retired to bed, she too knelt at her bed side and ask a kindly Heavenly Father, if he approved of her sister's idea. By now she had thought it out. She was warming to the idea. But only warming.

There were still aspects of this proposal with which she was not comfortable. But she had to admit, of all the eligible men she knew in the area, there was no one she respected more than Ben. He certainly wasn't the typical low skilled, penniless, morally bankrupt, occasionally sober cowhand whom Orrie was able to hire. They weren't without their good qualities, nor were they without their charming qualities. Few, however, ever went to church, read the Bible, or claimed to be a Christian.

Most would fit the description of having low moral character. They rarely had or wanted a wife and family. A trip once or twice a year to Jackpot, Nevada to gamble away their savings, and sample the available feminine wares was all they usually wanted. Little Feather had overheard some of the bunk house talk on the subject. It wasn't the kind of talk to impress a good girl. They never talked dirty to her, though. Orrie forbade it. Disrespecting Little Feather was grounds for instant dismissal.

One new guy who hadn't had the rules explained escaped being fired, but he was banned from eating with the crew. Two months of eating alone in the bunk house out of a can drove home the seriousness of the message.

Since Chenoa had brought up the subject, Little Feather decided to take inventory of her marriage prospects. She had always considered them slim, which is why she had never given them much thought. Why waste time thinking about the unlikely. Little Feather had thought the most likely scenario leading to her remarrying would be the arrival on the scene of some totally new prospect to the area. This would involve circumstances over which she had no control, so again, why think about it?

Orrie wasn't married, but Little Feather considered him too old. Who wanted to marry their grandfather? Besides, he was three times divorced already; not exactly an impressive resume. He was wealthy, but Little Feather was no gold digger. No, the only thing Orrie had to offer was what she already had, a job. She did enjoy his company fairly often, but in her position, she could enjoy the ranch social life with her clothes on. Why complicate their relationship by getting married. Besides, as the expression goes, "It takes two to tango", and Orrie had never hinted, he was the least bit interested anymore in women, or

romance. He fit the pattern of the old bulls, who are played out. Just content to lie in the shade of a hillside tree and watch life go by.

Little Feather thought there might be a couple other possibilities in Jarbidge or Mountain City, but she didn't know anything about them. As she thought about it, she found she wasn't much interested in finding out about them, either.

Little Feather came slowly to the conclusion Ben Walker was the only man in her life, currently, with whom a marriage possibility made much sense. He was a good man. They were both Shoshone. Although not in a romantic sense, she loved and respected him already. Little Feather was family to Ben and Chenoa. It gave a new twist to the expression, "Marriage made in heaven" if what Chenoa said was true, and her deceased sister was endorsing the idea. Little Feather fell asleep that night thinking about it, or as her English teacher on the reservation might have expressed it, "Pondering the possibilities." In fact, she dreamed about it.

It was in the early hours of the morning, after Little Feather had slept soundly for a few hours. Her mind began the sleep process of sorting out her unconscious thoughts when she dreamed she was sitting on a rock in a high mountain meadow, about to start eating a picnic lunch. She dreamed she heard a noise, looked up, and saw her sister riding toward her on a beautiful white horse. When her sister reached the rock where Little Feather was sitting, she asked what was in the basket? Little Feather removed the items one at a time from the basket to show her sister the special items she had prepared for herself.

Looks very nice commented her sister, but try what God has prepared for you. Abby handed her the basket she had brought for Little Feather on the white horse. Abby had ridden away with Little Feather's basket of food. Little Feather suddenly realized how very hungry she was. She started eating from her sister's basket. Never had she tasted such wonderful food. When Little Feather finished everything in the basket, she awoke. The words kept repeating in her mind, "try what God has prepared for you." It had been very delicious. Much better than what she had prepared for herself.

Chapter 9—Selling Horses

Ben was proud of the young gelding he had picked out to show the physician, Dr. Dean, and his horse-crazy daughter, Susie. She didn't want the usual older well broken horse. Susie wanted a young horse whom she could break herself. She had already experienced riding horses others had trained. She was a good rider and a veteran of the gentrified equestrian horse-show circuit. It was getting boring. What she wanted now was something more challenging, more exotic.

When Susie overheard some folks at a horseshow talking about a Shoshone Indian who raised the best Appaloosa horses available on a ranch near Jarbidge, she was hooked. She immediately started thinking about the possibilities.

Susie had long aspired to competing for the title of rodeo queen at the county fair. What greater strategy for separating herself from the other competitors than to be the girl who rode and had trained a beautiful Appaloosa. She envisioned adding some Indian accent to her attire, giving her horse a Native American name, and adding a few other touches to compliment the theme, she hadn't thought of, yet. When Susie told her father, he was sympathetic to the idea. Actually, he had heard of Ben Walker, and knew him, at least by reputation.

Susie was not an impetuous girl. She tended to be quite the opposite, very calculating. But in this case, she wanted to move ahead as soon as possible. Ben was not an easy man to get hold of, after all, he lived off the grid. But Orrie LaVal was. He or his ranch became the de facto answering service for Ben. It was Little Feather who usually

ended up taking and delivering messages to Ben. She had taken the call from Dr. Dean and arranged the appointment with Ben.

Susie was pleased with what she saw. Little Boy, Chenoa had given him the temporary name, was anything but little. He was, in fact, one of the biggest horses to come from Ben's herd in years. Ben had considered keeping him, but he needed the revenue.

Susie watched carefully as Ben showed her Little Boy. She had watched so many professionals do their job at horseshows, Susie immediately recognized a winner.

"Oh, Dad, he's perfect!" gushed Susie.

"I can see you are a far better judge of horses than a negotiator," kidded her father. "Can't you think of at least one imperfection to justify lowering the price?"

"Oh, sorry, Dad!" said Susie apologetically. "I'll keep quiet. But we have got to buy him. Riding him, I'm sure to win the Queen's contest!"

'Well, Mr. Walker, you heard her. There is no use beating around the bush. I am sure Little Boy will not leave here for a little price, so I will write you a check and sign it. Then, I will let you fill in the amount you think is right. I've heard you are a fair man, and I have no doubt you are."

"Thank you, Doctor. You don't know just how much wampum that complement just saved you. In exchange, I'd like to ask for just one favor: a picture with Susie when she wins."

"Deal!" cried out Susie in unison with her dad.

They were about to load Little Boy into Dr. Dean's Sooner brand four-horse trailer with living quarters in front when Susie gasped, pointed to the rim rock, and in awe asked, "Who is that?"

Ben answered quietly, but proudly, "My daughter and Sky Walker, Little Boy's sire!"

"Holy Cow, Mr. Walker, is he for sale?" asked Susie.

"No, Susie, I am afraid not. He is the one horse on this ranch who is not for sale at any price!"

When Chenoa descended from the rim rock, she rode up to Ben and his customers and dismounted. Dr. Dean's jaw was still hanging slack when Ben started his introduction.

"Chenoa, I'd like you to meet Dr. Dean and his horse-savvy daughter, Susie. Dr. Dean, Susie, I want you to meet my daughter, Chenoa, and

our herd sire, Sky Walker. Chenoa, we have just concluded a deal for Little Boy. Susie will undoubtedly ride him to success in a coming rodeo Queen's contest. Do you think they made a good choice?" asked Ben.

"Hi, Susie. It's so nice to meet you! Yes, I think Little Boy is an excellent choice. He has such a sweet personality and gentle disposition. I taught him to lead with no trouble at all," noted Chenoa. "Do you have any questions for me?"

"It is really nice to meet you, too," offered Susie. Her dad said nothing. He was staring, utterly speechless. Susie continued," Chenoa, I've noticed Little Boy seems nervous around us. I am not surprised since we are complete strangers, so I was wondering if you might be willing to introduce us? It would hopefully ease his anxiety."

"What a great idea!" replied Chenoa. "Let's do it right now." Chenoa took Little Boy's halter rope from Ben and handed him Sky Walker's reins.

Ben started leading Sky Walker to the barn. Chenoa invited Susie to start working with Little Boy by first petting his head. Susie let him smell her hand, then used that hand to stroke his nose, forehead, and behind his ears. Next she petted his neck and front quarters.

Little Boy was a bit nervous at first, even with Chenoa present. He gradually relaxed and let Susie pick up his left front hoof, then his right. Susie led her new friend around the yard and into the barn.

Ben handed Susie a small container of oats. It was as if Ben had handed Susie the key to Little Boy's heart. He quickly finished the treat, then pushed at Susie with his nose as if to say, "Ok, now that we are buddies, let's have some more."

This time, Chenoa handed Susie a few more handfuls of oats. When Little Boy finished the oats, Ben suggested the girls take him for a walk. When everyone nodded in agreement, Susie took her new horse by the lead rope, and followed Chenoa down the road to the creek. Susie was satisfied things could not be working out any better.

As they strolled along, Susie and Chenoa engaged in some casual girl talk, while Ben and Dr. Dean, who had only recently recovered his senses, ventured to discuss more pressing matters.

Ben commented, "I see your trailer is equipped with a camper. Since you have a long drive to get home, and it would be dark before you get there, would you care to stay over. Chenoa doesn't often get to

visit with other girls, and Susie seems like a real fine one. Got some fresh beef from my neighbor yesterday. I could cook us up some fine steaks, if you care to stay and spend the night."

"Ben, I would consider it an honor. Don't get out of the office as often as I would like, anymore. Perhaps you could tell me more about raising Appaloosas. I have to say, I don't know if I have ever seen a more impressive horse than your stallion. Confidentially, with your daughter riding him, I am still in awe. That was a vision I shall not soon forget; what a pair! I have been to most every horseshow within two hundred miles since Susie started competing. Never seen anything to compare with them," concluded Dr. Dean.

"If you think Chenoa is pretty, You should have met her mother. She set the hook in this old boy in one evening. Lost her in a botched surgery on the Duck Creek Reservation. Not one of the prouder moments for your profession, but I recognize, paraphrasing Forest Gump, crap happens!" said Ben resignedly.

"Forest Gump?" questioned Dr. Dean. "How do you know about him?"

"Videos," admitted Ben. "They stock quite a few at the Diamond Bar Ranch. We have a small DVD player and generator. When my sister-in-law finds a good one, she loans it to us."

"Yeah, the Public Health service isn't able to attract the best, nor the brightest, many times," admitted Dr. Dean.

By the time Chenoa and Susie returned, Ben and the Doc had the charcoal grill fired up and four steaks ready to go. Dr. Dean announced to Susie he had accepted an invitation to spend the night.

"Oh, that's wonderful", exclaimed Chenoa. "Maybe we can find time to ride over, and I will introduce you to my aunt Little Feather. She is so nice. You will really like her."

"I am game", agreed Susie. "I've got nothing going on tomorrow that won't wait."

"How does everyone want their steak cooked?" asked Ben. Everyone chose medium rare, so Ben didn't have the problem of keeping track of which was which.

Since it was too early in the season to have any food from their garden, Ben served up some canned vegetables to go with their meat and baked potatoes.

When they were finished, Dr. Dean leaned back in his chair, rubbed his tummy, and commented, "Maybe it is the altitude, but I can't remember having a more delicious steak. Thank you very much, and may I extend my compliments to the chef?"

"Pasture raised is the best beef in my opinion. In any case, you are very welcome. Buy a horse and get a free steak!" joked Ben.

"What do I get if I buy two?" kidded the Doc.

"Besides a second horse, I'm not sure," said Ben philosophically. "Have anything in particular in mind?"

"I bet I know what he would like," popped up Susie. "But if my mom heard him say it, there would be two new gelding at our place."

After that comment, Ben changed the subject.

"Doc, if you would like, since we cooked, we could let the girls clean up while you and I could fill out the application to get Little Boy registered," suggested Ben.

"Splendid idea!" agreed Dr. Dean. "Do you girls mind?"

"Not at all, any day you are willing to buy me a horse, I'm willing to do a few dishes," asserted Susie with a smile from ear to ear. "It is a cheaper price than you just paid."

"Don't remind me," cautioned her dad, jokingly, "or your next acquisition might be a long-in-the-tooth Welch pony."

"Not a chance, dad," rebutted Susie. "Admit it, you love me too much! You would never want your daughter to be seen in public on some old nag."

"I guess you know my weakness," confessed the Doc.

"I am just Daddy's Little Girl. I love and appreciate you, and every little thing you do for me; and that is a fact, Jack!" concluded Susie switching from a swooning to a commanding voice.

The doctor and Ben filled out the paperwork while the girls cleaned the whole kitchen. By the time the application was completed, Ben's kitchen was cleaner than it had been in a very long time. Chenoa was almost sad to finish the job, it was so enjoyable to have another girl with whom to work.

Susie and Chenoa left the house and began talking about Susie's experience going to horseshows. Chenoa had never been to one. They drifted toward the barn.

"Oh, you ought to go!" opined Susie. "You and Sky Walker would be unbeatable. No one has a horse as awesome as he is, and as beautiful as you are, you two would be the stars of the show."

"I don't know anything about horse shows," confessed Chenoa. We just raise horses and sell them. We are pretty simple folks and live a simple life."

"Chenoa, do you think I could have a look at Sky Walker? Is he a hard horse to ride?" asked Susie as she was already heading for his stall.

"I don't mind," said Chenoa, "but just remember, he is a stallion. They can be temperamental."

"Has he ever thrown you?" asked Susie, curious to know.

"Fortunately, no," asserted Chenoa. "He and I have sort of a special bond. If you can believe it, he is actually quite protective of me. My dad says he is more like my dog, than my horse. He has a very keen sense of our surroundings. He lets me know when he senses danger. He isn't like any other horse I have ever ridden. He is pretty amazing, for sure!"

Susie grabbed a handful of oats as she passed by the grain bin. She knew if anything could help a person get in the good graces of a strange horse, it was oats. The strategy worked.

Maybe it was because Chenoa was accompanying her, but Sky Walker accepted Susie and her oats like they were old friends. He let Susie pet him all over. After about 10 minutes, Susie asked Chenoa for permission to get on Sky Walker and ride him bare back around the paddock. It was an experience Susie would not soon forget.

As they left the barn, Susie expressed the hope that Little Boy would grow up to be half the horse his father was. If he did, she had no doubt she could earn her rodeo crown.

"Thanks, Chenoa! That was special. I really appreciate your kindness. Now let's go back in the house so my dad can stare at you some more," said Susie.

"Don't you think that is a pretty disrespectful thing to say about your father," asked Chenoa.

"It's true!" asserted Susie. "He is a man. You are undoubtedly the most naturally beautiful woman he may have ever seen and for sure in these mountains. Didn't you see how he stared at you? After a while, I worried I might have to take him in to get his jaw wired shut. For that matter, you should be glad I am not a lesbian!"

"A lesbian?" repeated Chenoa. "What is that?

"You don't know what a lesbian is?" asked Susie in surprise. "Girl, you have lived a sheltered life. Has your beauty ever proved to be a problem for you? I mean have men ever done more than just stare at you?

"No. My father taught me how to avoid white men. Indians are no problem. They all know my father would feed them to the buzzards if they harmed me."

"What a different world a few miles makes," mused Susie.

After breakfast the next morning, Susie and Chenoa decided to get Little Boy out, and work with him awhile. Another handful of oats worked its magic, and Susie was soon leading him around easily. He stood calmly as Susie used a currycomb to give him a thorough brushing.

Chenoa lent a saddle blanket to Susie with which she rubbed Little Boy down after he had been curried. The object was to get him used to the smell and feel of the blanket. Then it would only be a small step to put a saddle on him. Add some weight to the saddle to simulate a rider, lead him around for a few days till he accepts that, and you are ready for a rider.

It is a gentle way to break a horse. The alternative is the hard way; climb on and try to stay on. If you don't bounce well, the gentle approach has a lot to recommend it.

Chenoa saddled up Tumble Weed for Susie to make the ride over to the Diamond Bar ranch. Little Feather was surprised to see Chenoa riding Sky Walker into the yard with a strange girl on Tumble Weed.

Little Feather was excited to welcome another girl to the ranch; it was something she didn't often get to do. She lived in a world dominated by men. Chenoa was about the only girl she usually got to see.

Little Feather had just finished baking a couple of cherry pies for the crew. Susie and Chenoa accepted Little Feather's offer of a small piece of fresh pie with a glass of milk.

Little Feather wore just enough accent to her clothing customarily to suggest her Shoshone heritage. She had done this for so long, it was

where Chenoa had picked up the practice. This practice did not escape Susie's notice.

Thinking ahead to her intention of adopting an Indian motif for her costume when she ran for rodeo queen, Susie asked Little Feather if she might be willing to help her achieve a degree of authenticity when the time came. Chenoa thought it was a wonderful idea, and encouraged Little Feather to commit to the project.

After the last of the snack had been eaten, Little Feather offered to show Susie around the place. The Diamond Bar had a fine barn, a good set of corrals, and a shop equipped well enough to make most any needed repair. It had a comfortable bunk house, too, but out of respect for the privacy of the ranch hands, it was off limits to visitors.

Susie was fascinated by the rustic authenticity of the Diamond Bar ranch. Out of nowhere came the unbidden thought, what a great place for a wedding. Perhaps a little too far out of the way for a reception, but Orrie's flower garden was beautiful; no set up, no clean up, just show up! The girls sat and chatted under the big shade tree for most of an hour.

Sensing they would soon need to get going, Susie ask if she could show herself around a bit more to fix everything in her memory. Permission granted, she left Little Feather and Chenoa talking in the garden and retraced their path from the first perusal of the Orrie's ranch headquarters.

"Do you like her?" asked Chenoa. "Isn't she a sweet?"

"She is very charming," agreed Little Feather. "Too bad she doesn't live closer. I'm sure you two could be great friends. You could coach her in breaking and training Little Boy."

"I don't know," said Chenoa. "She is pretty set on the idea of doing it all herself. Now that we are alone, Little Feather, tell me what you think about what we discussed the other day."

"I have to admit, I was shocked," admitted Little Feather. "What a bombshell of a revelation! You aren't recanting anything you told me, are you?"

"Oh, no, never!" swore Chenoa. "I would swear it on my mother's grave!"

"That's good!" said Little Feather. "You know I love you and your father with all my heart. Your mother, my sister, and I had a great relationship, too. But because we were such good sisters, I would never want to do anything to hurt you! I can honestly say that I have never had any romantic interest in Ben. I respect him, I have always thought he was one of the finest men I have ever known. But in my mind, I have always thought of him only as my brother-in-law. Nothing more, ever.

I would never have any more thought of starting a romantic relationship with your father than my father. I have always simply thought to do so would be to cheat on my sister, like adultery. I have struggled with what you told me ever since you left."

"Oh, I am sorry. What we want is for you and my dad to be happy, together; happier than either of you could be alone. The Bible teaches, 'Neither is the man without the woman; neither the woman without the man, in the Lord.' You are both widowed. Why should either of you be denied the love of a spouse for the rest of your lives? It's just not right, it's not fair, it's not necessary, it's not what mom and I want for you. We don't believe it's what God wants for you, either." pleaded Chenoa.

"Who would have thought my own deceased sister would be my matchmaker?" mused Little Feather. "Have you talked to your dad about this? What has he had to say about it?"

"I have not discussed it with him yet. I didn't want to talk to him before I talked to you. Susie and Dr. Dean were there looking to buy Little Boy when I got back. I promised Dad I would tell him about Mom's appearing to me later," reported Chenoa. "I have no idea what he is going to think."

"If I know Ben," speculated Little Feather, "He will be just as blown away as I was. He was devoted to your mom; since then he has been devoted to you. He has never had trouble keeping his marriage vows, whether his wife was living or dead."

"I will let you know what he says," offered Chenoa.

"I just want you to know I am at peace with the idea. If your mom approves or is promoting the idea, I am sure I could be happy giving myself heart and soul to Ben and sharing his life till death do us part and I am reunited with John, my sweetheart, and husband of my youth," said Little Feather quietly.

"Thank you, Little Feather; I am sure my mom was hoping you would feel this way. Ponder all this in your heart for now. I will tell you when the time feels right," confided Chenoa.

Susie returned from her walk, convinced she would be back again. She and Chenoa bid farewell to Little Feather, mounted their horses, and rode back home at a fast trot.

When they arrived, Ben had helped Dr. Dean load Little Boy in the horse trailer for immediate departure. The Deans pulled away amid well wishes and promises of future correspondence.

Chenoa put Sky Walker and Tumble Weed up while Ben started lunch. In a few minutes they were able to sit down together to eat. Ben commented on his morning with Dr. Dean and asked how things went with Susie and Little Feather.

"We had a wonderful time," said Chenoa. "It feels as though Susie and I have been friends forever. She and Little Feather were immediate friends, too."

As Chenoa helped her dad clean up after their lunch, Ben quietly commented to her, "Ok, Honey, time to set down and tell me what really happened the other night with your mom."

CHAPTER 10—SOLO

It had been an unusually hot day in Southern Idaho, especially for June in the Jarbidge Mountains. Jake had thrown his back out jumping down from a hay wagon the morning he and Jerry were supposed to ride North Fork. Jerry asked Uncle Glenn if it would be ok for him to make the trip by himself. Jerry had made the trip with Jake enough times to know the routine. Uncle Glenn thought it over for a few minutes, then decided to take a chance.

"Ok, Jerry, but be careful; don't take any unnecessary chances, " instructed Glenn. "Try to make it back by dark, around 9:00. You'll need to be heading back by no later than 8:15. Any questions?

"I got it, Uncle Glenn, no problem. You can count on me!" assured Jerry. With that, Jerry loaded up Fleet and began his first solo trip to check the cattle grazing on North Fork. He was confident he was up to the task. He had made the trip with Jake at least once a week since the first week of May. They had never encountered any serious problem.

Old George had prepared a sack lunch for Jerry with an apple, a PayDay candy bar, and a couple of sandwiches. Jerry had his mouth watering for some cherry pie a' la mode. He hadn't had any for awhile, and his appetite would no longer be denied. He stopped off at the popular road side diner on his way through Rogerson.

A cute young waitress whose name tag read "Kim" took his order. She soon placed his pie in front of him. Lacking any other customers at the moment to worry about, she engaged Jerry in the inane banter typical of waitresses most every where. Jerry happened to see a notice on the wall announcing a reward for the first picture anyone could submit of the "Flower of China Mountain." Jerry had not been paying attention to what Kim was saying. Upon seeing the notice, though, Jerry interrupted Kim to ask about it.

"Its about a girl who lives up in the hills. People say she is really pretty. Mostly rumor, though, not too many people have ever seen her. The reward for a picture keeps going up. Oscar, the owner here, says he doesn't think he will ever have to pay off. Other folks just plain think she is a myth; our own urban legend, except, as you can see, there's nothing much urban about these parts. I see you gotta horse with you. Going up in the mountains? You are welcome to try your luck if you have a camera. You'll probably need a telephoto lens, though, because they who have tried, say it is not safe to get too close. Oscar, though, says his offer is good dead or alive. Says he will even make good on the reward posthumously, if you get a good picture, or for that matter, any picture. No one has yet submitted a thing," said Kim as her babbling finally concluded.

"You don't say?" said Jerry as he slipped Kim a ten to pay his bill.

Back on the road, Jerry left Route 93, crossed the Salmon Falls dam and climbed China Mountain to North Fork. He found and backed up to a mound of dirt to unload Fleet.

Jerry had in mind making the circuit of the pasture as he had done several times previously with Jake. He had considered bringing Thunder along for the company, and to get the cattle out of the trees and willows so he could check them. He hadn't, so now he had to make do without the dog. It took longer to get the job done, but soon enough he was heading back to the truck.

Jerry still wondered about the girl. In the previous visits back to North Fork since the cattle drive, he had yet to catch any glimpse of her. Jerry decided to take a look around. He started riding west from his truck. He was awed by the fascinating terrain. He rode on and on, not paying attention to the time or the weather.

The warmth of the weather had set in motion convection currents which in turn caused the development of a localized thunderstorm. By the time Jerry noticed he was about to be hit by a real nasty squall, he looked in vain for a place to take shelter. A sudden bolt of lightning hit so close to Jerry, his hair stood straight. Fleet was so startled, he lurched right out from under Jerry. Jerry fell to the ground, striking his head on a rock. The blow knocked him unconscious.

The rain started moments later. Soon Jerry was totally soaked, but the water didn't rouse him. Fleet stood at Jerry's side offering him some relief from the pounding wind and rain, but it was very little help. How long he had been there before a passing rider noticed his riderless horse, and found him was hard to say.

Helping the stranger went against her father's training, but some inner feeling prodded her on. They were miles from civilization. The only place she had hope of getting this stranger shelter was to some-how get him to her camp at Clark's Crossing.

But how? This fellow was a big one. She tried to rouse him. He was definitely knocked senseless. Not seeing another option, she tied his hands together with her rope, ran the rope over his saddle, and tied it to her saddle horn. She had Sky Walker step forward to tighten the rope. As her horse pulled, she lifted the unconscious stranger as best she could. He was soon lying across his own horse. She tied him to his saddle, and they were off to her camp.

It took two hours to get there. Chenoa left the stranger lying across his saddle while she built a fire in the camp stove. She didn't think there was anyway to get this unconscious man into the camp other than doing some sort of fireman's carry. She decided to lighten the load. She stripped off his boots and wet clothes, parked his horse in front of the camp door, then maneuvered him over her shoulder.

Chenoa was no weakling, but 200 pounds was no easy burden to carry up the steps of the camp entrance to throw him into bed. As the fire in the stove warmed the inside of the camp, Chenoa unsaddled the horses, watered them at the nearby spring, and fed them some oats and hay. She placed the saddles under a tarp, and brought extra firewood in side. She filled a pail with fresh water, and brought a pot of water to a boil. The camp was soon so warm Chenoa had to open the front door a bit to keep the place from overheating.

Chenoa was no stranger to wilderness first aide medicine. She retrieved her first aide kit from the camp storage locker, and went to work on the stranger. She cleaned his head wound, applied some io-dine, then a bandage.

Chenoa tried again to wake the man. He was still out cold. She stripped him of the rest of his wet clothing, and hung everything up to dry. Darkness was setting in, so Chenoa added fuel to the Coleman lantern, and lit it. She opened a can of soup, and savored it as it coursed down her throat.

As complete darkness settled in on the camp, Chenoa could hear the night sounds over the hiss of the lantern and crackling of the wood burning in the camp stove. It was such a contrast to the violent weather of the afternoon. She was always ready for foul weather, but even she had been surprised by the furry of this afternoon's storm. It was only by chance she had seen the horse with no rider. Sky Walker was the one who first took notice, and started going in their direction.

She was so far away, at first she had only noticed the horse, but not the saddle. As they drew closer, Chenoa could see the saddle, then some one lying on the ground. She fought the urges to both help and to flee. As frightened as she was, something inside her would not allow her to leave the seen; she was moved by some compelling impulse to help.

Now she had some near naked, unconscious stranger in her bed, and she was sitting, watching his clothes dry, listening to crickets, and eating soup. This was not what she had planned for the day. She had intended to drop in and spend the night with Little Feather. They had things they needed to talk about.

But for some reason Chenoa was happy. Her fears were gone. She had a feeling of calm. Her mind was as peaceful as was the evening.

Who was this stranger? Why was she helping him instead of leaving him to his fate? Chenoa didn't understand her feelings; she didn't understand what was going on.

Chenoa's clothes were wet, too. She closed the camp door to conserve heat, banked the stove fire, and hung her wet clothes up to dry. She wasn't about to climb into bed with this stranger, so she lay on top of the covers, pulled a blanket over her, and fell asleep, wondering why she felt the way she did.

It was midnight when Uncle Glenn rang Jake and told him Jerry had not returned.

"Gee boss, he knows how to take care of himself. He knows about the sheep camp for emergency shelter. He has food and water there if

that is where he is. We don't stand much chance of finding him in the dark if he is not there. I suggest we wait for daylight. If he is not back by then, I will take a few men and go look for him. That work for you?" asked Jake.

Glenn was worried. He didn't like Jake's plan but couldn't think of a better one. "Ok, Jake, but I want to be one of those who go with you, ok?"

"Sure thing, boss; want me to line up Doc Watson and his hounds in case we have to try to track him? Good contingency plan, Jake, see if you can make the arrangement!" With that, Glenn went back to bed but slept poorly.

Chenoa got up a couple of times during the night to stoke the fire in the stove. The last time, near the break of day, Chenoa heard moaning as she climbed back in bed. She froze. What a predicament. She wasn't naked, but he was. Well, almost. She had some clothes on, but not many. She had assumed he was out and would stay that way.

"Dumb, dumb, dumb!" thought Chenoa. She lay quietly, hoping without hope her rescued guest would not wake up before she was ready for him to do so. No such luck! Much to her chagrin, Chenoa next heard, "Where am I?" Well, thought Chenoa, as she had often heard Karl, Orrie LaVal's resident cynic, say, "No good deed goes unpunished." The next was, "Where in the heck are my clothes?" The next thing was even more embarrassing, "Who are you? Did you take my clothes?"

Ben had always counseled, "When you gotta problem, meet it head on."

"I am Chenoa, and yes, I took your clothes. They were wet. They needed to dry. They are hanging over there. Please put them on and get out of my camp so I can get up and get dressed," commanded Chenoa from under her blanket. Jerry's head was starting to clear enough to appreciate the uniqueness of the situation. I see some other clothes that aren't mine. Are you naked, too?"

"No, heavens, no!" exclaimed an obviously embarrassed voice. "Please put your clothes on and scram."

"Do I get to come back for breakfast?" teased Jerry.

"If you don't hurry, you can come back for another knot on your head," threatened Chenoa.

"Alright, alright, I'm just savoring the moment. You sure we couldn't just talk for a while. It is not every day a guy wakes up naked and in bed with a beautiful girl. You are beautiful, I hope? It would spoil the whole story if I had to go back and tell the guys I was in bed with an ugly girl. I will be so disappointed if you are plain." teased Jerry again.

"You aren't going to go back and tell anybody anything, or I'll cut your tongue out, myself," roared Chenoa more mad at herself than him. "And, no! We aren't going to lie here and chat. I have made geldings out of stallions many times. So get out of here before you tempt me to use my skills on you.

"Okay, okay, I am going to get dressed. Don't peeeek!" said Jerry stretching out the word.

"I should have left you out there for the buzzards," exclaimed Chenoa, kicking herself again for getting into this embarrassing predicament.

When Chenoa had finished dressing, she opened the camp door and invited the stranger back in. By then, her anger and embarrassment had cooled, and she was starting to see the humor in the situation.

"My goodness, you are beautiful!" a stunned Jerry exclaimed. "What did you say your name is? Athena? Helena of Troy?"

"My name is Chenoa. It means white dove or peace in Shoshone, my ancestor's language. I only know a few words, unfortunately."

"Chenoa," repeated Jerry. "It's a pretty name. I am Jerry. I don't know what it means; probably man who falls off his horse." They both laughed. Jerry noticed the sparkle in her eyes, perfect smile, and flawless beauty.

"I remember a sudden storm, but how did I get here?" inquired Jerry. "My Uncle has a sheep camp like this at North Fork on China Mountain, but it isn't equipped with anything like you."

Chenoa ignored the obvious compliment and responded, "I found you unconscious, lying by your horse about two hours from here, on Peter's Ridge. I wasn't there, so I can't tell you what happened before you fell off your horse and hit your head. I found you, I loaded you up and brought you here."

"And put me to bed?" added Jerry.

"I can assure you, your care was all very professional," asserted Chenoa. "No hanky-panky."

81

"I am sure I couldn't have been safer in my own mother's arms," affirmed Jerry. "But you can't blame me for fantasizing."

"Don't count on it," warned Chenoa. "I wouldn't want to have to shoot you after all the trouble I went to save you. So don't let your thoughts get you in trouble."

"I am a fairly heavy guy. How were you able to get me here and into bed?" asked Jerry.

"Trade secret," declared Chenoa. "I am afraid I can't tell you."

"Oh!" said Jerry. "Could you give me a hint?"

"No. Not a chance," parried Chenoa.

"Ow!" exclaimed Jerry in response to a sudden pang of pain from his head wound. "You don't have any Ibuprofen or other pain medicine, do you?"

"I think so. Let me look," said Chenoa sympathetically. Then, under her breath, she continued teasingly, "Whimp!"

"Heh, I heard that," said Jerry. "Thanks a bunch. So much for empathy, sympathy, and professionalism."

"It's not my full-time job unless you are a spotted horse," said Chenoa. "Here, let me look at that dressing."

"I have had at least a few dates think I was a 'stud,' claimed Jerry. "Does that count?" Jerry took a seat where Chenoa indicated.

"No, only if you are spotted," replied Chenoa, moving closer to look at Jerry's head in the cramped quarters. "I think this bandage ought to be changed."

"A spotted stud, huh," said Jerry. "I was spotted once; had the measles."

"Not big enough," said Chenoa

"I trust you are talking about the spots, and not, well…." said Jerry.

"Well, what?" asked Chenoa abruptly.

"Well, you are the one who put the words 'stud' and 'big enough' in the same conversation," argued Jerry.

"Watch your mouth," Chenoa demanded, stepping back and not too gently slapping his face. "Show some respect, or this filly will kick your teeth out."

"Sorry, just testing to see where the limits are. It's a male thing. You ought to know; you are the one who rides a stallion," Jerry said, excusing himself for his suggestive banter.

"My father says a man who respects a girl will set his own limits. The more he values and respects her, the higher he will set his standards. I know what kind of girl I am. What kind of man are you?" questioned Chenoa.

"Whoa! Wait a minute," said Jerry. "Tell me. Just what kind of girl strips off the clothes of a perfect stranger and then climbs into bed with him? Is that how nice girls around here make a new guy in the neighborhood feel welcome? Ouch!" cried Jerry as Chenoa purposely ripped off some bandage that took a chunk of hair with it.

"Oh! Really! Are you studying to be a lawyer? Who but a lawyer would be a big enough jerk to take an innocent set of facts and twist them into something vulgar? I saved your life by getting you onto your horse and hauling your ungrateful carcass back here. I cared for you all night. Then you have the gall to impugn my virtue, my character! I repeat, what kind of man does that?" asked Chenoa disgustedly.

Not realizing what his words would mean to Chenoa, Jerry humbly answered, "I am the man of your dreams; lightning doesn't have to strike me twice to know you are special. Please forgive me. I was just teasing. Thank you. I owe you my life; a debt I am willing to pay in full. Do you want cash, or will you accept credit?"

Chenoa had tears in her eyes as she compared Jerry's words to her mother's parting instructions. Both laughing and crying at the same time she quipped, "First, I will have to check your credit!"

"No problem. Could I please get a receipt?" asked Jerry.

Chenoa finished applying the new dressing, kissed her fingers, then used those fingers to pat his ouwee. "There, if that doesn't take away the pain and make you feel better, I am afraid your condition will require your mother to kiss it better." opined Chenoa.

"It is feeling better already," reported Jerry. "You mentioned breakfast."

"Yes, what would you like? You can ask for anything. I probably won't have it, but you can ask," joked Chenoa.

"What are the possibilities?" asked Jerry.

"I always carry bacon with me; it travels well. Can't say the same for eggs. I don't have the patience to pick the shells out of them when they get pre-scrambled riding through thick brush. I have butter, honey, flour, and Crisco; I could make some scones for us. I have syrup and pancake mix. Would you like pancakes or waffles? We have assorted canned fruit. Oh, and I do have eggs, but they are powdered. They are not bad, but they weren't laid anytime recently."

"Well, that is certainly more options than 'Coffee, tea, or me!'" quipped Jerry.

'Me' is not on the menu," said Chenoa with a smile. "But that reminds me; coffee, tea, or hot coco are possibilities.

"My parents were right," acknowledged Jerry. They always told me, "Son, 'Ya can't have everything."

"Well, what can I fix for you?" asked Chenoa, picking up a pen and piece of paper, standing with one hip cocked, and trying to imitate a waitress.

"I'll have to fall off my horse again sometime and see if 'Me' gets added to the menu by then," quipped Jerry. "For now, bacon, eggs, and scones ought to give me enough energy to make it back home."

"Careful there, fella," warned Chenoa. "I would hate to have to use the rolling pin on you, as well as the dough; it does a quick job of adjusting a guy's attitude."

All kidding aside, strong feelings were welling up with in Chenoa. She wanted to be on the 'Me' on Jerry's menu. She couldn't explain it; she didn't understand it. Here was a man, a white man no less. Hadn't she been taught to run from them, not to trust them, to hide from them? Yes, she had saved him from dying a lonely death on Peter's Ridge from an act of God. But how and why did she have such inappropriate feelings? How could she go against her father's warnings? As Chenoa cooked breakfast, she was wondering about these and other questions.

A thought finally settled in her mind like a spinning coin coming to rest. Maybe it was an act of God. Her mother said to be patient; someone was there for me. We would find each other. Now, here she was with Jerry.

A collection of quotes at the Diamond Bar ranch asserted, "God gives every bird its food, but He doesn't throw it in the nest."

Did the same apply to lovers or husbands? God had stopped this man in his tracks. Was it so she could throw him in her nest?"

Jerry was also wondering about this twist of fate, too. He had been thinking about trying to find the mystery girl, and she had found him. How amazing was that? Who would believe him if he went home and

told anyone why he had not returned as scheduled, that he had spent the night, albeit unconscious, in little more than his birthday suit inches away from the most naturally beautiful girl he had ever seen? No wonder there was a reward for a picture of her. Hardly anyone else had gotten to see her, yet he got to sleep with her. That would stretch credulity to the breaking point.

Jerry had met many pretty girls. Most tended to be stuck on themselves. Chenoa was different in so many ways. For starters, she had saved him. She was cooking him breakfast. She was the one who rode a Stallion. She was the one who had the values of an earlier era. Girls at college, more often than not, behaved more like the mares Sky Walker serviced. They had a moral code little better, if at all, than of a street walker.

Jerry found himself recognizing his feelings for Chenoa were different than anything he had felt for any other girl. The thought suddenly came to him, 'Flower of China Mountain' was the most appropriate nickname he could imagine for Chenoa. She was very beautiful; would take a blind person to miss that. She was rare; he had seen a lot of the world, but never before anyone as drop dead gorgeous as she was, even without make-up. She was a flower in another way, too; she definitely was protected by thorns. One wrong move and you were apt to bleed.

Jerry suddenly felt very protective of Chenoa. No-one was going to have to believe him. He wasn't going to tell them. She was his to think about. His memory of her was somehow too sacred to share with others.

He had come to China Mountain to find her; instead she had found him. Fate or something appeared to be guiding events.

Chenoa and Jerry didn't say much as they ate breakfast together. Both recognized feelings stirring deep within. Both recognized things were moving fast. Both felt the impression it was ok; if it is right, it is right. But were things moving too fast? What they were thinking; what they were both wanting was wrong. Maybe not by the standard of the world, but definitely by their standards.

Chenoa was the most beautiful girl he had ever seen, hands down. If her father was right, Jerry could not damage their possible relationship by disrespecting her. If he stayed here with her much longer, he did not know where youthful passion might lead or where it would stop. He would never forgive himself if he turned Chenoa, the Flower of China Mountain, into a cheap conquest.

"Thanks for breakfast, Chenoa. That was delicious! I have always heard some of the out-of-the-way places are the best. You have convinced me."

"You are most welcome, but please don't recommend us to anyone. Too many patrons, and there goes the neighborhood," kidded Chenoa.

"I understand," said Jerry in mock seriousness. "I was hoping you would at least allow me back."

"Certainly, kind Sir; you are welcome anytime we are open. As a guest you have been a knockout!" said Chenoa with a wink and a smile

"Very good. I couldn't live without hope," asserted Jerry as he ventured to take Chenoa's hand in his. "When can I see you again? My wound is bound to need further attention."

"I would hate to have your death on my conscience, so we ought not wait too long," said Chenoa in mock seriousness.

"I am sure you're right," agreed Jerry hoping for Chenoa to offer a suggestion when they might arrange a rendezvous.

"I think I can make it back here in four days," suggested Chenoa." Let 's say about noon. I'll fix us lunch; a guy has got to know if a girl can cook more than breakfast!"

"I'm sure I can be here then," agreed Jerry. "We will have the afternoon to get better acquainted, although you have a big head start on getting to know me."

"All in the line of duty; very professional," claimed Chenoa, a little embarrassed now, thinking about the last twelve hours.

"Chenoa, may I ask you one question before we go?" asked Jerry.

"What would that be?" asked Chenoa. "What are you so curious about that it won't keep for four days?"

"Other than I am so handsome, charming, and have other fine qualities of which no other girl has ever known, why me?" ask Jerry with sincere curiosity. "You have a reputation for being very shy, and reclusive to the point of being dangerous. So why is it different with me?"

"Let me think about that while we saddle up," said Chenoa. When the horses were ready to go, Chenoa walked up to Jerry and faced him directly.

"Well, do you have an answer for me?" ask Jerry.

"A fuller explanation is going to have to wait till we meet again." explained Chenoa. "But the short answer is because …." she paused, threw her arms around Jerry and planted by far the biggest, most passionate kiss on him of his lifetime. "…you are literally the man of my dream!" Chenoa turned, grabbed the saddle horn, vaulted effortlessly onto Sky Walker, and rode away.

Every circuit in Jerry's body seemed to have blown. It was almost as debilitating as had been the blow to his head yesterday. By the time he regained his senses, Chenoa was gone. Jerry had jokingly told Chenoa that he was the man of her dream. Apparently, it was true. How else could he explain her acceptance of him. He wasn't a novice at picking up girls at a social event, but Chenoa had never been known to give anyone the time of day.

His goal of meeting her had now been realized. She was undoubtedly the person he had seen at the conclusion of the cow drive. Mystery solved. Now what? The question played on his mind as he climbed on Fleet and rode north.

Jerry didn't exactly know where he was. Chenoa had reported he was two hours from where she had found him, probably south. Jerry reasoned he should ride north two hours to pick up his trail going west. The strategy worked well. It only took him a little over an hour to recognize where he had been caught in the storm. The rain had wiped out any tracks Fleet had made traveling west, but he recognized plenty of landmarks. The return trip to his vehicle at North Fork was also completed quickly. He made it before noon.

Jerry made sure to memorize all the landmarks he passed. What a tragedy it would be if he couldn't find his way back to Chenoa's camp at Clark's Crossing.

Jerry was surprised when he reached the ridge overlooking the entrance to North Fork to see a bunch of riders. They turned out to be the search party, organized in his honor. He should have anticipated it, after all he was supposed to have gotten home before dark yesterday. They had searched North Fork and were about to leave to go looking for him elsewhere, when he reached them.

Uncle Glenn was so relieved to see him, he didn't bother to get after him for not coming home on time. His tardiness returning home was partially explained when Jerry took off his hat revealing his bandaged head wound.

Everyone was all ears. Wild horses couldn't have pulled them away before Jerry divulged every detail of his misadventure. Almost every detail, that is. He wasn't a kiss and tell type. He edited his story to protect Chenoa's identity and roll in his rescue. No one would have believed him anyway.

Others had not even been able to get near her. Who was going to believe he had slept in her bed, albeit unconscious. Such salacious details would travel faster than a mid-August range fire in a high wind. He respected her too much to sully her reputation.

Besides, every cowboy in the county would be falling off their horse if they thought it would get them five minutes with Chenoa. He doubted he would ever get the North Fork assignment again, let alone in four days, if anyone knew the whole story. Jerry would keep quiet and ponder the details.

Aunt Martha took one look at Jerry, and insisted he be seen by the doctor. She drove him there herself. Dr. Kelly commented after seeing Jerry, how impressed he was with how well the wound had been treated. He wanted to know if Jerry had already been seen in an emergency room. Jerry answered evasively "You might say that Dr. Kelly, but not exactly. It was the best they had, though, up in the mountains."

Aunt Martha caught the obfuscation. Jerry knew she had, too. On the way home she made it clear that inquiring minds wanted to know more.

"Ok, Aunt Martha, I'll tell you. But please don't tell anyone but maybe Uncle Glenn. Not even Old George." Aunt Martha agreed.

"I saw her, Aunt Martha. I saw her!" said Jerry excitedly.

"Saw who, Jerry?" asked Aunt Martha. "Where did you see her?"

"The girl. The girl people have dubbed the Flower of China Mountain. Her name is Chenoa. She rides a big Appaloosa stallion and rides the Jarbidge Range keeping track of her father's Appaloosa horses.

When lightning struck, Fleet threw me off. My head hit a rock. You know all this. What I didn't tell anyone else, Chenoa is the one who found me!" whispered Jerry loudly. "I was unconscious. Somehow, she loaded me on my Fleet, and hauled me to a sheep camp; an emergency shelter like Uncle Glenn has for us on North Fork.

"How convenient," quipped Aunt Martha.

"She is as nice as she is pretty, Aunt Martha," attested Jerry. "She took care of me until I regained consciousness this morning."

"She was wonderful, Aunt Martha," claimed Jerry. "She made us a fire to warm the camp, dried our clothes, cooked breakfast, and dressed my head wound. She is the one who rendered the treatment Dr. Kelly was praising."

"Dried 'our' clothes?" asked Martha. "No wonder you left out this part of the story when you told the others!"

"Yah, I didn't want to give anyone the wrong impression," explained Jerry. "Besides, Aunt Martha, who would have believed me, anyway?"

"Let me get this straight, Jerry. You are saying the girl you thought you saw when the herd reached North Fork; the girl every cow hand, rancher, government agent, and curiosity seeker to visit the Jarbidge has been itching to catch a glimpse of is the girl who patched you up and provided other services we shall not mention for now?" asked Aunt Martha.

"Yes! That pretty well sums it up," declared Jerry. "A little hard to believe, wouldn't you agree?"

"A little, is putting it mildly," confirmed Aunt Martha. "If I didn't know you, I'd not believe it, either!"

"There is more, Aunt Martha," confided Jerry. "I agreed to meet her for lunch in four days. What do you think of that?"

Chapter 11—Rustlers

In the old days, the Bureau of Land Management, the BLM, had an emphasis on establishing grazing rights on government owned land; who got to graze where, and how much. A lot of under and over grazing occurred in the open range era. Livestock men who got individual allotments tended to think of their allotments as their land. At first this attitude was encouraged. The best way to promote the protection on the government land was to have those to whom it was allotted take responsibility, treat it as though they owned it, and take good care of it. As grazing rights issues were settled, another use of the public land came into focus; recreation.

When multiple use doctrines came into play, the BLM frequently had to make land use decisions which adversely affected grazing rights in favor of recreational uses of the land. Then environmental concerns became an issue, and grazing rights were further eroded. The result of this transition was the introduction of many non-local people to very remote areas. The Jarbidge Mountains are about as remote as an area can be. Over time, more and more outside traffic could be seen prowling the few roads into the area.

If prostitution is, as they say, the oldest profession, rustling may well be the second. In any case, rustling is a crime as old as is the owning of livestock. In the modern era, it has adopted newer technologies, but still comes down to a thief taking that which he wants from someone else to whom it rightly belongs through whatever means is available.

Old West movies frequently show gangs of rustlers stealing whole herds of cattle and driving them off. Circumstances have changed to where there are few opportunities for such large-scale theft. More common now are cases where small time crooks driving pickup trucks and pulling trailers, load a few head of livestock into the trailer, and can be gone in only a few minutes. They are hard to catch, and harder to track unless they are caught in the act.

Mike Jones was a low life with a love of horses. His favorite past time was hanging out at horse shows. He fancied himself a horse trader and would buy and sell horses when he had a chance. He was quick to notice when Dr. Dean and his daughter, Susie, appeared at a local horse show and took second place with a nice-looking Appaloosa gelding. People were very impressed. This was very good for a horse making his first appearance.

When Mike overheard a lot of chatter on the subject of Appaloosas, he started thinking there might be an opportunity to make a few bucks. He asked himself why not drive up into the hills, load up a trailer full of Ben Walker's Appaloosa horses, drive them to the Las Vegas National Horse Show, and sell them? Ben had lots of horses; he might not even notice if a few went missing.

When Chenoa left Jerry at the Clark Crossing camp, she intended to go home. She had things to discuss with her father. Her world was changing; fast. No longer was she plagued with the feeling something was missing. Everything felt like she was on a new course, the right course. It felt as when you leave home in the early morning before day light. It is still too dark to see well, but you know the general direction. You trust when the light of the new day dawns, you will be on the right trail.

Sky Walker had never taken her astray. She had faith her mother wouldn't either. All she had to do, she felt, was listen to and follow the whisperings of the Spirit as it spoke to her spirit. If it felt right in her heart, she wouldn't fear the darkness, nor wait for day light. Chenoa had questions, but she trusted they would be answered in time.

Chenoa navigated the vastness of the Jarbidge Range by knowing and referencing the prominent landmarks. If one knew and triangulated using those references, it was nearly impossible to get lost. Likewise, she was sure her happiness was assured by knowing with whom her future life would be coupled. She loved her dad, her childhood, Little Feather, and so many beautiful aspects of her past and current life, but it was time to graduate. The giant missing piece of her youth, her mother, had now been placed in her life's puzzle. Little Feather had been a good surrogate mother but had never really filled the void left by her real mother's death.

Chenoa had wanted to know her mother; now as a result of one night's dream, she felt she did. She had worried she would share the same fate as the beautiful cactus flower; here today, faded away tomorrow. Now she felt a new phase of life was about to blossom. She wanted to get home and confide in her father how she felt. Would he understand; she hoped so!

Chenoa's thoughts about life and her future came to an abrupt stop when she reached Gregg's Point. She saw a trailer being towed up Charlie's Creek toward Maggie's Campground. Maggie's was a popular place for weekend campers to set up. It had trees for shade, a creek for fishing, and a large meadow for playing softball or other games. Frisbee was very popular with small groups or those who had dogs who liked to run free and fetch.

What disturbed Chenoa were her observations which were inconsistent with normal campers. First off, it wasn't a weekend. Second, the truck wasn't pulling a camper, but rather a livestock trailer. There were possible reasons for these abnormalities, but she was, nevertheless, alerted to the possibility something was very wrong.

Chenoa reflexively pulled her rifle, and checked that it was fully loaded, and ready for action. She instinctively changed her plans from going home to guarding her horses.

Chenoa moved off the ridge line and out of sight. She surveyed the area to determine how many of her horses were in the area. Chenoa moved parallel to the road, but out of sight, to see if the truck did indeed stop, and set up at Maggie's campground. Not only did they stop there, but they also set up some mobile fence panels to form an enclosure, or trap with which animals could be forced into the trailer.

It also turned out the trailer was hauling two saddle horses. These folks might have come here to ride their horses, but that didn't explain the fencing. This was definitely looking like of some sort of nefarious operation.

Chenoa considered going for help, but she was too far away to get help before the suspects might load up and drive away. She rejected that option, and decided whatever she did, she was on her own. She would need to stay out of sight until their intentions were clear.

Chenoa turned Sky Walker toward Tommy's Butte. It was more than a mile away but offered a good view of the terrain for miles. From there she would be able to observe what these yahoos were doing. Being so far away would also lessen the chances the horses would give away her presence.

Chenoa did her best to hide Sky Walker out of sight when she reached the summit of Tommy's Butte. She retrieved her field glasses from her saddle bags and hid among the rocks. From her vantage point Chenoa watched as the strangers roamed the area around Maggie's Campground and gathered horses into the meadow. It was fairly obvious they belonged to Ben. No one else grazed horses in this area. Although they were too far away to see their spots clearly, Chenoa made the rather safe assumption they were Appaloosas.

The strangers locked the first few horses in their temporary enclosure, then rode off in another direction presumably to gather more. Chenoa tried to estimate how many horses might fit with in the trailer. She concluded they would likely have a full load if their second foray netted as many horses as the first.

Chenoa was shocked how quickly these apparent thieves would be able to strike and steal away with a load of horses. To her knowledge, there had not been this problem before. If these strangers were successful, she had no doubt they or others would be back. Chenoa reasoned she not only had to stop this attempt to steal their horses, she needed to make an example of them.

The morning faded to midday as the strangers continued their work. Chenoa was starting to feel hungry in the early afternoon, so she retrieved some of the dried food she carried in her saddlebags. The strangers returned with another bunch of horses and put them in the enclosure with the others. They loaded all the horses in their gooseneck trailer and prepared to leave. There was no doubt, now; these were definitely rustlers. She noticed they weren't loading up the fencing. Maybe they were planning to come back to steal more horses. That wasn't going to happen if she had anything to say about it. Chenoa realized, if the rustlers didn't take time to dismantle and load the fencing, they might leave any moment. They might get away.

Chenoa ran to Sky Walker, mounted up, and raced off to intercept the thieves. Sure, enough the truck and trailer began to move before Chenoa and Sky Walker reached them. The rustler weren't moving nearly as fast on the mountain dirt roads as Sky Walker could run. Chenoa and Sky quickly caught up to them. The truck came to a stop when Chenoa halted Sky Walker in the road ahead of them. At first the driver tried to act innocent.

"Excuse me, Miss. Can I help you," asked the truck driver.

"Welcome to our neighborhood, strangers" said Chenoa casually. "My name is Chenoa. Could I ask your name?"

"I am Mike, Mike Jones," responded the driver, immediately regretting he had given his real name.

"Care to explain where you are going with my horses?" asked Chenoa.

"Your horses?" questioned Mike. "These are just wild horses we gathered up."

"Appaloosas aren't wild horses; but in that case, do you have a permit from the BLM or forest service?" ask Chenoa.

"Permit? What permit?" asked Mike.

"The permit you need to catch wild horses," answered Chenoa.

"Oh, I didn't know I needed one," admitted Mike. "I'll be sure to get one next time."

"Were you aware stealing horses can get you sentenced to the state prison for 1 to 14 years," asked Chenoa to see if she could rattle Mike from his story.

"Stealing, don't be preposterous," said Mike in an attempt to bluff his way out of trouble.

"What do you say, Mr. Jones, why don't we let the sheriff decide whether you are rustling or not," demanded Chenoa. The tattoos he will find in the ears of these horses you are trying to haul off will confirm to whom they belong."

Mike Jones made the second real bad decision of the day; he pulled a gun on Chenoa.

"I don't think we are going to go that route, Miss," declared Mike. "That is a really fine-looking stallion you are riding. To show you there are no hard feelings for accusing me of stealing, I'm going to let you trade him for the horse of your choice in my trailer. Now get off him and stand aside."

"Do you mind if I keep my saddle?" inquired Chenoa.

"Not at all," answered Mike trying to act magnanimous, but focused on how much the stallion might fetch in Las Vegas.

Holding Chenoa at gun point, Mike removed Chenoa's rifle from its scabbard and stowed it in the back seat of his truck.

"Go ahead, take your saddle off, Miss," said Mike.

Sidling up to Mike, his companion in crime, Derek, suggested, "Hey, Mike! She is an awful pretty girl; couldn't we have a little fun with her before we head out of here?"

"Stealing horses is one thing, Derek. You want to chance getting pinched for sexual assault, on top of that?" asked Mike.

"Heck yes, Mike, I've never seen anyone quite so nice. I'd be glad to chance doing the time for something so fine!"

"Forget it, man, keep your pants zipped up. Let's get out of here, and over the state line as quickly as possible. With a bit of luck, we can enjoy a steak dinner in Jackpot tonight. Then you can get a little where it is legal, not 5 to 20 years.

Mike's hopes for a steak dinner were shattered, along with his right hip when he walked behind Sky Walker. Unbeknownst to anyone, Chenoa had taught Sky Walker to kick on command. He nailed Mike perfectly. Before Derek could figure out what was causing all the screaming coming from Mike, Chenoa had collected Mike's gun and was holding it on him.

Chenoa had heard Derek's suggestion about what he wanted to do with her. She would consequently rather have had Sky Walker kick the heck out of him, but Mike was the target of opportunity, not to mention, the one with the gun.

"Ok, lover boy. I want you to climb in that trailer and turn loose every horse with a Ben Walker tattoo in their left ear. You can keep all the ones with no tattoo. I'm sure you will agree, no mustang is likely to have a tattoo, right?" Chenoa motioned with the gun barrel for Derek to get in the trailer.

"Can't we do something for Mike, Miss?" asked Derek as Mike was writhing in pain.

"You can hurry," said Chenoa unsympathetically.

Within minutes, all of Ben's tattooed Appaloosa horses were set free. Only two horses remained; the two Mike and Derek had brought with them to commit their crime.

Chenoa had no way to contact the sheriff until she could get to Orrie's ranch. She re-saddled Sky Walker, retrieved her rifle from Mike's truck, and replaced it in its scabbard. She wanted to preserve as much evidence as possible, so Chenoa had Derek unhook the trailer and leave it at the scene of the crime. There wasn't much they could do for Mike other than let Derek put him in the truck, and head to the hospital.

"By all rights," Chenoa said threateningly to Derek and Mike, "I should shoot both of you, and leave you here for the buzzards!" She made them concede the point before she continued. Being the compassionate person I am, though, I am going to let you leave here to get help. However, if I ever see you in these parts again, I think I would be justified in shooting you on sight. Wouldn't you agree?" Chenoa again made them agree to her point.

"What about my trailer?" pleaded Mike.

"Your trailer," reiterated Chenoa. "Well, you have two options. You can send me the title or you can send a representative with $5,000, and I will let him bring it back to you with two Appaloosas in it of my choosing. They won't be the best I have, nor will they be the worst. If this deal meets your approval, I won't bother to call the law. If you think you can get a better deal from him, you are welcome to plead your case to the Sheriff."

"Deal!" exclaimed the two crooks nearly simultaneously.

"Ok, you two yahoos, get out of here before I change my mind." Chenoa watched as the pickup disappeared in a cloud of dust. She didn't think they would chance coming back for their trailer. Chenoa unsaddled their two horses and turned them loose. She put the saddles and bridles in the trailer for safe keeping. She decided to come back later with a sign which would read," FORMER PROPERTY OF TWO HORSE THIEVES!"

Chenoa patted Sky Walker on his neck and rubbed his nose. She spoke to him in a loving voice, "Thanks ole boy. You saved me once again." Sky Walker responded by tossing his head and gently butting Chenoa's arm with his nose. Their chemistry was inexplicable.

Chenoa climbed into the saddle, and without guidance Sky Walker headed for home. Now she had even more she needed to discuss with her father.

CHAPTER 12—HEART TO HEART

Ben was shoeing Tumble Weed when Chenoa and Sky Walker arrived home. ing was a talent Ben had learned as a young man. He had been taught by a farrier who frequented the reservation. Sharing his skill with a young brave such as Ben was not something he would normally have done, but he sensed in Ben an intense yearning to learn, to develop his talents and abilities, and thereby honor his ancestors by making of himself someone of whom they could be proud.

The farrier also recognized a young man with an exceptional ability to work with horses. He recognized a young man who had a genuine disgust for the decadence into which so many of his tribesmen had sunk. The farrier was advancing in age to where he knew he would not be able to endure the rigor of his profession much longer. He shared Ben's feeling of pathos for the social decay on the reservation. He found himself motivated to help a young man who was making every effort to help himself.

When he met and got acquainted with Abby, Ben's girlfriend, he was further impressed. If there were ever a couple who were bound to successfully escape the impoverishment which reservation life promoted, it was Ben and his very pretty fiancée.

To help Ben, the Farrier took him on as an apprentice and taught him the trade. It was a very valuable skill for a horse rancher. The last time Ben saw the farrier was at Abby's funeral. Not long thereafter, Ben heard the kindly man had himself passed on.

"Hi, dad, I'm glad to see you get Tumble Weed shod. I noticed when Susie rode her to see Little Feather the other day, she really needed it," said Chenoa.

"Yes, I have been wanting to get to her for a couple weeks," noted Ben. "Her hooves look a lot better now! Speaking of which, how are Sky Walker's feet?"

"I think they are ok," commented Chenoa "I think he likes going barefoot. Somehow, I think he is practicing horse chivalry; less likely to hurt the mares if he is not wearing metal s. I guess you might say a gentleman doesn't do rough sex. Sky Walker prides himself on always being a Gentleman, as far as I can tell."

"You and that horse," laughed Ben. "Have you ever wondered if you kissed him on his nose, whether he might turn into a handsome prince?"

"Not anymore. I already tried it. Didn't work," teased Chenoa playing along with her dad's idea.

"Well, it is probably the only way you are could find a prince around these parts," opined Ben.

"I won't need to kiss anymore horses, dad. I think I have found my prince just lying unconscious on Peter's Ridge. I didn't have to chase him down, rope, or hogtie him. I just snatched him up, hauled him back to camp, and put him to bed. Pretty much like the artists depict caveman courtship!" explained Chenoa.

"My, you have been busy. Care to share more detail? You have my attention!" confessed Ben.

"Well, where should I start? Do you remember, what I told you mom said, when I told you about her appearing to me?

"Tell me again, sweetheart. Frankly, my head is still sort of spinning on the subject," replied Ben.

"Mom said there was someone out there for me, to be patient, and I would be shown who it is. I told you I had been feeling as though something really important is missing in my life. Daddy, I love you, this ranch, and our life together with all my heart!"

"Well, I just couldn't bear the thought of riding off into the sunset with someone and leaving you and all this behind. I've been concerned about you. I know you love me every bit as much as I love you. How could we ever survive without each other? After all, if there were ever a "daddy's girl", you are looking at her."

"The call of nature is strong. I know I have to eventually answer it. But I have just not known how to do it without breaking both our hearts. Your wife, my mother, knows us. She watches over us. She knows our situation. She loves you and me, and she wants us to be happy. She brought us a message from God to answer my prayers. Unless I am mistaken, your prayers, too," opined Chenoa.

"You're right, Chenoa, I have dreaded the day I would lose you, since the day your mother died. Before you, she was grandest thing about my life. I have savored your presence for the last seventeen years. I would sooner die and rejoin her in some eternal realm than lose you.

To one degree or another, I have felt strongly, to the point of knowing, that our lives must eventually take separate paths. It is just the way life is!" said Ben with tears reddening his eyes.

Chenoa embraced her father, kissed his rugged checks, and confessed her love for him. "Dad, mom has a solution for us."

"What would that be, and who is this person you scraped off Peter's Ridge, anyway?" ask Ben with the curiosity and skepticism so characteristic of fathers with daughters being courted by suspect young men.

"Little Feather! It only makes sense, Dad. She has been part of our lives since I can remember. She has been my surrogate mom. She taught me about being female; about being a woman. She loves us deeply. Mom told me to tell you it was ok to let her be your wife; to fill the void in your life her death left. The void I have been filling for seventeen years as best as a daughter could, but one which mom now wants Little Feather to occupy. She is widowed, too. She has never wanted to intrude on the relationship you and mom had, but knowing it is mom's desire for the two of you to care for each other, she is prepared to respect mom's wishes and give her heart to you for the rest of your lives," confided Chenoa.

"I know you already love and respect her, as she loves and respects you. You two have never been disloyal to mom, nor Little Feather to John. Mom respects each of you for your fidelity, but the time has come to move on and adapt to an evolving reality."

"Dad, mom wants you to take Little Feather as your wife and love her until you and mom are reunited in the world of spirits. Marrying Little Feather is okay with mom. It is okay with me. It is Okay with Little Feather. Daddy, is it okay with you?" asked Chenoa.

"Don't you think I would be foolish to go against the wishes of the three most important women in my life?" asked Ben. "Not even a salmon would swim against so awesome a current. Am I supposed to court Little Feather or just show up at the wedding? I'm not exactly up on the protocol for arranged marriages."

"I think you ought to get off on the right foot, and at least take her a bouquet of flowers," counseled Chenoa. "I know you are a bit out of practice, so just remember the axiom, "Treat a girl like a thoroughbred, and she won't be a nag!"

"Got it, sweetheart, I'll dust off my courting manners and try not to take Little Feather for granted. She has always been a terrific girl." said Ben.

"Just remember, dad, every girl wants to loved, cherished, respected, and appreciated by the one to whom she gives her heart" said Chenoa. "That is not asking too much, wouldn't you agree?"

"Sounds like some familiar advice. If my memory serves me correctly, I may have imparted those words to a certain teenage girl once upon a time," said Ben.

"Aren't you pleased to know, I was listening," said Chenoa giving her dad another hug and kiss.

"Yes, very pleased! Now let's share a bit about this special someone you say you just happened to find and haul off of Peter's Ridge," insisted Ben.

He is Glenn Brigg's great nephew. He was knocked unconscious when lightning spooked his horse, and he was thrown off. I found him and was able to take him to our camp at Clarke's Crossing," reported Chenoa.

"Didn't I teach you to avoid white men?" Ben asked Chenoa.

"Yes, papa," admitted Chenoa. "But he was unconscious. There was a terrible thunderstorm that hit us with high wind and heavy rain. I was concerned he might die from exposure if I didn't get him to some shelter. Believe me, your words were shouting in my ears, but I just couldn't do it; I just couldn't leave him there. Daddy, something deep within demanded I help. I was able to load him onto his horse and take him to our Clarke's Crossing camp. Anyway, he was soaking wet. Plus, he is a big strapping guy. I didn't think I could carry him and all his wet clothing up the stairs and into the camp, so I decided to get rid of as much weight as I could."

"So how did you solve that dilemma?" asked Ben.

"Well, you taught me how to skin a deer," explained Chenoa. "Same principle. I figured I had a better chance of hefting him without his soaked clothing, so I stripped off all the heavy items I could and was able to get him into the camp bed. Then I took off the rest to dry everything. I fired up the camp stove and started drying clothes and cooking supper."

"After I got the camp warm, I put the horses away, then fetched enough water and wood for the night. I tried to rouse the fellow, but he was out cold. My clothes were wet, too, so I stripped off everything but my underwear to dry them too."

"What was your plan if he came to?" asked Ben.

"Dad, it must have been a mental block, but after I couldn't wake him up, it just didn't occur to me that he might wake up later," explained Chenoa. "I kept my panties and bra, but everything else got hung up to dry. Again, since I couldn't wake him up, it just never occurred to me, he might wake up later. I was very tired, so I got in bed, and went to sleep."

"So, if I have it right, you slept with an unconscious, near naked guy clothed in nothing more than your bra and panties. What were you thinking, sweetie?" asked Ben.

"That's the point, Dad, I wasn't," said Chenoa. "I was too focused on saving him; on keeping him alive."

Ben chuckled, "I know how young men think, sweetie. Seems to me you took an awful chance of giving him a heart attack, if and when he woke up."

"Well, he almost gave me one when he unexpectedly did wake up this morning," explained Chenoa. "Only thing I can say is, fortunately all is well, that ends well!

"So, what's this about finding your one and only?" asked Ben.

"Daddy, I think I have. When I talked to him this morning, I was so impressed that he is. It just felt right. Frankly I was tempted to give myself to him on the spot. It took every ounce of self-control I could muster to not act like one of Sky Walker's mares," confessed Chenoa.

"He was a gentleman, though, papa, he acted just like you said a man would who respects a woman; he set the limit."

"Good to hear," said Ben. "That says a lot for him. Given the circumstances, it would not have been hard for him to take advantage of the situation. A pair of panties is not a lot of deterrence for a two-legged stud."

"Yah, especially if the girl wearing them is willing to hang them up to dry, too," conceded Chenoa.

"Wow," said Ben, "I really do need to meet this young man. Where are things headed?"

"I have an appointment to meet him again in four days at the same camp," Chenoa informed Ben. "I'll know more after we have a chance to talk again."

"Sweetie, how do you know this guy is the one?" asked Ben sincerely trying to understand Chenoa's feelings.

"Daddy, somethings you know by your senses; seeing, hearing, tasting, touching, and smelling. Other things you know through feelings. Love for example is a feeling. Feelings might have certain manifestations, but they don't explain everything. The Holy Spirit is a Revelator of many things the senses cannot explain.

Mom said I would know. If the bolt of lightning which missed Jerry had hit me instead, I don't know if I could feel the answer any stronger." said Chenoa.

"How can you be sure it's not just hormones?" asked Ben.

"I have asked myself the same question," admitted Chenoa. "I have prayed about it, sincerely! I'm looking forward to our next meeting to shed more light on the question."

"Think he will show up?" asked Ben to tease Chenoa a bit.

"He is going to miss an awfully good meal, if he doesn't," declared Chenoa. "And you will have some very cold leftovers, by the time I get back here."

"How about if I just come with you," asked Ben. I'm trying to imagine what this Jerry's reaction would be if I confronted him with the question, 'So I understand you have been sleeping with my daughter. Don't you think you are rushing things a bit?"

"Oh, daddy, you wouldn't," asked Chenoa.

"We could find out real fast if he is a coward or not," said Ben. "I have never particularly wanted some chicken for a son-in-law."

"You can have your turn with him, when I bring him home to meet papa," said Chenoa. "For now, let me take my measure of the man."

"All right, if you insist," conceded Ben. "I guess I'll just have to cook a few more meals for myself."

"Well, you could pick some flowers and ride over to the Diamond Bar ranch, if you don't want to cook for yourself," suggested Chenoa.

"Now why didn't I think of that," asked Ben only half joking.

"You better watch it, though, Orrie and his crew might be more up set with you, losing their cook, than you are, losing yours," cautioned Chenoa.

"You are right, but it has been a long time since anyone was hung for rustling in these mountains," said Ben. "I think I will be safe."

"Speaking of rustling, I caught a couple of yahoos trying to haul off a trailer load of our horses from Maggie's Campground today," said Chenoa.

"No kidding, and you are just now getting around to telling me," said Ben surprised that Chenoa hadn't mentioned anything about this earlier.

"Sorry, dad. We just got off on a more important subject than horse thieves, and I forgot about them," confessed Chenoa.

"No problem, sweetheart, but would you please tell me now?" requested Ben.

"I was on my way back here. Around ten I reached Gregg's Point. I saw a dually pulling a gooseneck stock trailer up Charlie's Creek road toward Maggie's Campground. It struck me odd. I see mobile homes being towed up there frequently, but not stock trailers. Maggie's is a somewhat popular weekend camping destination, but it's not the weekend. I decided to hold up a bit and see what was happening.

Next odd thing they did was deploy a bunch of metal fence sections when they got to Maggie's. These guys were looking more and more like they were up to no good. Why would you drag a big gooseneck all the way to Maggie's, just for a couple people to go horseback riding? A two-horse trailer would make a lot more sense."

"I rode up to the top of Tommy's Butte, where I would have a good view of the whole area and watched. Sure, enough these two yokels set

about gathering up our horses. They drove them into the enclosure they had set up next to their trailer. It took them twice to gather up a trailer full of horses. They loaded them up and headed off. They didn't even bother to take their fence panels; just drove off and left them there. There wasn't time to go for help. I had to stop them before they got to a good road."

"They tried to play innocent when I stopped them; claimed they were rounding up mustangs. Their story didn't hold up long. Then one of them decided to have his way with me. The other one suddenly pulled a gun on me and took my rifle. It was all going their way until the man with the gun made the mistake of walking behind Sky Walker. He lost his grip when Sky Walker kicked him. I recovered his gun and did sort of a citizen's arrest.

I made the other one, the one who had wanted to have his way with me, unload and turn loose every horse with our tattoo in his left ear. It was all of them, except their two saddle horses. I gave them a couple options on how we might proceed. We reached what I believe would be called an out-of-court settlement. I had the one who could still walk unhook their trailer, and load up his ailing buddy, so he could take him to seek medical attention. They agreed to leave their trailer behind."

"Wouldn't surprise me if they turn right instead of left when they reach US 93, and high-tailed it for the border. I don't think they want to try to explain their problem to anyone in this jurisdiction," concluded Chenoa.

"No, I don't suppose they would," agreed Ben. "Why did you put yourself at such risk, sweetheart? Wouldn't it have been a lot safer, after you could see they were rustlers, to just shoot, shovel, and shut up?"

"Burying a couple of yahoos is not that hard, papa," kidded Chenoa, "but I just wasn't up to digging a hole big enough so no one would ask questions about their rig, besides I'm trying to develop a kinder, gentler side. This way maybe the word will get around that rustling our horses is a bad career move."

"Good point," agreed Ben. "I'd say you owe Sky Walker yet again for saving your hide, not to mention your virginity. Those two knuckleheads could have decided to kill you rather than let you go after they got tired of abusing you. By the way, why did Sky Walker kick the guy? I've never known him to be a kicker."

"It all started one day when we had been on the move for a long time. For some reason my behind was getting saddle sore, so we stopped to rest. After a while we started literally playing; horse play or horsing around. I was able to teach him to kick on command. We have practiced the kicking on command thing for long enough to where I can now say it is a skill. It proved quite useful when these jokers tried to kidnap me. I'll bet, if he ever walks again, it won't be within striking distance behind another horse," opined Chenoa.

"Amazing," exclaimed Ben. "I had no idea! What did you do with their horses if they left their stock trailer out on the Charlie's Creek road?"

"I turned their horses loose and left their tack in their trailer," explained Chenoa. "I told them they could have their trailer back by buying two $2500 Appaloosas. If they didn't like those terms, we could talk to the sheriff and see what he had to say. They both agreed to my terms."

"I am not sure I would have offered such generous terms, sweetie, but it does seem like some clever marketing. Wouldn't do us as much good to have them rotting in jail or under a few feet of dirt," asserted Ben. "If by chance they never come back, we can slap a For Sale sign on it."

"They abandoned some nice fence panels, too, daddy," said Chenoa. "Not sure how much it is worth, but we could either claim or sell it, too."

Ben took Chenoa by her hand and pulled her into his arms. He hugged her for a long moment, then kissed her cheek. "I am just glad you are ok, Honey. This incident could certainly have turned out a lot worse," said Ben. "I am not real comfortably with my little girl out there dealing with rustlers; from now on be extra careful, please!"

"Yes, sir! I don't know if you have noticed, though, but daddy's little girl isn't so little anymore," said Chenoa.

"You don't say, how could I have missed such a thing," asked Ben, giving Chenoa another big hug and kiss. "Note to self: Pay more attention to your family."

Chenoa gave her dad a gentle elbow in the ribs, "Good idea, pop. Very good idea! I need to go take care of Sky Walker." Chenoa turned to head to the barn. "Let me take Tumble Weed, and I'll put her away, too."

"Ok, then I'll start supper. What would you like me to fix?" asked Ben.

"What would you say to Sago Lilly soup?" asked Chenoa.

"You dig em, I'll cook em!" said Ben. "What has you thinking of sego lilies?"

"Oh, I've just been thinking about what I might fix for a particular, upcoming meal," confided Chenoa. "It has to be something really unique and special."

"May I assume the special meal is for someone special; anybody I know?" asked Ben with a big 'I know what you are thinking' grin.

"Uuum, would be a safe bet. Got any menu suggestions?" asked Chenoa. "What taste delight would be most likely to go from your mouth to your heart via your stomach?

"Well, let's think; what is in season? Can't do deer, waterfowl or game birds; they are out of season. You might be limited to rabbit, beef, or chicken, unless you want to go vegetarian. Little Feather might be able to fix you up with some fresh garden vegetables. I also know where you can find some watercress and asparagus. Of course, there are some nice rainbow trout being caught out of the Cedar Creek Reservoir, too. The Jarbidge is literally a cornucopia of possibilities; your choice," said Ben.

"Thanks, dad! The only thing worse than no choice, is too many," complained Chenoa.

"I agree. Some of my buddies who served in the military had the hardest time choosing the first time they were taken to an all-you-can-eat buffet," recalled Ben.

Ben and Chenoa took care of their evening chores, then settled down to a rather unspectacular evening meal of bread and milk. They ate quietly. It was their meal of choice whenever they were tired, just wanted to keep things simple, and hit the sack.

When they finished, they both helped clean up. Chenoa suddenly broke the silence with a question which betrayed her thoughts. "Daddy, what was the first meal you can remember momma fixing for you?" inquired Chenoa. "Was it memorable; were you impressed; was there anything about it you didn't like.? Did you enjoy it?" Chenoa was sincerely wanting to know any detail about her parents' early courtship.

"Well, sweetheart, I can assure you, as far as the food was concerned it was nothing grand. We were with each other; to us, that was all that mattered. It was early June. We had a lot of important things we needed to discuss; a lot of decisions we needed to make."

"We had already decided we wanted to get married. We knew we didn't want to live on the reservation. Much more than that, we still needed to figure out.

"Abby, and I decided to go where we could be by ourselves for a few days, and talk. We needed to go by horseback because we didn't have a motor vehicle. No one else I knew had one, either, that I trusted to get us where I wanted to go and get us back safely. So, we saddled up two good cow ponies, loaded our camping gear on Fred, a great pack mule, and headed for Jarbidge and Murphy Hot Springs."

"I frankly don't remember a lot about the food, except for the first night. We had a rather large wooden box for all the food. Most of it was canned, so we didn't have to worry about anything spoiling. When we camped the first night, I remember Abby fixed me a sandwich which consisted of two slices of white Wonder bread, liberally coated with Miracle Whip, covered with a layer of Van Camp pork 'n beans, and topped with, not one, but four sardines.

It was an especially juicy sandwich. She chided me for making a mess. I reminded her, she was the one who put so much in the sandwich. No one could have eaten it without stuff oozing out," reminisced Ben.

"We had a Border Collie at the time who fortunately would eat most anything. He dined well that night, too. Spared us a lot of clean-ups. We never picked a name for him, just called him Dog. He loved your mom; disappeared the day she died. Never saw him again," recalled Ben, his voice breaking remembering his double loss.

"Well, I don't think that history is going to help me much. My angle is probably pretty obvious; the idea of fixing something for Jerry like mom fixed for you. I don't think I would impress anyone with a pork 'n bean and sardine sandwich," said Chenoa.

"Might want to try it before you knock it," countered Ben. "It was certainly memorable, tasty, and easy to fix."

"It just sounds odd, dad, and besides I don't have a dog to help clean up," argued Chenoa. "If we are meant to be, I don't want to sabotage destiny with something which sounds so repulsive."

"You are the one who ask the question, sweetheart, I am just telling you the way it happened," concluded Ben. "I'll buy some Pork'n Beans and Sardines sometime and let you try it. Who knows, you may like it. With Little Feather's bread, it may be even better."

"Speaking of Little Feather isn't she supposed to be coming soon to bake bread?" asked Chenoa.

"Yes, I need to start firing the oven tomorrow evening," said Ben. "Thanks for reminding me!"

"Sounds to me like you don't need to go courting at the Diamond Bar, papa; just go pick some wildflowers, and let Little Feather come to you. This way you don't need to explain yourself to Orrie or his crew," observed Chenoa. "If you wanted to pitch in and help Little Feather with the bread making, no one would be around to interfere. I'm sure she would appreciate the help, not to mention the attention. Time to make your move, pop!"

"To say the least, I'm out of practice, coach," said Ben hinting that Chenoa's advice was welcome.

All the next day Chenoa continued to stew about what to fix for her man, as she now thought of Jerry. She knew she was being more than a little presumptive, but that was how she felt. She couldn't explain it, but she just knew he was. Several times she rode Sky Walker up to a little patch of trees about a mile from home where she could be alone. From there, there was a beautiful view of surrounding country at which she could gaze while she pondered and prayed for guidance.

She felt a comforting presence there of some unseen entity, some guardian angel, who her Heavenly Father had assigned to watch over her. She liked to assume it was her mother coming back once again to guide her through this critical stretch of her life. A few times, when she was praying, the feeling of some presence was so strong, she felt she would see someone, were she to open her eyes.

The little patch of trees was a special place to Chenoa, a sacred place. She had never taken anyone there. In fact, she had not even told anyone about it, except her father. Every time she left there, she had a clearer vision of the future. The doubt shrouding the next section of her trail was lifted. She knew with confidence what to do.

As Chenoa left her sacred grove of trees the next day, she began gathering items for the special meal she would fix for her man. She would do as her ancestors had done for centuries. They had lived off the land. To Chenoa this was God's country; he would provide for her meal and more. If a Shoshone squaw could feed her family hundreds of years ago, she could feed her man now. If her grandmothers could cook a meal over an open fire, she could do it in the confines of the camp at Clark's Crossing. Chenoa felt inspired. This was going to be fun.

Suddenly she broke out laughing. She had had the image of a trapper baiting his trap pop into her mind. Well, she thought, I suppose the differences aren't that great.

Ben was nervous; he had been all day. He had tried to calm himself by reasoning he had no good reason to be nervous. It hadn't worked. He told himself he had known Little Feather since she was a small girl. So why was he feeling so panicked? Ben's hands were visibly shaking when he started the fire to heat the big earthen oven. He just didn't understand it.

Ben first noticed his discombobulation during the afternoon, when he was scouring the vicinity for wildflowers. The product of his search was now safely displayed in a Mason jar on the kitchen table. It was a beautiful bouquet, in his humble opinion. Not a bad job for a guy who hadn't picked a flower in years. Chenoa was the one who always decorated their home with flowers. His only contribution was to throw them out when they wilted.

Now his mind was trying to figure out what to say when Little Feather arrived in the morning. In the many years Ben had known, loved, and respected her as a family member, he had always had an easygoing relationship with Little Feather. He had never been anxious around her; until now. Ben had always respected Little Feather as Abby's sister, his sister-in-law. There had never been any romantic aspect to their relationship; purely platonic.

Abby's message had changed everything. It was okay now. Okay to think of her as a woman; to be romantically involved; to marry her. Suddenly ways of thinking which had lain dormant for decades had sprung to life. In many ways Ben felt like a teenager who had just reached puberty. He was thinking like a teenager. It was as if he had just noticed Little Feather was a pretty, fine looking woman; a shapely, desirable woman.

Ben felt as awkward and apprehensive as a schoolboy trying to muster up enough courage to ask the girl he admired for a dance. Ben realized as he fired up and watched the oven get warmer, his fires, too, had been out for a long time. His new perspective regarding Little Feather had re-fired his long dormant libido. Bread making was going to be a labor of love this time for sure.

CHAPTER 13—BON APPETIT

Jerry respected Aunt Martha's opinion. She was from a different generation, but she was nevertheless a woman. She had insights into things which for Jerry were a mystery.

Jerry had had several quiet conversations with Aunt Martha to seek her advice. She knew about his invitation to lunch on the fourth day following his meeting Chenoa. She also knew about Chenoa's reputation for elusiveness. Aunt Martha didn't have an explanation for Jerry of the change in Chenoa's behavior. Why would she hide or run away from all others, but invite him to lunch? It was a mystery.

"You are going to have to help me out a little more, Jerry," said Aunt Martha. "What else did she say, which you haven't told me?"

"Well, she said a lot of things while we had breakfast," recalled Jerry hesitantly.

"Come on, Jerry, you can do better than that," prodded Aunt Martha. "What did she say, you don't want to tell me? You can't expect me to help you, if you don't tell me!"

"It is a little embarrassing; really personal, Aunt Martha," said Jerry.

"Ok , I understand, but I need to know," coaxed Aunt Martha.

"When we were having breakfast, I teased Chenoa that I was the man of her dream. Before we parted, I asked her why she was inviting me back. She said it was because I was the man of her dream. She wouldn't elaborate; said we could talk about it in four days. That's all, Aunt Martha. I was teasing; she was serious," concluded Jerry.

"Jerry, you just described the difference between boys and girls!" opined Aunt Martha. "It sounds to me, you were talking to a girl who for whatever reason has concluded you are the man for her because of some dream. What else would explain her acceptance of someone whom she had never met, handsome fellow, though, you may be?"

"Aunt Martha, I came to Idaho to spend the summer with you and Uncle Glenn. I was looking forward to learning about ranch life. I never had any idea of getting involved with a girl," asserted Jerry.

"If you wanted to learn about ranch life, welcome to it," chuckled Aunt Martha. "This is basic ranch life 101; boy meets girl!"

"Aunt Martha, what do I do?" asked Jerry.

"Young man, where this is going is a good question. You will have to figure it out for yourself. Your Uncle and I don't have the answers for you. But the two pieces of advice I'm sure he would agree with me on is keep your zipper up till you figure it out, and don't fall off your horse again. No telling what she would do to you next time," concluded Aunt Martha with a big grin.

"Why does the expression keeps coming to my mind, 'Going like a lamb to the slaughter'"? asked Jerry.

"If she is as beautiful as everyone says," responded Aunt Martha, "I suspect you are already lamb chops!"

By day 3 Chenoa had gathered all the supplies she needed. She headed to the camp at Clarke's Crossing. She felt impressed to stop in and visit with Little Feather. The two girls had a long heart to heart talk, the gist of which was that Chenoa was going to meet Jerry again to try and find out if he was indeed the man whom her mother had said she would meet.

The second point was that Ben was on board with Abby's wishes. He was waiting at the ranch to help her make bread and discuss their future.

Chenoa disclosed to Little Feather one other thing; her father was more nervous than she had ever seen him.

"Don't make him work too hard at this, Little Feather, he is out of practice," advised Chenoa.

"He need not worry," assured Little Feather. "I'll be gentle." Both girls laughed.

Chenoa made it to Clarke's Crossing by late afternoon and began making preparations for tomorrow's lunch. She had a lot to do.

Jerry, too, was anxious for day four to arrive. After a discussion with Uncle Glenn and Aunt Martha, Jerry left the morning of day three on horseback for North Fork. After Jerry had no definite answer to his question, "When will you be back?", Uncle Glenn suggested he ride Fleet instead of driving there as usual with a truck and horse trailer.

Uncle Glenn would need of his equipment for other assignments, and didn't want it sitting idle at North Fork. Plus, he thought the ride would give Jerry time to do some thinking and clear his head. He frankly had not been of much use during the last few days, anyway.

Everyone had noticed how distracted Jerry was. Most of the hands had attributed Jerry's strange behavior to his head trauma. Uncle Glenn suspected the real reason and Aunt Martha knew it. His problem wasn't with his head, it was his heart. Cupid had, from all appearances, scored a direct hit.

When Jerry rode away from the stable at the ranch headquarters, he was prepared for a long ride. Old George had fixed enough food to last Jerry for days. Jerry retraced the route the cow drive had taken shortly after his arrival. Fleet was fresh. Unlike the slow pace of the cow drive, Jerry and Fleet covered the miles quickly. The scenery was different. The green grass of spring had dried. The air now smelled of sage brush and grease wood, aka, rabbit brush. The wildlife babies of spring were babies no more, but nearly as big as their parents.

Jerry noticed a small, burned area near the Salmon Falls Creek Dam where a range fire had been started by a lightning strike, reportedly from the same squall which nearly got him. Thanks to the quick response from the fire fighters of the Bureau of Land Management, the fire was extinguished before it could do much damage. Had it started in a more remote area, the fire might have burned hundreds, or even thousands of acres of the now dry grass and brush before it could be put out.

Riding across the dam, Jerry mixed with some vehicular traffic which this time of year generally consisted of fishermen headed to their favorite reservoir where they could try to catch the rainbow trout Fish and Game kept stocked there. He wondered momentarily if that might be what would be on tomorrow's lunch menu.

Jerry checked his watch. The time to reach the dam from home had only taken a little over an hour and a half. When he started up the road to North Fork, Jerry let Fleet walk for a while. There was no need to hurry. The day was still young with plenty of time to check the cattle before dark.

Jerry's plan was to ride North Fork today, spend the night at Uncle Glenn's sheep camp, then leave in the morning to meet Chenoa at Clarke's Crossing.

Jerry was thinking about tomorrow as he and Fleet ascended China Mountain. What an unexpected summer he was having. How different from city life. He wondered what Chenoa would think of Philadelphia. He imagined what a stir it would cause were he to walk across campus with her. Pretty girls were everywhere at his university, but Chenoa was in a class by herself.

The girls he would previously have rated as a ten, would likely not fair better than an eight when compared to Chenoa. Jerry wondered how she would do in a university environment. Most coeds had to spend hours putting on makeup to achieve anything above an eight. Chenoa was a natural ten. Jerry doubted she even owned any makeup. Her hair was black, as were her eyes. Her hair was long, easily reaching her waist. It wasn't what you would call curly, but it wasn't straight either. It could best be described as having a gentle wave to it.

Jerry tried to quantify Chenoa in the normal ways. Not too tall, not too short. Not too big; not too little. Simply put, she was perfect; one of a kind. Jerry had the thought; after God made her, He broke the mold.

Jerry was very near the entrance to North Fork when he saw it. In full bloom, an exquisite cactus flower. He later learned it was called Opuntia polyacantha, but he instantly knew it had to be the flower from which Chenoa got her nickname. It had to be. No other flower could possibly fit the description.

Jerry had been riding this range for months and never seen a cactus like this in bloom. He dismounted Fleet to have a closer look. It was beautiful. Jerry tried to fix in his memory every detail of how it looked. He didn't expect to chance upon another one in full bloom again.

Jerry wished he had a camera with him, but he didn't. A camera would be nice for tomorrow, too, but then maybe not. Jerry kept having the feeling that Chenoa was too special to share with the world. Would sharing her image with the leering masses be sacrilege. Jerry didn't feel he had the maturity to judge such matters, but he nevertheless felt it would be.

After spending a few minutes admiring the cactus flower, Jerry remounted Fleet and began his inspection of the cow herd. He was impressed how fast the calves were growing. North Fork was good pastureland judging from the health of the cattle grazing there. Calves who had barely been old and strong enough to endure the cow drive from Holister to China Mountain were now a hundred or so pounds heavier and looked in extremely good condition.

The cows patiently endured the punishment as their growing calves head butted their udders to strip every possible ounce of milk from them. Fortunately, the calves' diet was fast changing to a more vegetarian one. North Fork abounded in green succulent vegetation. The plants at the elevation of North Fork didn't die and dry up like the grass on the lower elevations from the Salmon Falls Creek Dam to Rogerson or Holister.

Jerry found not a single sick cow or calf as he rode through the herd. Every animal appeared in good health. The calves were lively. The cows had shed all of their winter hair and were looking great. The bulls were all young and strong enough to be about what bulls do without having to retire to some hill side to rest up.

By late afternoon Jerry had completed his work and arrived at the North Fork shelter camp. His work no longer distracted him from thinking about Chenoa. Now he was free to think about her and where his future was heading. Questions were flooding his mind. Answers were illusive and needed some serious contemplation.

Jerry unsaddled Fleet and placed him with some oats and hay in the stable. He built a fire in the camp stove to warm up a 24 ounce can of beef stew. Old George's sandwiches were good, and had hit the spot during his workday. Now, though, Jerry wanted a warm meal. Uncle Glenn kept the camp stocked with the best brands. Anyone who needed to spend a night at this shelter need not want for good food if they knew how to light a fire and use a can opener.

When Jerry had finished eating and cleaning up, he retired to bed. The mattress was surprisingly comfort. He might have noticed this

factor a few days earlier, but his attention had understandably been diverted following his night at Clarke's crossing. He now needed to decide if he wanted to wake up with that distraction in his bed every morning as he strived to live 'happily ever after'.

Jerry had often heard the opinion that for a marriage to be successful, it helped to have as many things in common as possible. He had trouble thinking of anything he had in common with Chenoa. The big differences were big. He was white; she was Shoshone. He was a city boy; she was a country girl. This was bound to have a big impact on their lives.

Jerry remembered watching the Donny and Marie Show in which she sang, she was a little bit country, and Donny responded he was a little bit rock 'n roll.

Jerry was university educated; he didn't know about Chenoa's education, whether she could even read. He found it unlikely she couldn't. It was a big plus she spoke English, in fact she seemed to have a good command of it. She had demonstrated she could cook breakfast. She had promised to cook lunch tomorrow. Jerry wasn't sure what other domestic skills were needed for a happy relationship; he had never given it any thought.

Jerry was still pondering the question when he drifted off to sleep. He had not yet met Chenoa's father, but he nevertheless dreamed about him. In his dream Jerry conjured up a rather stern, intimidating figure as Chenoa's father whom he had to meet in order to get permission to call on her. When the father figure in his dream asked Jerry why he wanted to call on his daughter, the only reason Jerry could come up with was because she is cute.

In the dream her father didn't find his reason to be very compelling. He had thundered, "here are lots of cute girls, why my daughter?" In the dream, Jerry could not think of a single solitary reason; good or bad. His knees were shaking, and to his further embarrassment Jerry wet his pants. Chenoa's dad ordered, "No coward is calling on my daughter!" In the dream Chenoa came to Jerry's rescue with the statement to her father, "but, daddy, he is the man in my dream!" The dream turned nightmare was so upsetting to Jerry, he woke up and couldn't go back to sleep for a long time.

Chenoa finished the last of her preparations just before she needed to light the Coleman lantern. She loved the sound it made. It was hard to explain, but it just created a comforting feeling; a feeling that you were home. Everything was coming together nicely for tomorrow. She looked forward to the opportunity to feed her man and visit with him.

Suddenly, the most awful thought attacked the peace of mind she had enjoyed all day. What if he didn't come? Chenoa was nearly paralyzed by the thought. The idea was so demoralizing, she fell to her knees and wept as she prayed to God for relief. For the last three days her heart had enjoyed the feeling of hope of a girl falling in love. Now this dark, evil, depressing feeling of despair had robbed Chenoa of her confidence in her mother's assurance. Tears flowed freely as she begged God to free her from the fear and doubt which had overcome her. She at length ask God if he would send one of his angels to comfort her; her mother, if possible. After all, hadn't he done that for His Son as he endured his suffering in Gethsemane. When she could no longer bear the evil feeling which was depressing her to the point of despair, Chenoa fled the comfort and safety of the camp and ran to Sky Walker. She threw her arms around his big muscular neck, buried her face in his shoulder and sobbed uncontrollably.

By small degrees Chenoa began to feel better. When she was finally able to release Sky Walker's neck, step forward, and stroke his head, he responded by nuzzling Chenoa's arm. She in turn took his head in her arms and petted him from his ears to his nose.

"You know, big boy, anytime you are ready to turn from the most magnificent stallion in these hills to my Prince Charming, I'll be glad to plant a big kiss square on that handsome nose of yours," stated Chenoa. She was trying to find a handkerchief in one of her pockets to deal with her running nose. Chenoa continued, "Thank you, my four-legged hero, I guess you without a doubt have the biggest shoulders around here for a girl to cry on; I love, my big buddy!" Feeling she could manage now, Chenoa started back to the camp. Sky Walker quietly returned to eating.

Before she reached the camp, Chenoa heard the words so distinctly, she wasn't sure she had heard them with her ears, or in her mind, "He will come to you!"

The peace of mind for which Chenoa had been praying suddenly came over her. It was as if night had turned into day. The depression and despair were gone. Joy swelled her heart as the thought filled her mind, "God does answer prayers." Chenoa went to bed with a bright anticipation of tomorrow. She pulled the covers up around her neck as she said a silent prayer of thanks to her Heavenly Father for relief from the evil thoughts which had so sorely troubled her.

Unlike Jerry, she slept peacefully for the rest of night. Chenoa had endured her hour of trial and met her test well. She was beautiful inside as well as out.

Ben fired the oven on time. When Little Feather arrived the morning of day four it was heated to perfection. Ben had read a National Geographic article once about the way the Lebanese Mountain people cook bread. They have small dome shaped ovens with a large opening in the side of the upper half. A fire would burn down to coals in the bottom of the oven. The dough would be flattened out like a thin crust pizza, placed on a round pillow, and slapped on the oven wall. When the bread was baked, it would be peeled off the oven wall. The bread was so thin it was used as wrapping paper where rotisserie chickens were sold. When the bread was eaten as bread, it was often torn in pieces and used like dipping chips.

In contrast, Little Feathers bread was formed into loaves and cooked in a separate chamber from the fire.

Ben had finished his chores, shaved, and cleaned up by the time Little Feather arrived. The flowers had been placed in fresh water in the only vase Ben had been able to find. Ben's home was cleaner and more tidy than Little Feather had ever seen it. Ben formally offered his services to help Little Feather make bread. After a few perfunctory comments about not getting in her way, Ben's offer was accepted, and they started mixing dough.

The horse play started after Little Feather accidentally hit Ben with a cup of flour. By midday they were laughing at each other's silly antics, and engaging in some serious rough housing. By the end of the day Ben had attempted to place a kiss on Little Feather, and she let him.

When the bread had been divided up, and they were saying "Good night" to each other, their pent-up need for each other led to a heart to heart discussion. They both expressed their affection for each other. They were both on board to join their lives together as Abby had requested. In summary, they wanted each other, they needed each other, and they loved each other.

Possibly as important, they just felt at home with each other; they were a good match for each other. They decided to get married as soon as they could make the arrangement. Going off to Jack Pot, aka, eloping, would have been the fastest, but it just didn't seem right.

Little Feather agreed to come back as soon as she could get some time off, but in the meantime give Orrie notice he would need to be hiring a new cook. Ben and Little Feather engaged in some intense good bying before she left. It was Ben who suggested they ought to "save it" after he recognized some old, but familiar feelings emerging. Little Feather agreed, whispering to Ben "I haven't felt like this since I was eighteen, and John and I sneaked out of a school picnic."

"Many a forest fire has been started from a smoldering ember," commented Ben.

"It has been a wonderful day, Ben! Thank you for the help. You are hired," said Little Feather with a parting kiss and a smile.

Ben watched as Little Feather departed. He hadn't felt this satisfied in years. He wondered how they ought to proceed. He was convinced they ought to proceed, without a doubt. He never would have indulged in such intimacy were he not convinced Abby approved.

After his nightmare, Jerry slept poorly. He knew it was only a dream, but it may as well have been real. He dreaded the thought of meeting Chenoa's father. Fathers had always frightened him. They had a way of looking at you which simply took all the fun out of knowing their daughters.

Jerry remembered one of his friends telling her dad that Jerry didn't think he liked him. Without argument or contradiction her father had simply said, "That's my job." Jerry supposed if he ever had a daughter, especially a cute one, he would cop a similar protective attitude when boys were around.

Jerry gave up trying to sleep at about 4am. He got up, dressed, slapped some unheated wash water on his face, and combed his hair. He had been letting it grow longer than usual this summer. Holister had no barber of which Jerry was aware, consequently, everyone was a barber or offered to be one. Old George offered his services to Jerry, but after seeing how Uncle Glenn's hair cut had turned out, Jerry decided to let his hair grow longer, and see if he liked how it looked.

Jerry considered letting Chenoa cut it today, if she wanted. The thought of her fingers running through his hair had discombobulated Jerry so severely, he had thrown some more cold water on his face to calm down. He waited till after breakfast to brush his teeth. He didn't try to shave. A little stubble was the style nowadays. After Jerry was satisfied with how he looked, he curried Fleet to where his coat glistened, then saddled up.

Jerry cleaned his saddle to make sure nothing need embarrass him when he met with Chenoa. By 8Jerry was ready to ride. He had gotten up, dressed up, cleaned up, and was ready to go to get to know Chenoa better. He couldn't think of any young man in the county who wouldn't jump at the chance to trade places with him. He considered himself lucky beyond words. Every lottery had a winner; he still didn't understand; why him?

Jerry closed up the camp making sure it was ready for its next guest, then headed for Clarke's Crossing. He didn't want to be late, not today. It was a beautiful morning. Jerry quickly reached the trail going west. As Fleet climbed to the crest of the ridge overlooking the entrance to the North Fork pasture, Roger and Hammerstein's words and music from the musical *Oklahoma* flooded his mind, "Oh what a beautiful morning; oh what a beautiful day, I've got a wonderful feeling, everything is going my way." Jerry couldn't agree more. He turned Fleet west to discover his future.

Jerry's concern about finding his way back to Clarke's Crossing proved to be no problem. He had no difficulty recognizing the landmarks which indicated the way back to Chenoa. The miles past quickly. An inner excitement grew; his pulse quickened. A feeling of anticipation grew until he was reminded of how he felt on Christmas morning, waiting for his parents to let him in to see what Santa had brought. Jerry's excitement continued to grow. It reached a peak when he spotted the smoke rising from the camp stove chimney.

Jerry stopped to gaze upon the scene before him. All of a sudden, Fleet let loose with a loud whinny which Sky Walker answered immediately. As a result of the commotion, Chenoa slide open the camp door and looked out. Chenoa smiled broadly and waved vigorously upon spotting Jerry.

"You must be hungry; you came early," observed Chenoa.

Jerry stopped a few feet from the camp and dismounted. "Places where a guy can get a good meal around here are a little scarce, so I have come to collect on a promise," said Jerry.

Chenoa descended the stairs at the front of the camp. "It is almost ready," said Chenoa as she took a step forward and gave Jerry a quick kiss. "I hope you won't be disappointed."

Jerry's reaction to even a little kiss was electrifying. He stammered something about taking care of his Horse, and lead Fleet behind the camp. He tied Fleet near Sky Walker, but far enough from him so they couldn't get in a fight.

Jerry returned to the front of the camp, and waited for Chenoa to invite him in. Jerry was simply in awe of how beautiful Chenoa was. It was a raw beauty. She obviously hadn't spent any time this morning primping, yet she was nevertheless a knockout. It was just astounding that anyone could be so beautiful.

The image of the cactus flower flashed into Jerry's mind. Her beauty was even more rare than that of the flower. The many thorns surrounding the flower had effectively dissuaded Jerry from trying to pick it. Jerry wondered what the thorns were which guarded Chenoa.

"Did you have any trouble finding your way back?" asked Chenoa

"Would you believe I have been wondering around looking for this place for hours and hours?" kidded Jerry.

"I wondered if I might have to come looking for you. The cute fellows are sometimes not very smart," asserted Chenoa.

"So, was finding my way back here is some sort of test, your own personally designed intelligence test?" asked Jerry.

"I hadn't thought of it that way," said Chenoa. "But I suppose that would be one way of thinking about it!"

"Well against all odds to the contrary, I am here," said Jerry. "Now what do we do first; talk or eat?"

"Oh, eat. Food would all be cold by the time we could finish talking," said Chenoa.

"Suits me," said Jerry, "What is on the menu?"

"It is a secret," Said Chenoa.

"Secret, how so? asked Jerry.

"It is going to be a sensual, trust building meal. You are going to be blindfolded, and I am going to feed you," said Chenoa. "If you want to really enjoy what I have fixed, you are going to have to trust me! I want you to focus on how the food tastes, not how it looks."

This was interesting, thought Jerry. "Can I trust you," asked Jerry. Smiling he continued, "The first time we met, one could argue you took advantage of me."

"We both know you might have died a lonely death had I not come along. I didn't say 'happen along' because I don't think I just happened along. I think I was guided to you as surely as God placed you in my path."

"You mean to say, God arranged for us to meet?" asked Jerry.

"I think so," said Chenoa. "That is what I am here to find out."

"You mean you don't make a habit of rescuing guys with poor riding skills?" asked Jerry

"You are my first, and probably the last," said Chenoa.

"Why do you think God is behind all this?" asked Jerry.

"Because he loves me; because he loves us, and wants us to be happy," answered Chenoa sincerely.

"Sounds like some sort of answer one might hear in a Sunday school class," opined Jerry. "There has got to be more to it than that. What else haven't you told me," pressed Jerry.

"Enough talk; the food will taste better warm," asserted Chenoa. "Here put this on," handing Jerry his blindfold.

"Ok, once again I am putting my life and safety in your hands," said Jerry teasingly. "If I die before this day is over, I will have the satisfaction of claiming no one has ever been the victim of a more beautify woman."

"Oh, you are dramatic, aren't you," claimed Chenoa. "Here, let's start with this." Chenoa pressed a warm, fresh baked roll to Jerry's lips.

"Wow, that tastes great! I recognize bread when I taste it, but what was on it?" asked Jerry? "Am I supposed to be guessing what I am eating?"

"No, just enjoy it. You have just tasted choke cherry jelly, compliments of the trees of Three Creek Canyon, and my aunt, or soon to be stepmom," answered Chenoa.

"What a delicious spread" declared Jerry. "Do you have more surprises as amazing as choke cherry?"

"You will just have wait and see," said Chenoa.

"Ok, I am in your hands, what is next?" asked Jerry.

"This," said Chenoa as she pressed a spoonful of soup to Jerry's lips.

Jerry was surprised at the difference it made to just rely on his sense of smell and taste to appreciate what he was eating. Being blindfolded forced Jerry to pay more attention to his other senses. The result was to actually enjoy his food more. This was how lunch progressed from one course to the next.

Chenoa refused to tell him what he was eating. He just had to pay attention to how it tasted. It was a new experience. Never had Jerry enjoyed the taste of a meal more. Never had he tasted and enjoyed more unfamiliar foods.

Finally, Chenoa announced the meal was finished. She removed the blindfold, and gently wiped his face with a damp cloth. "Now we can talk," said Chenoa.

"First, I have to pay my compliments to the chef," said Jerry. "That was honestly a most enjoyable experience. You really have proved you can cook more than breakfast. I have no idea what I just ate. There was nothing familiar, but everything was enjoyable. Thank you, it was wonderful."

"You are welcome," said Chenoa. "Would you like to find a more comfortable place to set and visit? I'll come back and clean up later."

CHAPTER 14—THE CHAT

Jerry and Chenoa left the camp and walked to a small patch of trees with an adjoining meadow.

"Where shall we start?" asked Chenoa.

"You promised to answer the question, why me?" reminded Jerry. "From your reputation, you have avoided contact with most everyone who comes into these mountains. Then I fall off Fleet and everything changes. Again, why me, why now, and how am I related to your dreams?"

"A whole bunch of questions," acknowledged Chenoa.

"Okay," said Jerry. "Let's take the questions one at a time. First, who are you? I don't even know your full name?"

"I am Chenoa Walker. My father is Ben Walker. We raise Appaloosa horses. I ride the range to kept track of our horses. My father was born and raised on the Duck Valley Indian Reservation, which is about 60 miles west of here. We are Shoshone. My father didn't want to live or raise his family in the environment on the reservation, so he decided to leave the reservation and make his way in the white men's world. He changed his name from Walkingbull to Walker. He bought out an old Jarbidge rancher and has been raising Appaloosas ever since. My mother, Abby, died as the result of a poorly performed medical procedure years ago at the reservation hospital. He has been a single parent since then."

"Why the elusiveness?" asked Jerry.

"You might have noticed, I am a Girl," joked Chenoa. "Ever since I have been old enough to ride a horse, my dad has needed my help to

watch our stock. He is not oblivious to the danger of a girl being alone out on the range. His concern grew into near paranoia after a couple of men tried to molest me one day. He felt awful for exposing me to such danger, but he didn't have the means to hire someone else. So, he taught me to protect myself by staying out of sight. He was especially concerned about white men. He especially wanted me to be a ghost when they were in my area."

"You might have noticed, I am a boy," parroted Jerry. "How come this white man gets a pass?"

"The answer to that is a bit of a long story," admitted Chenoa "I really was conflicted when I found you. If I had followed my training, I would not have gotten involved. Something overrode all caution. I simply had to help. I have always been happy with my life till recently. Lately I have developed an uneasy feeling causing me to know something was missing. I have made it a matter of prayer. I have spent hours pondering what I should do.

My mother came to me recently in a vision or dream. She told me of her love for me and my father. She told me there was someone out there she wanted me to meet. However, I should be patient; I would be shown who. I have faith her message is true, because I have been at peace ever since. I have had not a doubt God loves me, wants me to be happy, and would lead me to find the someone my mother told me I'd meet."

"It would be hard to meet anyone, if you continued to avoid everyone," commented Jerry.

"So, you see how providentially our meeting is," agreed Chenoa. "How else could we have met? As I see it, God sent a lightning bolt to facilitate our meeting. Even your horse played a part. Do you have any doubt, we were meant for each other?"

"It certainly is a possibility," answered Jerry in a tone which indicated he was not yet convinced. "Tell me more about you, please."

"When we were having breakfast a few days ago, my anger melted away as I started to realize the hand of the Lord in our meeting. He did everything but a formal introduction. What were you looking for when you went riding that day?"

"I was looking for you. I was looking for the pretty girl people call the Flower of China Mountain," answered Jerry very honestly.

"Why?" asked Chenoa as she took Jerry's hand in hers. "I am here. What do you want?"

"I want to get to know you," said Jerry.

"Why?" repeated Chenoa, as she moved closer to Jerry and placed her lips on his.

This didn't clear Jerry's thinking. He was transformed into a babbling mound of humanity. Chenoa had no experience getting intimate with a young man. She hoped instinct would take over where experience was lacking. She and Jerry wrapped themselves in each other's arms and kissed for a long time.

They both considered what each really wanted. She wanted to know if Jerry was the partner who would be the man of her dream. She was looking for her true love, not just any male who would happily count her as one of his conquests.

Jerry wasn't sure what he wanted, but holding Chenos in his arms and kissing her was convincing him real fast he wanted her.

"Tell me more about yourself," requested Jerry "I want to know more about you. It is obvious you are incredibly beautiful. Tell me about the subtle aspects of your life?"

Chenoa was not sure where to begin, so she just started talking. Sharing this personal information didn't come easy, but she knew she would have to trust Jerry and his good intentions, if they were ever going to build a deep relationship.

Jerry knew his blood pressure was undoubtedly off the charts from making out with such a beautiful girl for any length of time. He needed a break before his cardiac system blew.

"I love my father. He is a kind gentle man, who loved my mom with all is heart. When she died, I don't think he was prepared to raise an only daughter, but he never shrank from the challenge. He shared a lot of the challenge with his sister-in-law, Little Feather. She has lived for many years on the Diamond Bar ranch, not far from our home. Her husband was a foreman for Orrie LaVal, the owner of the Diamond Bar. Tragically, her husband, John, was killed by an out-law horse."

"Afterward, Little Feather accepted a job from Orrie as the ranch cook and housekeeper. She has been my surrogate mom ever since

I can remember. She taught me the things about being a girl, my father couldn't."

"My father was so respectful of my mother; he never pursued the obvious opportunity to build a relationship with Little Feather. He always felt it would be disloyal to his deceased wife, Abby, to even consider a life with someone else. He felt it was his primary obligation to raise me, not to get involved with another woman, albeit his widowed sister-in-law."

"All that changed as I have grown to maturity. I think we all realized I can't be daddy's little girl forever. Eventually, I must leave the nest and make a life with my own man. As any loving daughter would do, I have fretted about what would become of my father when I rode down my own trail. It would likely leave him with a giant heart ache."

The longer I have delayed riding my own range, the more discontented I have become. This has driven me to my knees to seek guidance from Heavenly Father frequently in past few months. Recently my mother came to me by night, and answered a lot of questions. She brought a message from God to guide us in directing our lives. She said she was proud of my father and how well he had raised me, but it was time for me to move on."

"She told me to not worry about leaving my father; he would be ok. My mom told me that it was ok for my dad to marry Little Feather; for them to forge a life together. It made so much sense. They have always had a good relationship, respected each other, and gotten along well. With my leaving the nest, why not get together? They are in the process of courting each other."

"I am in the process of finding out if you are the man my mother told me I would find. I think you are. If I find out you are not, I will return to being the ghost you have heard about. You said you were the man of my dreams. Do you really believe that or was that just talk? If you are, if you honestly believe you are, I am yours. My body, my soul, my love, my hopes, my dreams, my heart, all of me; I am yours. Jerry, do you want me?" asked Chenoa.

"How could I not want you, the embodiment of the Flower of China Mountain?" answered Jerry in all sincerity. "You are the most beautiful creature I have ever laid eyes on. I believe you are not just beautiful on the outside, but through and through. I didn't come to Idaho in search of love, nor to be struck by lightning, but I have been struck by both. Yes, Chenoa, I want you! First, though, I think we need to get to know each other."

"I agree," said Chenoa. "I have told you a fair amount about myself, I would love to know more about you!"

The weather was pleasant. There were lots of white billowy clouds floating from west to east along the Jarbidge range. Jerry and Chenoa lay in the meadow for most of the afternoon sharing information about themselves. Now and then they would spot and point out a cloud which looked like some familiar object. A bond developed quickly between them. At first Chenoa and Jerry lay near each other. Soon Chenoa moved closer to Jerry and laid her head on his outstretched arm. They found it easy to talk to each other. What they discussed didn't offend one another but deepened their affection for each other. They talked about nearly every aspect of their background that came to mind. The breeze which flowed gently over them was a bit cool when they were in the shadow of a cloud. When they were once again having the sun beat down on them, it warmed them pleasantly. When they were in the shadow of a cloud for a particularly long time Chenoa became chilled. She turned on her side and snuggled close to Jerry. He felt comfortably warm. In fact, she realized everything about Jerry felt comfortable. She felt feelings of love swelling within her.

The feelings of disharmony which had attended their first banter filled conversations were gone. Chenoa found everything about Jerry pleasant, charming, and likable. Yes, he was a bit of a tease, but in a friendly way. His way of teasing was not mean or hurtful but displayed a fine sense of humor.

Jerry was impressed with Chenoa's personality. She exuded love. It radiated from her like warmth from the intermittent periods of afternoon sun. When Chenoa snuggled in next to him, he felt great. For a brief moment he couldn't breathe. The words ran through his mind, 'died and gone to heaven'. The next phrase he heard in his mind was 'heaven on earth'. Jerry wasn't sure exactly what was happening to him, but he was ready to let it happen. As the gambling expression goes, "He was all in!"

When the sun was getting low in the western sky, Chenoa paused in her efforts to learn everything she could about Jerry, swirled her index finger on Jerry's chest, and asked seductively, "Eat, drink, or me? Or keep talking?"

"How could you possibly respect a man who was all talk, and no action?" asked Jerry. With that he aggressively rolled on to her, took Chenoa in his arms, and kissed her first on her lips, then on her neck. "Consider this as making permanent my choice."

Now it was Chenoa's turn to find herself breathless as Jerry kissed her neck passionately. "Ok, ok, I'll never accuse you of being all talk."

Jerry rolled off Chenoa and onto his back. She followed his move by rolling onto her side again and snuggling up to Jerry. "Chenoa, I likewise think you are the girl of my dreams. Having said that, how do we proceed from here? In Philadelphia I would arrange a meeting with your father, ask for your hand in marriage, then we would start planning a formal church wedding. I haven't the slightest idea of the customs here in the Jarbidge mountains, or amongst the Shoshone."

"Well, it is customary," said Chenoa as she snuggled closer to Jerry, "for you to go hunting for a big fat buck, so when you go to see my father you will have a present for him; something to trade for me. You are getting his daughter; he is getting a buck."

"Doesn't sound like a very fair deal! What if I can't find a deer?" asked Jerry.

"I will have to bear the shame of people knowing my husband to be is a poor hunter," teased Chenoa.

"Ya, I have heard the joke," declared Jerry.

"What joke?" asked Chenoa.

"The joke which asks the question, where does the word vegetarian come from?" said Jerry.

"What is the answer?" asked Chenoa. "Where does it come from?"

"According to the joke," stated Jerry, "it is an old Indian word meaning poor hunter."

"Maybe it is no joke," suggested Chenoa.

"I am starting to think that" said Jerry as he stroked Chenoa's hair then pulled her closer. "I thought deer were out of season, this time of year."

"They are, except for you," stated Chenoa. "There is a little known and seldom used provision of the 1863 Treaty of Ruby Valley, that allows for the taking of game off the reservation in exercise of traditional Indian customs."

"What? Are you some kind of Indian lawyer?" asked Jerry. "What does that which you just said, mean?"

Chenoa rose on her elbow to look Jerry face to face and gently rubbed his face. "Simply put, my darling, it means you can go hunting any time you want, if it is for the purpose of seeking permission from my father to marry me."

"Swell, but I've never shot anything in my life; not even a bunny rabbit," admitted Jerry.

"Not a problem, my handsome city slicker, I have," said Chenoa as she kissed Jerry's cheek. "This will be one of the easier of the many problems we will need to solve, if we are to live happily ever after. I know just where to go to find a four-point buck. I see him just about every time I check on our horses in the upper Cedar Creek drainage. He would be perfect!"

Jerry still seemed a bit panicked. "Chenoa, honey, I have never shot a gun. I don't know how!"

"So what, I have never had sex, but I think I can learn how," said Chenoa.

"I can help you there," admitted Jerry.

"I can help you with the buck, too," offered Chenoa. "My father will not know who pulled the trigger." Chenoa threw herself into Jerry's arms, kissed him for a long moment, then continued, "I believe there is nothing we can't accomplish together."

"Does that include supper," asked Jerry with his focus switching from one appetite to another.

"Oh, my goodness," said Chenoa realizing how time had flown by. "I can fix supper for you in just a few minutes. Will you please throw the horses some fresh hay while you are waiting?"

Jerry helped Chenoa to her feet, and they walked hand in hand back to the camp. Earlier today they had walked away from camp knowing little about each other. They had covered so much during the course of the afternoon, they now felt like old friends; friends who were in love.

"Do I have to wear the blindfold this time?" asked Jerry.

"Not unless you catch me in my underwear again," joked Chenoa.

"How long before that won't matter," asked Jerry.

"Let's figure that out on a full stomach. I just realized, I am hungry, too," confessed Chenoa.

Chenoa paused as they reached the camp, turned to Jerry, and gazed up into his steel gray eyes. "I am convinced," she whispered as she closed in for another kiss.

"Convinced of what, my little Shoshone dove," ask Jerry as soon as he could catch his breath.

"You are the man of my dreams; the man my mother told me I would meet. Jerry, I love you with all my heart already; my darling, I am yours. Now go feed the horses, before I give in to doing something we shouldn't do, yet," said Chenoa trying to be honest about her feelings, while struggling to stay 'a good girl'.

Jerry agreed with Chenoa's desired standards. They were his standards, as well. He had never spent a more amazing afternoon. He recognized he was falling in love with Chenoa; completely, hopelessly, without question. Everything he had learned about her in the last few hours had chipped away at any reservations he may have had. His original reasons for wanting to meet her may have been to satisfy some sort of curiosity, but that was no longer the case. He wanted to be her husband. If that necessitated presenting some unfortunate deer to her father, so be it. The deer would not go to waste. It couldn't be for a better cause.

Supper had a couple items which tasted familiar; Jerry wondered if he was being fed leftovers. Chenoa congratulated him on his fine sense of taste and memory. Jerry was surprised at how seeing the food affected how it tasted. He still had no idea what it was. They ate slowly and continued their discussion of things past, present, and future.

They were both 'all in', no going back, no hesitation, no reservations.

Chenoa remembered the words of her father, "A pair of panties is not a lot of deterrence." When it got dark, they kept talking for hours. When they were both so sleepy, they could no longer stay awake, they slept in each other's arms, on the camp bed, but this time fully clothed sans boots.

They awoke early, ate some breakfast, saddled up, and were on their way to bag a buck as day light broke in the eastern sky. They made their way south and west toward Cedar Creek. They were riding into a slight breeze. Chenoa explained to Jerry this was good since the wind would not carry their scent toward the buck with his keen sense of smell.

Chenoa and Jerry arrived on a ridge overlooking Cedar Creek as the sun started to cast shadows in the bottom of the canyon. The wind shifted a bit, but not enough to alert the buck. They watched from the ridge for a few minutes, then Chenoa suggested to Jerry a strategy for taking the buck.

Jerry listened intently then headed north per Chenoa's instructions. Chenoa was impressed Jerry was so willing to do as she had counseled. Few fellows would have been willing to follow the instructions of a girl without hesitation. Chenoa had heard how hard it was for the male ego to fully cooperate.

Jerry rode Fleet quietly north for about one mile, then turned west to cross Cedar Creek. He then turned back south to approach the buck's suspected location on the west side of the canyon down which Cedar Creek flowed.

Jerry could see Chenoa had dismounted Sky Walker and had taken up a secluded firing position in a cluster of rocks. She had a good view of the patch of trees where she had often seen the buck on other occasions. Jerry rode Fleet to a spot directly downwind from the buck's suspected location, then per Chenoa's instructions started not so quietly into the canyon. About halfway down to the creek, Jerry was startled when as predicted a nice sized four-point buck burst from the brush. It started up the hill away from Jerry, but right into the kill zone of Chenoa's location. For Chenoa, it was an easy shot.

Jerry didn't know anything about hunting or what needed to be done after you pull the trigger. Chenoa explained how they would need to take the buck down the hill where they could hang it in a tree to 'dress' it. After Chenoa explained what that meant, Jerry asked why they didn't call the process 'undressing'?

"Just don't tell my dad, you 'undressed' a buck for him," warned Chenoa, "And when he asks how long the shot was you took to get the buck, just say something like, "You would have to ask Chenoa; I wasn't paying much attention. Or I'm not a very good judge of distances."

"Don't you think we should just tell him, sweetheart?" asked Jerry.

"If you aren't embarrassed to reveal you can't hunt and didn't shoot your own engagement deer, at least don't make me reveal that I am in effect buying myself," laughed Chenoa.

"Ok, I see your point," agreed Jerry. "You don't want people to think of me as a vegetarian."

Chenoa showed Jerry the fundamentals of dressing a deer. She also explained the more graphic term was gutting. She supervised, but let Jerry experience the process. Without its entrails, the buck was considerably lighter.

Jerry and Chenoa had a short discussion on how they were going to proceed. They needed to decide if they were going to pack the buck on one horse, and ride double on the other, or carry the buck on the horse one of them was riding. Didn't take a lot of consideration, before Jerry offered Fleet to pack the buck. He could see instantly, he would rather ride hugging Chenoa rather than a dead buck for miles to her home.

Jerry hefted the buck onto Fleet, and Chenoa tied it down. Fleet didn't seem overly pleased to be carrying the buck, nor did Sky Walker seem to like Jerry riding double behind Chenoa. In Jerry's opinion that was tough. He was pleased with the chance to hold Chenoa in his arms. It was yet another indescribable, sensual thrill. He tried to balance the need to hold on tight enough he didn't fall off another horse, and the need to be gentle with Chenoa. He didn't want to hurt her by squeezing too tight. She nearly shorted out his nervous system, yet again, when she clasp her free hand over his hands which he had around her slim waist. Her every touch was an ecstatic experience.

Jerry didn't know how much of this ecstasy he could handle before he suffered a stroke, heart attacker, or some other system failure. Her touch was as exciting as was her beauty.

Jerry asked himself whether he would ever have had a chance with Chenoa sans the intervention of her mother. Lots of guys hated their mothers-in-law, and the feeling was mutual. He owed his good fortune to a special woman he would never meet this side of heaven.

By noon they were still a long way from Ben's ranch headquarters. For the last few miles Chenoa had leaned her head back against Jerry's chest. She had succeeded in conveying to Jerry she enjoying being in his arms.

Sky Walker now seemed more accepting of him; much less like he would just as soon buck him off. That was a good development, because Jerry had no idea of how to charm a stallion if they hadn't hit it off.

"How is your butt? asked Chenoa.

"Starting to get a little sore," admitted Jerry.

Chenoa suggested they stop for a few minutes by another creek which flowed out of the Jarbidge. They watered the horses, then sat on a grassy steam bank.

"I have some dried food in my saddle bag," said Chenoa. "Are you hungry? I would be glad to share."

"I could cut a few strips of meat off that buck, I suppose," said Jerry, "if you have something a little less raw, I accept."

Chenoa grabbed a few chunks of her dried food and gave it to Jerry.

"Humm, not bad," said Jerry. "Sort of a cross between granola and jerky. Did you make this yourself?"

"Not alone," said Chenoa. "My papa and I make it together in batches big enough to last for months."

"What is is made of," asked Jerry.

"It varies," admitted Chenoa. "Dead horse is the only ingredient I can assure you we have never used!"

"Well as assuring as that is, horses do wind up in dog food. Maybe that is why dogs age seven years for each year we do," speculated Jerry.

"Here, if you don't like it, don't force yourself," advised Chenoa.

"I'm good," said Jerry.

"Your backside feeling any better?" inquired Chenoa. "If not, I'll let you have the saddle for a while, and I'll ride in back."

Jerry was hesitant to accept, but Chenoa assured him it would be ok. On the next leg of their journey, they traded places. Sky Walker could walk amazingly fast. Fleet would occasionally break into a trot to keep up.

Jerry's senses were again fired into overload when Chenoa squeezed him much more tightly than was required for someone with her riding skills to keep from falling off. Her touch was awesome. No matter in what manner she touched Jerry, it was magic.

They crested a hill and saw a large ranch headquarters lying in front of them.

"Your spread?" asked Jerry.

"No," said Chenoa. "Welcome to the Diamond Bar ranch, owned and operated by Orrie LaVal. This is our closest neighbor, and where my Aunt, Little Feather, works as the cook and housekeeper. That is until my dad steals her away and makes her my stepmother."

"Is he going to have to shoot a buck for Orie, or just take her?" asked Jerry.

"He is a bit worried the hands might come after him for rustling," admitted Chenoa, "if Orrie can't find another good cook."

"Want to stop in and meet her?" asked Chenoa. "You will love her!"

"It is not deer season," said Little Feather when she saw the buck laying across Jerry's saddle. "So, is this what I think it is?"

"As a matter of fact it is," confirmed Chenoa with a happy smile and an enthusiastic hug after she dismounted from Sky Walker.

Chenoa introduced Jerry to Little Feather, and then the two women disappeared in a frenzy of girl talk. Sensing his duty, Jerry lead the two horses to a water trough, then tied them to a hitching rail outside the building with a sign over the door which read 'Cook Shack'.

Jerry decided to take his chances, wander in, and see what kind of grub might be available. It just had to be tastier than dried saddle bag food, no offense to Chenoa or her papa's cooking.

To his great pleasure Jerry found a fresh loaf of bread along with some butter and jelly. He learned later the bread had been recently baked by Little Feather with Chenoa's father's help at Chenoa's home. Jerry recognized the delicious taste of the jelly. He had been introduced to it the day before by Chenoa. It was Choke Cherry.

Jerry was eating his third slice of bread when the girls found him in the cook shack. Chenoa finished off the slice of bread Jerry he was eating.

"Um, love fresh bread," said Chenoa.

"This is especially good," agreed Jerry. "Homemade bread has always been my favorite."

"Even if you didn't like this particular bread, I wouldn't say so," chuckled Chenoa. "It was baked by your soon to be mother-in-law and father-in-law."

"No problem, it is great," asserted Jerry. "Want to share another slice?"

"Yes, thank you," agreed Chenoa, taking Jerry by his arm and snuggling close to him."

"Ok, but I'll need this arm, unless you want to fix it," said Jerry to Chenoa.

"I'll gladly trade you an arm for another half slice," answer Chenoa cheerfully.

"Hold onto your man, and never let him go!" advised Little Feather with a wink and a smile, "I'll fix it."

Little Feather fixed an extra slice for herself, then asked, "Anybody care for a glass of milk, too?"

"Sure," said Chenoa, "We'll get three glasses." Chenoa used the arm she was holding to guide Jerry to the cupboard, then the refrigerator. They worked together to pour three large glasses of cold milk. They set them down at the table where Little Feather was preparing the third and last slice of bread.

Chenoa, Jerry, and Little Feather enjoyed their bread and milk while discussing their plans. They finally decided Jerry and Chenoa would go ahead to introduce Jerry to Ben. Little Feather would come later after she finished her work for the day.

Ben was repairing a corral fence when he saw riders appear on the ridge above the ranch headquarters. It was immediately obvious the lead rider was Chenoa on Sky Walker. She was followed by a big man riding a nice-looking sorrel horse with a white striped face and three white stocking legs. It was interesting how far away one could see these distinguishing markings. The horse was a very impressive gelding.

It did not escape Ben's notice; the man was leading a pack horse over which was tied a buck. It was not yet deer season, so some distinct possibilities crossed Ben's mind to explain why he would be packing a deer.

Ben stopped his repair work and watched as he waited for the riders to complete their descent. He was impressed with how well the stranger sat a saddle.

Chenoa met Ben at the barn door. She stepped down and gave her dad a long embrace.

"Papa, I would like you to meet Jerry. I brought him home to meet you!" said Chenoa.

Jerry stepped off Fleet, shook Ben's hand, and handed him the reins to the pack horse.

"This is for you. I have come to ask you for Chenoa's hand. I'd like to marry her with your permission, Sir.

Ben was anticipating Jerry's request but was taken back by his directness. Jerry didn't waste any time, which surprised Ben.

"Thank you, young man! Would you be offended if I reserved my answer till I have a chance to talk to you and Chenoa. I would like to get to know the man to whom I am giving my daughter's hand."

"Sure, I understand." said Jerry.

"Papa, we can help you hang the buck in the barn, if you want," suggested Chenoa.

"Thank you, I would welcome the help. Say isn't this Orrie's pack animal?" asked Ben.

"Yes," answered Chenoa. "We stopped in to see Little Feather. She let us borrow him. She should be coming by later and will take him back home."

"That was nice of them to loan you the pack animal," said Ben. "That gives us a while to get acquainted before she comes."

Ben, Chenoa, and Jerry worked together to hang the buck in the barn where it could cool and cure for a few days before it was butchered. Working together gave them a chance to interact with each other, and take a measure of one another.

When the buck was properly hung, and the horses put away for the evening, Chenoa offered to cook the heart and liver for their supper. Ben was pleased at the idea, since he had not had any venison since last fall during the regular hunting season.

Little Feather arrived early enough to join Ben, Chenoa, and Jerry for supper with its venison menu. Chenoa had cut the heart into thin slices and breaded it and the liver in flour. Ben loved venison, especially liver.

Ben invited Chenoa to go for a walk after supper, because they hadn't had a chance to visit since her return.

"Tell me what you are thinking, sweetheart," requested Ben.

"I think Jerry is the one mom said I would find, dad," said Chenoa

"So, you want me to say yes?" asked Ben.

"Yes, papa," said Chenoa. "Want to make it a double wedding?"

"Do you?" asked Ben.

"I think it is worth considering. Let's discuss it with the others," suggested Chenoa.

Ben invited Jerry to take a walk next to discuss matters. Little Feather volunteered to help Chenoa with the clean up of the supper dishes so the two could talk, also. The two impending brides needed to decide what they wanted; how they wanted to proceed. The guys would likely care little about the details.

Ben had a routine way of checking to see if things were secure for the evening before turning in. Jerry paid close attention as he accompanied Ben. Jerry was impressed with the similarities he noticed between Ben and Uncle Glenn. After telling Jerry he had Ben's blessing to marry Chenoa, Ben proceeded to ask Jerry a few questions about his plans for the future. It soon became apparent, there were no plans, yet.

Ben recommended to Jerry, he and Chenoa figure out a lot of things before they proceeded to get married. Ben's questions had already brought Jerry to the same conclusion. He and Chenoa needed to think things out way beyond the point of "I do."

Ben went for a walk with Little Feather after he returned to the house with Jerry. Little Feather shared the ideas with Ben which she and Chenoa planned. They all seemed reasonable to Ben. Jerry likewise had a chance to talk to Chenoa who explained them to him. Jerry didn't oppose the ideas. He was now more focused on the need to plan for the long term. He explained to Chenoa what her father had asked him.

Their earlier conversations during the last two days had not really dealt with question of how they would 'live happily ever after', only if they wanted to try with each other. They needed to write the rest of the story. Just how would they live happily ever after. They recognized they were from two different worlds. Would he join hers, or would she follow him.

Chenoa had not been oblivious to this dilemma. She raised the question if there were a third option; could there be a 'their world'?

Jerry and Chenoa spent quite some time speculating what a 'their world' might entail.

Jerry suggested Chenoa ought to meet Uncle Glenn and Aunt Martha. They finally came up with the following plan. They would spend time first with Ben and Little Feather, letting Jerry get to know them, then go to spend some time with the Briggs. Jerry pointed out how Uncle Glenn was approaching an age where he needed to be considering retirement.

Forging a 'their world' option might entail eventually taking over his operation. In the meantime they might work for them. There were a lot of options. They just needed to be explored.

Chenoa was excited to meet Uncle Glenn and Aunt Martha. From what Jerry had told her, they were great people. As ranchers Chenoa anticipated it would be easy to relate to them.

Little Feather and Ben sat with Jerry and Chenoa to discuss the ideas they had been considering. Just before dark Little Feather left for the Diamond Bar ranch taking Orie's pack animal with her. Ben, Chenoa, and Jerry sat together and talked late into the evening.

Jerry spent several hours explaining what life was like in Philadelphia. Ben spent time explaining what life had been like on the reservation followed by his description of how life was different in the white man's world. They talked about the possibility of Jerry and Chenoa working for or with Ben. Part of Jerry's college curriculum had been in the field of marketing. They brainstormed the idea of Jerry and Chenoa becoming the marketing arm of Ben's ranch.

There were lots of possibilities; the more they talked the more ideas they came up with which seemed viable in a 'their world'. In a short time, they had been able to come up with answers to most of the concerns Ben had expressed in his conversation with Jerry. Chenoa and Jerry felt confident there was a way forward which would serve them well. Their union would not be an exercise in recklessness.

CHAPTER 15—WEDDING PLANNING

The cowhands of the Diamond bar ranch couldn't have been happier for Little Feather when Orrie announced to the crew she would be leaving to marry Ben Walker. It was as though she were the little sister of each of them. Every man came to Little Feather when they had an opportunity to privately congratulate her and express their best wishes. A common sentiment was how happy they were Little Feather would still be living in the neighborhood. A cheer went up when Orrie announced he had negotiated an arrangement for Little Feather to continue supplying bread to the Diamond Bar ranch. A couple men joked if they had known Little Feather were willing to consider marriage, they would have proposed. Her usual response was to give the cowhand a kiss on the cheek, a smile, a hug, and say, "Now you tell me!"

As luck would have it, Orrie just happened to know of an old maid from Mountain City who had been working in Jack Pot for years. Word was she was tired of the gambling scene, wanted to move to the Jarbidge area, but hadn't found a job. Fortuitously, she had been a cook for one of the casinos for several years. The crew joked about how the menu might change, when Orrie announced he had recruited her. What is her name, the crew all wanted to know?

"Sadie," replied Orrie.

Weddings were rare in the Jarbidge mountains, given how few people inhabited the area. Ben and Little Feather didn't bother to send out wedding invitations. They didn't need to. Word spread faster than a wildfire. Within days, everyone in the zip code knew. The idea of a

joint wedding had been scrapped. Ben and Little Feather were ready to marry and had no need or desire to wait. Social calendars weren't crowded for local residents. A local wedding easily trumped all else. At the invitation of Orrie LaVal, Little Feather and Ben chose to hold the wedding at the Dimond Bar ranch. It had room to accommodate a larger crowd than Ben's ranch.

Sadie arrived a week before the wedding to assume the duties of her new job. She willingly agreed to help with the wedding preparations, as did all the cowhands. Some of the ranch work suffered a bit for a week or two. The cowhands paid more attention to the wedding preparations than their normal work. The 'little sister' syndrome was in full effect. Every cowhand was seen working on the project with an attention to detail as though it was his own kid sister who was tying the knot. When Orrie saw how well the ranch was looking, he joked to Sadie, having the wedding at his ranch was the best idea he could remember having had in a long time. Orrie learned to his great surprise and pleasure; Sadie had been a confection baker at one time. She was able to plan a menu for the guests which was better than anything seen in the area ever.

The crew constructed a BBQ pit for the wedding and picked out a fine steer to cook in it. As luck would have it, one cowhand was from Texas, and a veteran of BBQ cooking. After the menu leaked out, no one wanted to miss the wedding.

Little Feather found herself with a dilemma. She sought Chenoa's advice. Chenoa was equally conflicted and asked for time to think about it. They would have asked Ben for his opinion, but this was a girl thing. They needed to decide which dress Little Feather would wear. She had two principal choices: she still had her dress from when she married John, and Ben still had Abby's dress in a trunk of keep sakes. Unable to decide, Little Feather finally sought Ben's opinion.

The decision was easily made when Ben asked a simple question, "Have you tried them on?" When they knew Ben would be away, Chenoa and Little Feather met in semi-secret to see how the dresses fit. Abbey had gotten married when she was considerably younger than Little Feather had been. As a result, she had been tinier than Little Feather. Abby's dress proved to be uncomfortably tight, but her own dress still fit beautifully.

"Why don't you wear your mom's dress?" suggested Little Feather.

Chenoa eyes watered, and she had to fight to keep her composure as she thought about wearing her mother's dress when she married Jerry.

"I would love to," replied Chenoa choking back tears.

Seeing Chenoa's tears caused Little Feather to choke up also. Soon they were both crying and hugging each other; what might be described as a good ole fashion 'blubberfest'. In the midst of this, Jerry walked in and was totally at a loss to understand what was wrong. He did the manly thing and made a strategic retreat.

"Excuse me, but I should probably go check on Fleet," said Jerry.

He said it with such timidity, and departed so quickly, both girls switched from crying to laughing. Some men's lack of understanding of women was sometimes very humorous. They probably would understand a lecture on interplanetary geometry better. Jerry had heard Jake confess in frustration on their trips to North Fork one morning, "It is fortunate you don't have to understand them, to love them." He and his wife had gotten married young and were having some challenging times in their marriage.

Ben owned a suit but had worn it exactly three times. First time when he and Abby had gotten married; second, when Chenoa was christened; and the last time to Abby's funeral. It fit a bit tight when he tried it on for size, but he judged it would be ok for the fourth usage. He decided to indulge in a bit of vanity and fast a day or two before the wedding. Losing a few pounds couldn't hurt. He also wanted to have room for the BBQ without busting out at the seams.

Jerry continued his efforts to get to know Ben and Chenoa better as preparations for the wedding progressed. Chenoa and Jerry had decided to wait till after Ben's wedding to go see Uncle Glenn and Aunt Martha. Jerry had invited them to the wedding when he had called to check in from Orrie LaVal's phone at the Diamond Bar ranch.

Aunt Martha had been glad to get the call, since they hadn't heard from Jerry for an uncomfortably long time. She admitted they were starting to get worried. Aunt Martha confirmed she and Glenn would be at the wedding. This would be an opportunity for them to meet Chenoa. Uncle Glenn was well known in the Jarbidge mountains. Attending Ben's wedding would be a chance to see a lot of old friends. Although Ben and Glenn had never met, they knew each other by reputation.

Aunt Martha agreed to search Jerry's one bag of clothing to find a clean and nicer shirt and pair of pants. She also agreed to come a little early to deliver them in time to wear to the wedding. Jerry wished he wasn't traveling quite so light, now. He hadn't envisioned attending a formal events. On the day of the wedding, Aunt Martha surprised him by having purchased a real nice cowboy shirt.

Chenoa had washed his one pair of pants and had loaned him some of Ben's boot polish. She teasingly told Jerry, "You clean up real nice, fella!"

What Chenoa planned to wear to the wedding became a topic of discussion when they all got together again a few days before the big event. Bride's maids were sometimes had in Shoshone Indian weddings, but they were more of a cultural appropriation, than traditional. Ben's practical side came out again when he suggested they keep it simple. Little Feather agreed readily. In spite of making a concerted effort to keep things as low key as they knew how, things seemed to be getting more complex with each passing day. Besides there was no time to make special dresses.

To honor her heritage, Chenoa announced she would be wearing her favorite white, deer skin ceremonial dress. Nothing would more clearly telegraph Chenoa's message to the assembled crowd, "I am Shoshone and proud of it!"

As Jerry would later see, the dress complemented Chenoa's beauty perfectly. In it, she was not just pretty, she was absolutely stunning. Little Feather asked Chenoa if she would be her one and only bride's maid? Chenoa graciously accepted the honor.

Quicker than anyone was prepared, the wedding day was upon them. Ben had gone out the night before and picked a bouquet of wildflowers. It was his way of denoting how special this day was to him. He didn't want anyone thinking he was taking this day or Little Feather for granted.

It may have been Abby appearing in a dream or vision to Chenoa to get things started, but he was all for it now. Ben thought of himself

as one lucky guy to have had Abby as his wife, and now to be marrying her sister, two of the finest women he had ever met. He indeed was going to love her with his whole heart and soul now and forever. He felt sure Abby would want and expect nothing less of him.

Loving Little Feather more was not loving Abby less. It was going to be a love triangle reaching across the veil of death. How this would all work out in the afterlife was not a thing to worry about now. In the wisdom and love of God, Ben had faith it would all work out. He had talked to Little Feather on the subject, and knew she felt the same.

How God would deal with them and John in the hereafter, was a question for another day. Ben shared his feelings with Chenoa, too. She was happy for her father and Little Feather. She could work out her future with Jerry, and not have to feel she had somehow abandoned her father to a life of loneliness. He would be just fine; more than fine. Ben would be happy.

Chapter 16—The Wedding

The guests started arriving early on the big day. The aroma of roasting beef filled the air. Picnic tables had been set up all around the new BBQ pit, not far from Orrie's flower garden. As was customary with mountain folks, people treated get-to-gathers as potlucks, and brought pies, cakes, and casseroles or other dishes to help feed the masses. For special occasions like a wedding, people didn't just throw in a bag of chips, they brought the tastiest fair they knew how to make. This was their chance to show off a bit. When the affair was over, if your dish was empty, that was considered a high compliment. It meant folks liked what you fixed. If folks scraped your dish clean, it was an even higher honor.

The wedding vows were scheduled for high noon. Was an easier time to remember for most folks than something like 2:15. The invitation to the wedding was also designated a BYOFC event (Bring Your Own Folding Chair). The cowhands had set up some crude seating with planks and blocks of wood, but those seats were mainly for those who didn't own a folding chair. Folks who wished to pamper their butt, knew to bring their own chair.

Ben had arranged for the "Bishop of Jarbidge" to conduct the wedding. He was also the postmaster, the mayor, and the head of public works. He had also been the fire chief, but decided to give up that post in favor of a younger man after the citizens started murmuring, he was getting too old for the job. He preached a non-denominal version of Christianity which taught if you accepted Jesus, you were saved. Most of his sermons were heavy on forgiveness, and light on calling anyone to repent. He couldn't afford to offend anyone in his little flock. Anyway, the price was right, so Ben hired him. Praise the Lord, he was on time, too.

Most of the population of Jarbidge was present at Orrie's ranch when the sun stood at high noon. Not everyone in Jarbidge owned a watch; which was another good reason for the choice of the start time. The real attention getter was when Chenoa and Jerry arrived.

Jerry was only memorable in that he took up the position of the Best Man. Chenoa on the other hand was beautiful beyond description. When she rode in on Sky Walker dressed in her white deer skin dress, she had the attention of every man there, and most of the woman.

Here again, most folks had heard about Chenoa, but few had ever seen her in person. She met and surpassed all of the superlative's folks had heard about her. Chenoa took up her position in front of the preacher and waited patiently for the bride and groom to take their places.

Uncle Glenn and Aunt Martha had planned to arrive early for the wedding. Unfortunately, there was another unanticipated union on this special day. Uncle Glenn got a flat tire when he picked up a nail. It had been a long time since this had happened. By the time Uncle Glenn was able to find a jack, a tire iron, and get the spare tire on, it was too late to be early. This was an embarrassment to a couple who were rarely late to anything, let alone something as important as a wedding. By the time they arrived, Little Feather was already approaching the 'Bishop'.

Orrie got the honor of giving the bride away. Sadie had helped Little Feather with her hair. It looked great. Turns out Sadie had also been a hairdresser, too. Apparently, Jack Pot was a good place to go to develop your hidden talents. When the preacher declared Ben and Little Feather husband and wife, it was Ben who was overcome with emotion. It was as though Abby had returned from the dead. Now he had someone again to whom he could devote his attention as well as his long pent up desires, appetites, and passion. He had been without Abby for years. Now he had Little Feather. Now they had each other.

Jerry and Chenoa were busy in the reception line. For most it was the first chance they had ever had to meet Chenoa. Many had heard of her, but only a few had ever met her since she was a young girl. More than one wife hustled her husband on down the line when they lingered too long with this young beauty. The first chance Jerry had to greet his aunt and uncle was when they came through the receiving line. After he introduced them to Chenoa, Aunt Martha and Uncle Glen both whispered the same message to Jerry during their embrace, "Wow!"

Two surprise guests were Dr. Dean and his daughter Susie. They had heard about the wedding through what Susie later described as the Appaloosa Grapevine. Susie was glad to report the training of Little Boy was going well. Dr. Dean reported Susie seemed nearly obsessed with him. She spent hour after hour working with and training Little Boy. They were especially pleased how well he picked things up. The first thing Dr. Dean expected to hear when he came home every evening was about the latest thing Susie had been able to teach him. He was not only exceptionally smart, but trainable.

Susie summed up with the comment to Chenoa, "Little Boy and I are bonding like you and Sky Walker."

Many folks were engrossed in visiting with one another. It had been a long time since so many residents of the Jarbidge Mountains had gathered together. Some hadn't seen each other in years.

A natural flow developed. Folks would visit in small groups till it was their turn to enter the reception line, extend their congratulations to Ben and Little Feather, then proceed to the food line to load their plates with BBQ beef and a variety of other appetizing foods.

No one went home hungry for lack of enough food. Since BBQ cooks on the outside faster than the inside, the chefs cut away at the outer layers to supply diners a continuous supply of perfectly done meat. By late afternoon, the steer was little more than a skeleton.

Sadie had saved enough to feed Orrie's crew for a few days, or weeks. Nothing would be wasted.

Jerry, Chenoa, Martha, and Glenn all sat together to eat and talk. When Chenoa volunteered to go fetch Aunt Martha more of a particularly delicious dish before it was all gone, Jerry asked Glenn and Martha if they could stay long enough to have a serious private discussion.

"Is this about what I think it is? asked Aunt Martha. "She really is everything you said she was, and more."

"I have spent the last 2 to 3 weeks getting to know her and her father, Ben. Aunt Martha, her personality is on par with her beauty. She is simply wonderful. Likewise, Uncle Glenn, there is so much Ben and you have in common, I find myself wondering if you two could be long lost brothers. You two define the expression, 'good ole boys'. You are both 'salt of the earth' types, who would be best friends if you were closer neighbors.

Chenoa returned with the food for Aunt Martha. The get acquainted conversation continued. The affectionate way Chenoa and Jerry treated each other left no doubt in Glenn or Martha's mind what needed to be discussed. It was fairly obvious where their relationship was headed.

"Do you think these two could successfully merge a Shoshone with a Philadelphia background," Glenn asked Martha when they were alone.

"Yes, my aging love. Look at her. Leaving me out of the conversation for the moment, have you ever seen someone as gorgeous and gracious as the creature with whom you just had lunch? If Jerry finds the rest of her personality equally as attractive, trust me, he is hooked. I don't mean it in a negative context, either. I think he will sacrifice whatever he needs to of his world, to have her. From what little I know of Chenoa; I think she will also."

"They met through the near miss of a lightning strike. The lightning may have been a near miss, but she was a direct hit. You know every marriage is a merger. Even we can testify to that. The strongest glue keeping every marriage together, is the conviction the union was not a mistake." "Chenoa is going to have an incentive few others have; the assurance she has her dead mother is her guardian angel and guided her meeting, Jerry. She is unlikely to let anything or anyone get in her way. With that kind of determination to make it work, petty differences will not matter so much as in most relationships," asserted Martha. "Mark my word, my aging lover, these two want to talk about getting married."

"Well, I suppose we could make room for a teepee in the backyard," kidded Uncle Glenn poking Martha gently in the ribs.

"Very funny," retorted Martha. "Don't believe me; just wait. You'll see."

The last of the wedding guests didn't leave the Diamond Bar until high noon had faded to sundown. Visiting with old friends was the main activity which kept folks there, but BBQ and all the food was the other. Guests going to see what food was left over were heard to offer a variety of reasons to explain their healthy appetites. Sayings like, "My pappy taught me to never pass up a water hole, waste not, want not, my waste or go to waste." Once people were through eating, it was back to visiting.

Comments on how good the food had been on everyone's lips as they bade farewell to their host. Orrie had harvested an abundance of goodwill and publicity from hosting Ben and Little Feather's wedding.

Orrie gave some thought to using his ranch as an exotic wedding venue. There might be some good money in this aspect of dude ranching. So many people had had such a good time, Orrie intuitively knew such a venture would be well received.

Sadie had proved to be a great asset; she had so many hidden talents. She was amazing. No one left till late afternoon when Ben and Little Feather thanked Orrie and his crew again for hosting their wedding, then slipped away.

Chapter 17—The Evaluation

After hours of tending to the guests, and after Ben and Little Feather had slipped away to be alone, Jerry and Chenoa found an opportunity to meet privately with Uncle Glenn and Aunt Martha. They soon found Chenoa to be as likable and charming as Jerry had asserted. They could see where this was headed, and silently endorsed it. The elderly universally wish their loved one's happiness in matrimony by finding someone nice to marry.

Glenn and Martha had seen their share of marriages both succeed and fail. The factors which spelled doom to most marriages were various aspects of selfishness. The two partners need to love each other enough to sacrifice what they individually want for that which is best for the marriage. Selfish people can't or won't make those sacrifices. If both parties to the marriage are selfish, that marriage may not last beyond the honeymoon. If only one party is unselfish, the marriage will likely last as long as they are willing to remain so. Few unselfish people are willing to suffer the inevitable abuse of a selfish spouse forever.

Glenn and Martha had not observed a problem with selfishness in Jerry's personality. It didn't take long for them to discern a giving spirit in Chenoa's personality. As they visited Aunt Martha recalled Jerry claiming Chenoa was as beautiful on the inside as out.

Uncle Glenn was smitten by Chenoa in short order. He was struck by the impression she could charm the rattles off a snake. For a girl whose dominate reputation was for reclusiveness, he found her to be remarkably social. She made you feel you were the only, or at least most important person in the room. When she drilled into you with her coal black eyes, you got the feeling there was nothing about you she was not seeing. Her voice was so melodic, you hoped she would keep talking. Some pretty girls were

frequently stupid, air heads; the mentality which gave rise to blonde jokes. Uncle Glenn was impressed with Chenoa's apparent practical wisdom. She was obviously a country girl with rare intelligence.

Aunt Martha was a harder sale. Being what she frequently called herself, 'an experienced old broad', she had the analytic advantage of not being influenced by testosterone. It took her awhile to overcome her skepticism of another pretty face, especially one who was so extraordinarily beautiful, but Chenoa proved to be everything Jerry promised she was and more.

Chenoa was not unaware she was being sized up. She had nothing to hide nor any desire to do so. She didn't want to present herself as anything other than herself. Jerry had talked frequently about Martha and Glenn. She trusted Jerry's opinion. Chenoa quickly agreed with his assessment of how nice Martha and Glenn were. It took a special breed of people to succeed at ranching.

People of poor character didn't last the years of hardships faced by people like Glenn and Martha. The good years were too few, and too far apart for people of weak character to survive. For example, if people couldn't trust you, sooner or later they would stop doing business with you. Survival in agriculture required one rancher helping another. You needed to negotiate what are commonly called win/win deals requiring a lot of trust.

Trust substituted for a lot of fine print in contract law. A handshake deal between someone like her father, and Glenn was always honored. If you ever welched on a handshake deal in the world of the good ole boys, you didn't go to court; your reputation went to hell along with your chances of doing further business with your neighbors. People needed to trust your word was your bond. That was essential to success in places such as the Jarbidge Mountains.

Any air of skepticism quickly dissipated. A willingness to aide Jerry and Chenoa achieve their goals replaced any doubt Glenn and Martha may have had. They were not too young to think about marriage; they just needed to think about marriage. Where would they live? What would they do? One look at how Chenoa was dressed convinced anyone with eyes how she felt about her heritage; she was a proud Shoshone. Ben had a reputation for being a successful Appaloosa breeder.

Glenn recognized Chenoa was riding an especially fine stallion. Would their future involve Appaloosa horses. Would Chenoa accompany Jerry at the fast-approaching end of the summer if he decided to go back to Philadelphia. Would they be willing to wait a few months or maybe even a year to get married, if getting married was what they were wanting to do? There was seemingly no end to the questions which needed to be considered.

Their available discussion time ran out before the questions did. They all considered when and where to continue their talks. Not wanting to disturb Ben and Little Feather, Ben's ranch was quickly dismissed as an appropriate venue. In the end, it was decided Jerry and Chenoa would accompany Glenn and Martha back home to continue exploring ideas.

Chenoa and Jerry rode their horses back to Ben's, put them away, and changed clothes. Ben and Little Feather graciously tolerated the interruption but were visibly pleased when everyone left. This was their special day, and they were in no mood to spend more of it with anyone.

It was dark by the time the foursome left Chenoa's home for Glenn and Martha's. The four of them had a pleasant drive lasting a little over two hours because Uncle Glenn asked as they drove through Rogerson, if anyone wanted to stop for a bit to eat. He received the expected groans he anticipated from his companions who all felt like bloated ticks. Suddenly Jerry burst out, "Yes, yes, yes! I want to stop. Trust me, you'll love this!"

Somewhat shocked by Jerry's exuberance, Glenn pulled in and stopped at the roadside diner. Glenn had never been told Jerry had visited this diner months earlier. Kim, the waitress who had been Jerry's server on his first visit, was on duty. She told the party of four to sit where they like.

The girls took the inside seats with the guys on the outside. Jerry asked Chenoa to hide behind her menu if she wanted to have a little fun. When Kim approached to take their order Jerry casually asked how the photo contest was coming.

"No one has submitted a single entry, yet" reported Kim. "I'm coming more and more to the opinion she doesn't really exist." Showing a remarkable memory, Kim asked, "How about you, mister? You see anything when you went up in the mountains?"

Kim grew curious when everyone at the table started chuckling. "Well, I think I may have seen her," claimed Jerry. " But no camera, no picture; but I do have some proof."

"Proof? What proof," asked Kim.

No sooner had Kim asked about Jerry's proof, than Chenoa lowered her menu, and addressed her with, "Hello!"

"Kim may I introduce you to Chenoa; some people around here refer to her as "The Flower of China Mountain", said Jerry. "I am truly sorry I won't be able to qualify for your contest under the standard rules, but is presenting the person as good as submitting a picture?"

"Oh my gosh!" exclaimed Kim. "You are real? I wouldn't believe it is you, except you are so unbelievably beautiful. Oh, wow! Nobody is going believe me. The Flower in my Diner. Can somebody pinch me to make sure I am not just dreaming this?"

Uncle Glenn spoke up, "Young lady, how would you like to win your own contest? Do you have a camera?"

"Yes, I do, Mr. Briggs. If you all would pose for me, it would be my honor to dish you up some pie a' la mode, on the house. What will it be: apple, cherry, berry, or pecan?"

Kim was so shaken and excited, she appeared to be a nervous wreck. She discovered she was out of film but couldn't calm down enough to get a fresh role threaded into the camera on the first two tries. With a little help from Jerry, the third try succeeded.

A trucker who was enjoying his own slice of banana/coconut cream pie offered to take the picture. It was a house specialty, but Kim explained the trucker was eating the last piece. Kim felt obliged to explain why she hadn't offered Mr. Briggs and his companions the cream pie option. Glenn tried to calm Kim's nerves by explaining they all preferred cherry pie, anyway.

The picture was taken, the pie was eaten, and the trucker departed at the same time as the Briggs, party of four. As they departed, Kim was talking to Joe, the night cook, recruiting him as a witness that the elusive "Flower of China Mountain" had been right there in their diner, and had had her picture taken with Kim.

The Briggs party managed to make it home eventually and park in the underground garage. Uncle Glenn said he was tired and without ceremony headed straight to bed. Aunt Martha took time to show Chenoa to their guest room, after which Chenoa and Jerry took a stroll around the Briggs' home. It was late now, but when Chenoa saw the swimming pool, she was very impressed. She reached up and whispered into Jerry's ear, "Would you like to go swimming?"

"Yes, if you do," Jerry whispered. "Do you know how?"

"You can show me how," teased Chenoa.

"What about a swimming suit," asked Jerry.

"I have never needed one," teased Chenoa. "Do I need one here?"

"I would recommend one," advised Jerry. "Too many old folks around here with insomnia. We wouldn't want to offend Aunt Martha or give Uncle Glenn or Old George a heart attack."

They went to their rooms where Jerry put on his swim trunks and returned to the hallway to meet Chenoa. She was waiting for him wrapped in a large bath towel. She embraced Jerry with an enthusiastic hug and a tender kiss. They walked arm in arm to the pool whereupon Chenoa pushed Jerry unexpectedly into the deep end. By the time Jerry was able make his way to the surface, Chenoa had shed her towel and was treading water which covered her up to her neck. They had purposely not turned on the pool lights, so Jerry was not able to see what Chenoa was wearing, if anything.

Jerry found himself wishing he and Chenoa were already married, that they had chosen the double wedding option. But they weren't married. They would just have to wait to enjoy the benefits of commitment. He found himself saying in his mind, "You can wait, you can wait, she is worth waiting for for a while longer!"

Just about the time his pulse had slowed to normal, Jerry felt Chenoa surfacing next to him from deep water. She managed to come to a stop snuggly in his arms. Again, she sent his nervous system into a frenzy by making out with him there in the pool in the dark.

Jerry relaxed considerably when he was able to discern that at least she wasn't skinny dipping; the essentials were covered. With what, he had no idea, but she was being discreetly modest. They need not have red faces, if someone flipped the lights on.

After making out for a few minutes, Jerry followed her as Chenoa started swimming laps. Much to his surprise, it became plain, not only could Chenoa swim, but it was also hard to keep up with her. When and where this girl learned how to swim like a fish were two questions Jerry really wanted to have answered.

At length Chenoa stopped. Jerry was shocked when he noticed she was not even breathing hard. The list of amazing things he was learning about this girl who was stealing his heart just kept getting longer and longer.

Jerry knew enough history to know about the extraordinary athleticism of Jim Thorpe. The guy had amazing ability; he was one of a kind. What's more he was an American Indian. Chenoa was from a different tribe, but equally one of a kind. That they were so different from their peers was hard to understand. They were simply genetic freaks of nature.

When they tired of swimming they returned to their rooms. It was eventually obvious Chenoa had been swimming in her underwear. There was little difference wearing a bra and panties in the dark and wearing a two-piece swimsuit.

For modesty reasons Jerry had been given a pair of pajamas to wear around Aunt Martha's home. Since her underwear were now wet, Jerry donated his PJs to Chenoa. After a couple more minutes of saying "Good night" to each other, they went to bed in their rooms.

In spite of the long day, Jerry was not especially sleepy. He lay in bed mentally reviewing every detail he could remember of the day. He was happy for Ben and Little Feather, but more than a little envious. He found himself laughing quietly to himself when he remembered how much they had acted like over sexed teenagers after taking their wedding vows. He figured thy must have repressed their sexual desires for so many years, when it was okay again, it was like an emotional dam bursting. They wanted each other, and they wanted each other, now!

Just as Jerry was about to go to sleep, he heard a light knocking on his door. Before he could respond, the door opened. Chenoa entered, quietly shut the door behind her, walked over to Jerry, and announced, "I am cold. I've got the shivers. Can you help me get warm, please?" Without waiting for an answer, she climbed under the covers. It took about ten minutes of cuddling before her body stopped shaking. Jerry found himself sexually aroused, but then a protective instinct washed over him so strong he only wanted to hold Chenoa in his arms, and never ever let her go.

They feel asleep in each other's arms, and didn't wake up till morning when Old George knocked on Jerry's door and announced

breakfast in thirty minutes. Chenoa was trying to sneak back to her room when she ran into Aunt Martha.

"I got chilled last night after going swimming," offered Chenoa in the way of an explanation.

"I am sure the two of you were able to solve the problem together," said Aunt Martha. "I think we need to get you two married, ASAP. Do you agree?"

"Oh, yes, Aunt Martha. Would today or tomorrow be too soon? I am free both days," said Chenoa unabashedly.

"So am I, darling. So am I," said Aunt Martha with a maternal grin.

Old George treated everyone to another of his spectacular breakfast feasts, but no-one ate as much as usual. They hadn't yet recovered from all the wedding food from yesterday.

Martha and Glenn excused themselves after only a few minutes, and met in the den to talk. They soon invited Jerry and Chenoa to join them. Glenn started off the conference with a rather direct but simple question.

"Well kids, what are you thinking?"

Ignoring the obvious, Jerry asked, "About what, Uncle Glenn?"

Patiently Uncle Glenn responded, "About your future. Martha tells me you two were sleeping together last night. Don't you think you are getting your cart hitched up in front of your horse?"

"I know it looks that way Uncle Glenn, but I respect Chenoa too much do what you are concerned about."

"Listen son, you may respect her, but trust me, you warm yourself next to the fire too close for too long, and you get burnt," warned Uncle Glenn.

Looking at Jerry and Chenoa as they sat holding hands on the den sofa Aunt Martha spoke up, "I think the real question here is, is there any doubt in your minds that you two want to get married? If there is, don't be tempting yourselves. If not, I recommend you get hitched before you lose the chastity battle."

"I want to do things right," offered Chenoa. "I have not the slightest doubt, I want to be Mrs. Jerry Briggs. I want to give myself to him, I want to love him with all my heart and soul, I want to make his bed my bed, I want his trail to be my trail, I want his challenges to be my challenges, I want his family to be my family, I want his God to be my

God, and I want his fate to be my fate. I never want us to be separated in life or death." Chenoa had tears in her eyes when she finished.

"I don't think I could ask for much more than that," said Jerry. "Just for the record, though, Chenoa will you marry me?"

"Can I think about it for a moment," asked Chenoa with a smile and a twinkle in her eyes. After about five seconds, "Yes, yes, a million times yes, my darling!

"Well, I think this calls for a toast," offered Uncle Glenn. He stepped to the den door and called out to Old George. "Bring us that pitcher of orange juice left over from breakfast, and five glasses, please!"

Old George brought the orange juice and poured five glasses half full. Uncle Glenn lead the way and invited everyone in the room to drink to Jerry and Chenoa and their engagement.

Old George was not exactly surprised at the announcement, but asked the logical question, "When?"

Now it was Aunt Martha's turn to lead the conversation. "As I see it, you two have two basic choices; now or later. If you want to wait for a big affair such as was put on for Ben and Little Feather, we could offer our home here to host it. If you want my advice, don't wait if you are going to be sleeping together. Do it now. We can hold whatever you want later."

"Glenn thinks you ought to wait, and do it right, but Jackpot is 30 minutes away, and you could cuddle up tonight as husband and wife. It is up to you. We will leave you alone to talk it over," concluded Aunt Martha.

Old George, Aunt Martha, and Uncle Glenn left the den. Jerry and Chenoa were left to consider their options. Ben and Little Feather had had a wonderful wedding and been honored by the well wishes of almost everyone in the community, people they knew and respected.

On the other hand, Jerry knew virtually no one, and Chenoa cared little for the prospect of having a big wedding. What she wanted was here in Glenn's den. She didn't want the dark, empty feelings she had endured before her mother had guided her to Jerry. A thousand wedding flowers didn't appeal to her as much as his embrace. He was the man of her dream, and she was ready to wear his brand; his ring! The thought of sleeping in his arms again tonight as his wife was more desirable than Christmas morning to a child. Chenoa's choice was now, no doubt about it.

Jerry had not as yet thoroughly thought things out, but he had faith everything would work out well. He was for sure smitten by Chenoa. She was a rare find in the realm of woman. He seriously doubted he could do better. Weighing his options he had to consider whether there was wisdom in Uncle Glenn's counsel to wait and do it right. In the end impatience and testosterone tipped the scales. He decided now was right.

He found Aunt Martha with Old George working on some baking project in the kitchen.

"What are you working on?" asked Jerry.

"Tell me what you decided, and I will tell you if it is a wedding cake or desert," said Aunt Martha laughing at her own cleverness.

"Then it is not desert," asserted Chenoa.

"I didn't think it would be," confided Martha. "I contacted our attorney to see what is required to get married in Nevada. He says you don't have to be a resident, take a physical, a blood test, or anything like that. But you do need a marriage license. To get that you both will need to appear before the county clerk with proper identification. Chenoa, do you have a driver's license or other photo ID?" asked Aunt Martha.

"No driver's license, but I do have a BIA ID," said Chenoa.

"Ok, with those and about seventy-seven dollars you should be able to get a license. Only problem is you will need to go to Elko to get it," said Aunt Martha. "Elko is a bit over two hours from here.

I'll have Old George pack a lunch for you. If you leave by 10:30, you should be able to reach the clerk's office by the time the clerk is returning from lunch. If we allot an hour to procure the marriage license, you could be back on the road by 2:00. You could easily be back to Jackpot by 4:00.

While you are gone, I will make arrangement for a justice of the piece to be ready, and Mr. and Mrs. Jerry Briggs can spend the night at Cactus Pete's in downtown Jackpot, Nevada.

If you prefer, you may take your time, and stay the rest of the week, compliments of your family and loved ones."

CHAPTER 18—ELKO

It was a quarter past ten AM when Jerry and Chenoa left the ranch in Glenn's old 57' Chevy. It only left the garage on special occasions. Today qualified. They looked festive as they set out for Elko.

Uncle Glenn and Aunt Martha stood arm in arm gazing after them from the elevated front lawn of the ranch house. They themselves had spent time on many special occasions driving around in Lily, Glenn's name for his classic old Chevy. Watching Jerry and Chenoa drive away from the ranch in Lily brought years of treasured memories flooding back to Martha and Glenn. They were both incurable romantics as was evident from their red eyes.

Riding in an automobile was a rare experience for Chenoa. She had probably ridden a horse many times more miles than she had ridden in a car. Jerry and Chenoa were prepared this time with their own camera.

Their first stop was in Rogerson. Kim was enjoying the lull between the breakfast rush and the soon to start lunch rush. She was delighted to see her new friends. She was even more thrilled when Chenoa confided in her that she and Jerry were on their way to Elko to get a Marriage license. Jerry and Chenoa had a schedule to keep, so after a few quick pictures, they were back on the road with a couple of fresh donuts, compliments of the Rogerson diner.

Nineteen miles further down US 93, Lily attracted some approving smiles from car buffs as Jerry and Chenoa crossed the Nevada border and cruised through Jackpot. The gas gauge still read full, so there was no need to stop. As soon as they reached the edge of the unincorporated community, Jerry pegged the speedometer at five miles over the speed limit, where there was one, and focused on getting to Elko by lunch time.

US 93 was a two-lane rural highway. This was new and scenic country for Jerry. For Chenoa, it was new, but very similar to the country to where she had always lived. When they reached Wells, they left US 93 and proceeded to Elko on Interstate 80, a divided four lane highway. Chenoa had never seen such a big highway before, except on television. Jerry told her this was nothing compared to the highway system in Philadelphia.

As they neared Elko, Jerry asked Chenoa if she would break out the lunch Old George had prepared. Jerry was getting hungry, and since they were running ahead of schedule, they decided to stop off at a rest area to eat. Old George had not only fixed some great sandwiches, but he had also sent them off with some fried chicken. It was so delicious, it got polished off first.

Chenoa wasn't a big fan of soda pop. She had been warned by her father it would rot her teeth. Ben had seen how the introduction of soft drinks to the reservation had led to an epidemic of dental problems, not seen previously. She prized her perfectly aligned, cavity free teeth. Chenoa liked nothing better than cool, mountain spring water. She credited her good health in large measure to the quality of the drinking water she had always consumed in large quantity.

Chenoa was happy. She felt well. Life was going smoothly. She could think of nothing she needed, which she didn't have, or was soon to get, ie., Jerry. She no longer suffered from the dark feelings which plagued her prior to her meeting Jerry. He had proved to be the remedy for all that had been lacking in her otherwise idyllic life.

Jerry couldn't believe his good fortune. Here he was with Chenoa, heading to Elko to get a license to marry her, the most wonderful girl he had ever met. He couldn't imagine a more stunning young woman. He had always heard beauty is only skin deep. Maybe for some. Jerry thought Chenoa had shown herself to be beautiful to her core.

Jerry had come west hoping to sample western life for the summer. Marriage was perhaps the last thing on his mind. Now it was the first. Sitting next to him was more than the girl of his dreams. Here was the closest personification of perfection he was likely to meet in this life. A negative thought swept over him; what had he ever done to deserve her. He suddenly felt totally unworthy of Chenoa. How could he, an ordinary guy, consider himself a suitable husband for such an awesome creature? At that moment of doubt, Jerry was brought back from his stupor of negative thinking by the pleasant voice of Chenoa happily, dreamily contemplating their circumstance.

"Just think; tonight, I will be Mrs. Jerry Briggs, the happiest girl in the world," cooed Chenoa. "It's high noon. Let's go find this clerk's office and be first in line when they reopen after lunch."

How could he think of himself as unworthy, if Chenoa felt he was the one for her? He decided he would just have faith he could meet her expectations and muster up the courage to press on.

They jumped into Lily and proceeded to Elko, determined keep on schedule. The words of a Broadway song suddenly came to Jerry's mind which he modified to fit his own thinking. Chenoa giggled as Jerry burst out with, "Tonight, tonight I'll be with my wife tonight; tomorrow will be the first day of our married lives." The words didn't fit the music well, but Jerry pressed on till Chenoa interrupted his serenade. She literally jumped him, and exclaimed,

"I didn't know you could sing. On the way back, let's sing to the music on the radio. I love to sing!"

Jerry's reaction was to think; *what do you bet; she sings like an angel. What an amazing girl. I wonder if there is anything she can't do.*

Jerry took the Elko exit from the Dwight D Eisenhower Highway, aka I-80, then took a left turn on to E. Jennings Way. It led them to Idaho Street where they needed to turn right. They followed it past a Pizza Hut, Wells Fargo Bank, Sears, Wendy's, Tesoro, Garibaldi's Restaurant, and host of other businesses to #571 Idaho Street. They parked Lily in the courthouse parking lot and asked directions to the clerk's office.

The ink was still drying on their marriage license when they returned to the parking lot thirty minutes later. Their only delay had been when two young male courthouse employees had crashed into each other, watching Chenoa, instead of where they were going.

One half hour ahead of schedule, Jerry merged Lily into light traffic on I-80. They had chosen the Tesoro to top off the gas tank and use the restroom.

It was unwise to travel the lonely roads of Nevada with less than a full tank. You never knew what might happen; running out of gas in the middle of nowhere could be your last mistake. Most people carried an emergency kit in case they got stranded, and needed, food, water, common repair items, or a way to stay warm during the cold weather months.

True to her word, Chenoa found a radio station playing enjoyable music and encouraged Jerry to sing along with her. The miles seemed to go by more quickly than before as they sang karaoke together until the radio reception faded out.

Afterward Chenoa fell asleep with her head on Jerry's shoulder. She had been asleep for 20 or 30 miles when Jerry noticed a sign which had escaped his notice on their way to Elko.

Chenoa awoke when Lily slowed, asking, "Why are we stopping?"

"Look at that sign, sweetheart," responded Jerry. "It says there is a ranch for sale here. Why don't we check it out?"

"Do we have any money to buy a ranch," asked Chenoa, trying to shake off the deep sleep into which she had fallen.

"No, but that doesn't mean we couldn't find some," suggested Jerry. "We are going to have to do something to make a living!"

Jerry and Chenoa turned up a narrow lane near the sign, followed it for about a mile till they crested a low foothill into a beautiful little valley whose prominent feature a was a picturesque, modestly sized ranch house. It was nestled between a number of hay fields. The hay had been harvested, stacked next to a classic style red barn, and some black Angus cattle were now grazing on the hay stubble. The scene before them was beautiful; fit for a picture post card. As they approached, they noticed a woman working in a garden on the sunny side of the ranch house. She came close to greet them as they stopped the car.

"Welcome folks, welcome to the Crooked Creek ranch. I am Merna Marchant. How may I help you?

Chenoa spoke first, "We are the Briggs. We saw your "For Sale" sign on the highway. We were wondering if you could tell us more?"

Chenoa had not wanted to indulge in a lengthier introduction than necessary, so she had taken the liberty of presenting themselves as already married. It wasn't too much of a misrepresentation, after all, they did have a license. By night fall, it would be completely accurate.

Merna explained she and her husband, Gerald, owned 160 acres of deeded land, rented another 80 from relatives, had grazing rights on two sections of BLM land, and leased a school section from the State of Nevada. All told the ranch raised Angus on 2,160 acres. Of that total, they raised hay on 200 acres of the deeded land.

Jerry had no clear understanding of what Merna had just said. It was Greek to him. Chenoa, on the other hand, understood every word having listened to her father discuss the business of ranching her whole life.

"How much are you asking for it," asked Jerry, not knowing what a fair value would be.

"All we can get," kidded Merna with a smile. Actually, we are waiting for an appraiser to submit his report.

We are getting old enough, we need to retire. Working the land at our age wears you down. Without our kids to help out, we just can't do it anymore. Our kids didn't want anything to do with agriculture.

They all admit growing up here was a great way to spend their childhood, but they have all opted to get a good education, and a job in the city.

Merna explained, "Our oldest son, who served our country as an Air Force pilot, now flies for the airlines. Our second was able to get a scholarship to Harvard, then went on to get a law degree. Smart kid; very disciplined.

Third one came the closest to staying in agriculture. He got a degree in Agriculture Economics and worked for Del Monte for a couple years as a scheduling coordinator. He had a fine experience there; learned a lot about corporate management, but I didn't think it was the right fit for him. I told him to go into dentistry like my youngest brother. He eventually specialized in endodontics.

"What is that?" asked Chenoa.

"Doing root canals," explained Merna.

"What is that?" asked Chenoa who had never been in a dental office.

Merna, who had heard these questions countless times before, was ready with an answer. She replied, "If you have a tooth start hurting, sometimes you can fix it by removing decay, and placing a filling. Other times you have to remove the nerve from the tooth and place a special filling that reaches all the way down to the tip of the root. That is what endodontics is all about. If a general dentist can't or doesn't want to do a root canal, he can refer the case to an endodontist.

"Oh," said Chenoa still not understanding the whole concept as well as she would like.

"My son never dreamed he would end up doing what he does. He was the one his father thought was most like to take over the ranch when he retired. Life takes a lot of unexpected turns. But he enjoys his work now. Says it is like spelunking in miniature."

"Spee-whating?" ask Chenoa.

Jerry had this one. He had spent one school break doing it with some college friends. "Spelunking is a fancy word for cave exploring, sweetheart," explained Jerry.

"Oh, so doing root canals is like exploring very small caves. Is that right?" asked Chenoa. " I think I like that word. Spelunking, spelunking, spelunking! I found a cave once, very near North Fork. I had no idea I was spelunking. I will show it to you sometime, and then we can go spelunking together."

Jerry was amused by Chenoa's exuberance at learning a new strange word. He was beginning to understand how she could have been raised in such rural isolation, and yet be as well educated. She loved learning.

Merna continued her narrative, "Fourth child had a somewhat troubled childhood, probably because he was too smart for his own good. He finally found himself, and eventually became a well-known shrink. If I ever go crazy, I expect treatment at no charge."

"Fifth boy got an appointment to the Naval Academy. He resigned to serve a mission for our church, got a degree in civil engineering, then did a tour with the Marine Corp flying those big helicopters with two rotors. He went back to school again, got an MBA, and has been running a construction company ever since."

"Poor boy lost his wife to cancer, a tragedy for our whole family. He has since remarried a really nice, fun-loving girl, who is one of the smartest lawyers you will ever meet. We love her so much, if for no other reason than she has spared our son from a life of loneliness."

"My sixth son served our country in the navy keeping all those spooky electronic gadgets running. Afterward, he went back to school to study I.T. He was probably the most soft-hearted of all our children. Used to grow a full, naturally white beard in recent years, and loved doing his impression of Santa Claus."

"We lost him to cancer, too. He left a really wonderful family. As much as we love this ranch and all that it has meant to our family, and as sad as it makes us to part with it, it is our family which we count as our greatest blessing. We will cherish them most now and forever."

"People sometimes ask me what I did to motivate my six sons to get good educations and become professionals outside of agriculture. I just tell them that my boys grew up working hard harvesting and hauling hay in the summer and feeding to the cattle in the winter. They decided when they grew up, they didn't want to do that anymore."

Chenoa asked, "Didn't you have any girls?"

"Oh, yes," responded Merna, "After six boys, I finally got a girl. The caboose. I enjoyed raising my sons, they were good boys, and have become fine men, but I wanted a girl. One of my sons was afraid I would not know how to care for a girl since I had only been raising boys for so long."

"After all these years, I'm not so sure but what his concerns were well founded. Gerald and I are empty nesters, our kids are all grown and gone. On the whole, I would say we did a pretty fair job, but I think raising daughters is not as easy as raising boys. I once proclaimed that raising six boys was about as much trouble as raising one girl. I think I still agree with myself."

"Girls are different animals than boys. When you hear a fight in the other room, if you call and ask a bunch of boys what's going on, they will tell you. They will say something like, "Johnny hit Donny, so Donny threw Johnny's cat down the clothes shoot, so Johnny fed Donny's goldfish to his cat." Next day they all go fishing in the pond. All is forgotten, all forgiven."

"With girls, if you hear a commotion and ask what is going on, they will probably answer, "Nothing!" Girls hold grudges. They can be mad at each other for weeks. Then when the hormones kick in, Lord help you, they don't even understand themselves. I love a cartoon I saw once. The caption read, "Finally, a book has been published on how to understand women." The picture above the caption showed a man standing next to an open book that must have measured 18"x 24"x 4'.

When my sweet husband ask why I was laughing so hard and long, I showed him the picture."

His only comment was, "Ya, probably volume 1 of 3!"

Merna continued, "He struggled to understand what had struck him when our one and only daughter reached puberty. She went from a sweet little daddy's girl to an incomprehensible human being overnight. It was like being hit by one of our afternoon thunderstorms, if you know what they can be like."

Jerry stole a glance at Chenoa, smiled broadly, and said to Merna, "Oh I was caught in one once, very violent. Was literally life changing!"

"Thank you, Merna. It has been a pleasure making your acquaintance. You have been most kind and informative. If we leave you with our contact information, would you be so kind as to let us know when the appraisal is finished. We really have been impressed by everything we have seen. We would love to meet your husband, too," added Jerry.

"Well why didn't you say so. You needn't come back to meet him. He is in the barn sharping mower blades. Come with me, I'll introduce you," invited Merna.

They all walked to the barn and into the little shop where Gerald was just finishing the last blade. Merna beamed as she gladly introduced her husband of 55 years to their guests. The foursome chatted for another half hour.

It became obvious Gerald was a quiet, hardworking man, and Merna was the chatty Kathy of the family. When Merna took a long enough breath occasionally to let Gerald get a word in, he made it plain he would welcome the opportunity to show this young couple around the property.

Jerry and Chenoa left the Marchants feeling they had made new friends. They had to hurry now or risk being late to their own wedding. Jerry pushed Lily a little harder now to make up for their extended visit. Chenoa fed Jerry morsels from the last of their lunch as he drove.

Feeling so excited, she could resist no longer, Chenoa leaped at Jerry, throwing her arms around his neck, and kissing him again and again.

"I love you; I love you, I love you," repeated Chenoa over and over. "Can you drive faster, I want to be your wife, and I don't want to wait any longer!"

Jerry pressed Lily even harder, and cautioned Chenoa, "Careful, Honey, give me a little warning before you jump me. I don't want to get married in an ambulance on our way to the hospital and spend our honeymoon in traction. I want to be your husband, hold you in my arms, and whisper in your ear all the reasons I will cherish you now and forever."

Chenoa gently rubbed against Jerry this time, and whispered in his ear, "Ok, ok, I'll be more careful. How much longer to Jackpot? I just hope Aunt Martha has been able to make the necessary arrangements. I have never felt like this in my whole life. I heard a word for it once."

"Horny?" asked Jerry.

"Yes, that's it," admitted Chenoa. "But it sounds like a word a nice girl wouldn't use!"

"How about sexually excited?" suggested Jerry.

"Yes! said Chenoa. "I am very excited! Drive faster, please."

Jerry dared not drive any faster. It might well prove counterproductive. Prudence paid off and Lily cruised into Jackpot at precisely 3:55. Jerry parked next to Uncle Glenn's dually which he spotted in the parking lot of the Horseshu Club. Jerry wasn't sure what to do next; wait for someone to come back to the dually or go looking for them.

Chenoa remembered, "On the TV they always advise, 'If you are lost, stay with your vehicle!' Are we lost?"

Jerry pulled Chenoa into his arms and said softly into her ear, " Does it really matter as long as we have each other?"

Chenoa answered, "Yes, it does! Now that we have each other, can you blame me if I want to know you?"

"What do you mean?" asked Jerry. "Why would you ever marry me if, you don't know me? Haven't we been learning about each other this last few week? I know it has been a short courtship, but I think I have learned enough about you to marry you."

"I want to know you," repeated Chenoa.

"Ok, what would you like to know? Ask me anything. We have a few minutes. Go head!" invited Jerry.

"What does the Bible say, 'And Adam knew Eve his wife and she conceived, and bare Cain, and said, I have gotten a man from the Lord.' Genesis: chapter 4, verse 1. I want to move from being with you, to getting to know you; in a Biblical sort of way."

"Just out of curiosity, Chenoa, can you tell me what the next verse is?" asked Jerry.

"Sure!" replied Chenoa. "Verse two, 'And she again bare his brother Abel. And Abel was a keeper of sheep, but Cain was a tiller of the ground.' I am sorry I can't tell you what verse three is. It has a water stain and someone spilled ink on it, too. It is a very old Bible. Would you like to hear about verse 4?"

"Later, Darling, another time. Holy cow!" thought Jerry. He was beginning to realize he was about to marry a girl who had a photographic memory. He was flabbergasted. The superlatives that he would have to use to describe Chenoa were mind boggling. Jerry had thought her to be a freak of nature. Now he would describe her as a miracle of nature; a rare, beautiful flower of humanity, if ever there was one!

The next moment, the question were they lost, was rendered moot. Aunt Martha suddenly appeared next to Lily's driver's door window and tapped. Jerry and Chenoa were both startled. Her first question was, "Did you get the license?"

Chenoa was beaming when she answered by holding up the precious piece of paper.

"Fantastic! Any problems getting it?" asked another voice.

"Daddy" screamed Chenoa as she jumped out of Lily to embrace her father and his new bride. "You came! How wonderful. How did you get here?"

While Chenoa, Ben, and Little Feather were engrossed in their joyous reunion, Aunt Martha brought Jerry up to speed on the arrangements she had organized. Bottom line was they were scheduled to meet at the Jackpot Baptist Church at 1795 Piersanti Street at 6:00. Reverend Bowcut would perform the ceremony followed by a private banquet at Cactus Petes. The bridal sweet had been reserved for them at the Horseshu Club.

Jerry was curious. "Why not at Cactus Petes where we at eating?"

Aunt Martha explained, "Ben and Little Feather are booked there. I didn't think you would want to share your honeymoon night with them, would you?"

"Doesn't Cactus Pete's have a second bridal suite?" asked Jerry thinking it odd they would only have one.

Aunt Martha blushed a bit then confessed, "Yes, but Glenn and I have that one reserved; for sentimental reasons, if you can understand."

Aunt Martha's voice trailed off at last, feeling more embarrassed at having to divulge this particular detail than she needed to be. Apparently, there was going to be more than one guy in Jackpot tonight doing a little "getting to know you" with his wife.

Little Feather took Chenoa aside with Aunt Martha and discussed getting the bride ready and the fact she had brought Abby's dress for Chenoa. They needed a private place for Chenoa to get ready.

"No problem," declared Aunt Martha. "I have the bridal suite reserved for the happy couple. Let's just go get them checked in!"

By 4:20 Aunt Martha had the future Mr. and Mrs. Jerry Briggs checked in to Room 624 at the Horseshu Cub, downtown Jackpot, Nevada, and by 4:35 Little Feather was helping Chenoa into her mother's wedding dress.

They were pleased to find it fit perfectly. It was a white, plain, but pretty dress which had suffered a tinge of yellowing over the years, since it was first worn. The effects of aging were faint: only noticeable under bright lights. It was a modest dress with long sleeves, and a lace collar. There was no train to drag through the ever-problematic high desert dirt. Another fortuitous discovery was Chenoa didn't need to adjust the hemline. Abby must have been the same height as her daughter.

With a little guidance from the Horseshu desk clerk, Jerry was able to find a small rental shop and rent a Tuxedo.

Chapter 19—Jackpot Nuptial

As planned Chenoa and Jerry walked through the doors of the little church at 1795 Piersanti Street at precisely 6pm. Aunt Martha had been consulting with Little Feather and worked out the following plan.

Little Feather would be Chenoa's bride's maid. Ben would do the traditional thing and give his daughter away. Old George agreed to be the Best Man, and Reverend Bowcut would perform the ceremony. He had the easy role, having done hundreds of weddings. He had his part down pat. His little chapel was decorated so appropriately, one would have thought this event had been in the works for months.

What really surprised everyone was the size of the audience. Jerry wondered, if these were like paid funeral mourners, who Reverend Bowcut could pull from his pocket any moment, ready to appear like the flowers, to adorn any occasion.

Turned out Kim had invited virtually every customer of the Rogerson Diner to come and see that not only did the Flower of China Mountain exist but watch her get married. At Chenoa's urging, Aunt Martha increased the bride's maids by one, and invited Kim to stand in with Little Feather. She accepted. She drafted Joe, the night cook, to take pictures. These photos would win for sure. How could they not be the best pictures of the formerly elusive mystery girl. Chatter around the diner would never again be the same.

When they were ready, the organ music began to play courtesy of Thelma, the preacher's wife. Chenoa headed down the aisle on the arm of her father. Both had tears in their eyes, and the inescapable feeling they weren't walking alone. When they reached Reverend Bowcut, Ben

took a seat, and Jerry took his place. When the Reverend started to lead this most unusual couple through their vows, Little Feather suddenly had the same feeling come over her, too. She felt the presence of Abby so strongly, she thought she might see her, if she looked around.

When the "I do's" were done and the ring ceremony started, Jerry and Chenoa realized they didn't have any rings.

Seeing the situation developing, Ben stepped quietly forward and handed a ring to Jerry.

"This was her mothers," whispered Ben.

The ceremony proceeded. Chenoa was a little surprised, the ring fit perfectly.

The situation was only partially resolved. Chenoa still didn't have a ring to place on Jerry's finger. Problem was temporarily solved, when the ever-resourceful Reverend Bowcut, surreptitiously dug into one of his pockets, selected one of several rings, and discreetly slipped it to Chenoa. Jerry thought it was a little too big when Chenoa slid it on his finger.

The Reverend later explained, he didn't want to chance disrupting the ceremony by choosing a ring, that might be too small. When in doubt, he advised, go large, and fix it later. It was obvious the Reverend really did know his business. Whatever he was charging for his services, he had earned it.

Jerry and Chenoa were ecstatic. They were warmly congratulated, first by family and friends, then by a ragtag collection of guests. Kim got her pictures, and the Rogerson Diner crowd left for home in utter disbelief of how fortuitous they had been to attend this particular nuptial.

The celebration moved next to Cactus Petes. Ben invited the close friends and family who attended to order from the menu due to the impromptu nature of things. After everyone else was seated in the small banquet room, Uncle Glenn and Aunt Martha noticed Old George was missing. His whereabouts was soon learned when he came whooping and hollering into the room like a drunk'n cowboy.

"I won, I won, this dinner is on me, I won!" shouted Old George at the top of his lungs. "I played the dollar slot on my way here, and sweet Mary, Mother of Jesus, I won! I won more money than I have ever won before. I can't believe it. This just about makes up for all the times I have lost previously!"

The last admission set everyone to laughing. He was not a gambler. He just liked pulling the lever and watching the slot machines whirr. He had a strict entertainment limit, he never played more than ten dollars; never. When it was gone, he was done.

Tonight, this town was appropriately named; he had hit the jackpot! While Old George was pondering what he was going to do with his money, everyone else was contemplating what to order for dinner.

Just about everyone ended up ordering prime rib, medium rare. Jerry was seriously of the opinion a small chunk of prime rib soaked in Au Jus, dipped in horseradish sauce, and eaten with a bite of loaded baked potato was one of the most perfect blends of tastes known to man. The new Mrs. Briggs, not wanting to get off on the wrong foot by arguing with her husband, simply told their server, "Make that two!"

The stories of how the day had unfolded dominated the table conversation for as long as it took for the orders to start arriving. Aunt Martha had moved heaven and earth to pull things together to make this day as special for the Jerry and Chenoa as possible. She knew Ben would want to be there for his only and beloved daughter's wedding. Martha tried in every way she could think of but sending out carrier pigeons, to contact Ben.

Finally, Orrie had taken it upon himself to deliver the message. Ben wasn't home, but Little Feather felt she could find him. Orrie had offered to drive them to Jackpot if he could have an invitation to the wedding.

"Yes, oh yes, you are invited and thank you again for all you did for Ben and me. We love you for all your many acts of kindness. In our hearts you couldn't be more family," proclaimed Little Feather as her eyes began to redden from the tears she was shedding.

Orrie figured they were roughly an hour from Jackpot. He promised to return for them at 3pm. Little Feather started the water heating for a bath, then headed to the barn. With Sky Walker's help, she did find Ben, then returned ahead of him to get ready to go.

She placed the heated water in the tub, then more water on the stove. While it was heating Little Feather removed Abby's wedding dress from the trunk where it had lain safely for years. She did her best to freshen it up. She would take it to Jackpot for Chenoa to wear when she made her vows to Jerry. Sitting next to the dress, she also found Abby's wedding ring. She knew Ben would want Chenoa to have it.

Little Feather next went to her own trunk and carefully removed the negligee she had worn only twice, once for John, and once for Ben. She would take it with her in case Chenoa didn't have one. It was important for a girl to have something beautiful to wear on her wedding night, even if she didn't wear it very long. After two weddings, this attire by rites should still be considered brand new. It had only been worn a total of about twenty minutes.

Little Feather had stripped and was just getting into her bath when Ben walked in. How could she do this to him, when they needed to hurry, thought Ben? Oh, well, he could make up the time by not shaving. Two clean and happy people were ready when Orrie arrived.

The drive to Jackpot went smoothly with Ben and Orrie talking shop, and Little Feather thinking ahead to all the little details with which she might need to assist Chenoa.

Orrie's travel time estimate was nearly spot on. They had only been waiting a few minutes, when Ben spotted the bride to be. Ben and Little Feather immediately went to see how they might be of service.

Desert for the wedding dinner was cake. Aunt Martha had brought the one she and Old George had baked. Cactus Petes provided a complimentary cake when someone booked the bridal suite. Ice cream also came compliments of the house, too. There were a round of toasts to the newlyweds.

Ben made a touching speech about his love for Chenoa, his years of dreading the day she would find a husband and leave him. Ben mentioned how grateful he was to have had a loving wife, who though she had been taken from them much too early, never-the-less had watched over them these many years. At the appropriate time had step in to lead Chenoa to her now husband for whom he was very grateful. As Ben put it, he felt he was gaining a son, rather than losing his daughter. In addition, he was grateful to Abby for guiding him to Little Feather, to whom he was recently and most happily married. Ben concluded by recalling a statement he had recently heard, "Love is not love, till you give it away!"

Uncle Glenn stood and spoke on behalf of the Briggs family, expressing how happy they were to welcome Chenoa into their midst,

and testifying to their belief and confidence she was indeed a special person, beautiful through and through. He concluded by wishing Jerry and Chenoa a long life of happiness together.

Among the impromptu wedding guests were Jake and his wife. Over the summer Jerry and Jake had become good friends. As the post wedding dinner was breaking up, Jake and his wife, Jessica, had slipped quietly from the revelers and tied several strings of tin cans to the back of Lily. Then they took some water-based chalk markers, and adorned the windows with "Just Married" and other cute public notices of their nuptial status. Jessica was a talented artist who was able to turn Lily into the best decorated car to be seen in Jackpot in a long time.

When Jerry and Chenoa exited Cactus Petes, everyone in their company was impressed, and insisted on having a picture of the bride and groom standing by the "Just Married" masterpiece. For old time sake, Aunt Martha and Uncle Glenn had their picture taken standing by Lily. This started a trend. First, Jake and Jessica then Ben and Little had their pictures taken, too.

Orrie wasn't escorting anyone, so Chenoa invited him to have his picture taken with her. She decided to ham it up, and had one picture taken with her embracing Orie as though he were the groom. Responding to the positive crowd reaction, Chenoa posed for another picture with Orrie by inviting him to pick her up as though he were carrying her across the threshold. Everyone though it was a fantastic way of showing appreciation to Orrie for all that he had done to contribute to Ben and Chenoa's weddings. When Orrie finally put her down, Chenoa gave him another hug and kiss, then told him as much.

Orrie smiled and said teasingly to Chenoa, but loud enough for everyone to hear, "One kiss from the most beautiful girl ever is payment in full. I got two. You now have a credit on your account!"

Jerry stepped forward and addressed Orrie, "I too, would like to thank you for your many acts of kindness, Mr. LaVall, you have been most gracious. Would you mind, though, if I reclaimed my bride?"

Everyone laughed. Chenoa suddenly kissed Orrie again, and exclaimed, "Now, I have two credits on my account!" She then jumped into Jerry's arms, and shouted, "Horseshu Club, here we come. Mr. and Mrs. Jerry Briggs are on their way!"

Jerry opened the door for Chenoa, Lily's motor roared to life, and they were off dragging some very noisy tin cans! What was left of the wedding party clapped until Lily disappeared from sight.

"I am so happy, darling!" whispered Chenoa to Jerry as they rode a crowded elevator to the sixth floor. Since Chenoa was still wearing her wedding dress, and Jerry his tux, it was not too surprising, people were paying them special attention and congratulating them. Moments later, Jerry carried Chenoa across the threshold of Room 624.

Chapter—20 Honeymoon

Chenoa had been in a bit of shock when she saw the luxurious furnishing of the bridal suite. It was nothing like the rustic homes of the mountains. Chenoa was fascinated. She began roaming around the suite checking out everything with the curiosity and exuberance of a little girl. When she opened a small refrigerator stocked full of all sorts of goodies, she let out a squeal of delight and invited Jerry to come see what she had found. She had enjoyed a candy bar, and two bottles of juice, apple and cranberry, before Jerry was able to advise her, "Its not free, sweetheart. Everything you eat will go on our bill."

"Oh, I thought it was complementary," confessed Chenoa, having never stayed in a hotel before.

After inspecting the premises, Jerry and Chenoa refocused on the subject of the day.

"Who did you say you are?" Jerry asked Chenoa as he took her in his arms and hugged her tightly.

"Mrs. Jerry Briggs!" said Chenoa enthusiastically.

"Who do you love?" asked Jerry.

"Mr. Jerry Briggs?" replied Chenoa.

"For how long?" Jerry continued.

"Now and forever," asserted Chenoa planting kisses across his face with each word of her answer.

"And just why are you here?" asked Jerry.

"Getting to know you, getting to know all about you," answered Chenoa singing the words to the famous tune. "Which reminds me!" Chenoa took a small bag and headed to the washroom.

"What's that?" asked Jerry.

Chenoa stopped, turned, gave Jerry a broad seductive smile, and said, "A little wedding present from Little Feather. It's not much, but what there is, I'll show you in a moment."

In the period between Abby's appearance to Chenoa and Little Feather's marriage to Ben, Chenoa had had a couple chances to discuss marriage with Little Feather. Chenoa was a little nervous about the whole idea. These girl talks were the closest thing Chenoa would have to a mother/daughter chat. She had seen enough movies depicting honeymoons to know about the brides wearing sexy nighties on their wedding night. Her question to Little Feather was simple, "Why, why not just wear pajamas?"

Little Feather thought for a bit before trying to answer. Then she tried to help Chenoa with an analogy. "Have you ever gotten a present?" asked Little Feather.

"Sure, every birthday, and Christmas," answered Chenoa.

"What did they look like?" asked Little feather

"It had a pretty wrapping with a bow, recalled Chenoa.

"Exactly, its is customary to wrap a gift. When you get married, you are a gift to your husband. You are giving yourself and your love to your husband, not to mention your body. Usually, the fancier and more costly the gift, the prettier the wrapping. Think of the sexy nightie as your gift wrapping. Just as you unwrap your birthday or Christmas presents soon after you receive them, husbands typically don't waste much time unwrapping your gift to them.

Waiting for Chenoa, Jerry's heart started beating hard and fast. When she reappeared, he thought for sure he was going to have a heart attack. He said a quick but fervent prayer, "Dear God, help me. I don't want to go to a hospital; not tonight, please!"

Jerry would have said she looked like an angel, but somehow, he couldn't imagine God letting one of his angels out of heaven in a negligee, let alone this one. His eyes nearly popped out of their sockets. Jerry took Chenoa in his arms and caressed her tenderly.

"I have to be the luckiest guy on planet earth," proclaimed Jerry. "Promise me again you will love me forever; for time and all eternity!"

"Yes, darling, for time and all eternity. More than that, well, I'll have to think about it!" said Chenoa with a wink and a smile.

Jerry's pulse rate finally slowed to a safer range. True to its historical average, after ten minutes the negligee settled gently to the floor, atop a pile of Jerry's clothes by the side of the bed. It had been a long day since Chenoa awoke in Jerry's room. They had spent a day to remember. Now they needed to wait no longer. Now they belonged to each other. They had been true to the goal of chastity by which they had lived since their meeting in the sheep camp at Clark's Crossing.

Chenoa stirred every desire and passion known to young men, but she was and would continue to be the girl of his dream. He respected her too much to disrespect her in the past, present, or future. She made getting to know her well worth the wait.

About 4 in the morning exhaustion overcame passion, and Mrs. Jerry Briggs fell asleep once again in the arms of the man of her dream. Chenoa was confident this was a night Mr. Briggs would never forget. They had talked about many things as Jerry and Chenoa got to know each other. Jerry was taken back when at one point Chenoa quietly ask him, "Darling, do you believe my mother is my guardian angel, and she engineered our meeting?"

"I don't find that hard to believe," conceded Jerry.

Chenoa continued her thought, "Then does it bother you my mother might be with us now?" The idea gave Jerry a sudden attack of paranoia, chasing away, at least temporarily, his desire to know Chenoa better.

Normal check-out time from the Horseshu Club is 11 AM. Shortly thereafter, a knock at their doorway was accompanied by the announcement, "Housekeeping!"

Chenoa sprang from the bed and hustled to the door dressed, as Jerry would later recall, the same way she came into the world. "We wish to keep the room at least another day," said Chenoa through the door.

"Ok, no problem. I'll inform the front desk!" said the maid.

Chenoa had hoped to not wake Jerry. The commotion had nevertheless done so. Chenoa climbed back under the covers and snuggled up to Jerry.

"Good morning, darling. Did you sleep well?" asked Chenoa.

"Never better. How about you? replied to Jerry. "Are you hungry?"

"Yes, what will you have? Coffee, tea, or me?" asked Chenoa, throwing back the covers to again reveal her 'to die for' figure. It was the easiest decision of Jerry's life.

"I would hate to see you catch cold," said Jerry. As he pulled her to himself, he continued, "You better get back under the covers with me."

"I want to have your baby, darling," proclaimed Chenoa. "Do we need to get to know each other more?"

Jerry was a bit shaken by the statement and question. After seven hours of sleep though, Jerry was up to the challenge, and ready to go again.

"Definitely more, my darling! Never say I wasn't willing to do my part. Boy or girl?" inquired Jerry.

"Yes, boy or girl. I think I will let God choose," responded Chenoa with wisdom beyond her years.

Jerry did his part again, but he was running out of steam. He fell back asleep. Chenoa slipped on a hotel bathrobe, and called room service to order breakfast, which was available 24/7. While Jerry slept, Chenoa took a bath. Jerry had graciously offered to wash her back and whatever else she needed, but as the old saying goes, "You snooze, you lose!" She would have waited, but was sure he would have other opportunities.

Chenoa got a phone call from Aunt Martha, inviting her and Jerry to dinner, if they were so inclined. They tentatively agreed to dinner at 8 PM at the main Horseshu Club restaurant. Aunt Martha added before she hung up, "Ben and Little Feather have accepted our invitation, too, in case that makes a difference." For Chenoa it did.

Room service delivered their breakfast promptly at 2:00. Chenoa had requested they knock softly in case her husband was asleep. When the food was all laid out, and the server had left, the robe met the same fate as the nightie. Chenoa descended yet again under the covers to invite Jerry to breakfast. Faced again with whether to satisfy his appetite for food or sex first, Jerry and Chenoa's breakfast was eaten later at room temperature. The odds of Chenoa getting her wish, though, were getting significantly better.

Not wishing to distract Jerry from doing his part, he ate his first breakfast as a married man served bite after bite by a mostly naked wife. Chenoa had retrieved the bath robe to keep her warm, but she wore it in such a manner as to leave nothing to Jerry's imagination.

Chenoa was not worried about getting too chilled. She could count on Jerry to keep her warm.

Jerry could not believe a girl could be so beautiful. That, he was now married to her, was, for him, one of the wonders of the world. Jerry could scarcely believe the good fortune the last few months had brought him. Who would have thought when he stepped off the bus at Henstocks, he would soon be the husband of the Flower of China Mountain?

Jerry and Chenoa continued to do what honeymooners do till 6 PM, then started getting ready for diner. They decided to go to the casino gift shop and add to their wardrobe. When they reemerged, they had both purchased T-shirts, cutoffs, and flip-flops. Jerry was again impressed at Chenoa's beauty; he was convinced she would look good in a gunnysack.

Since the three couples were all on time, they met each other at the restaurant entrance. A slightly overweight hostess with a charming smile and delightful personality, showed them to a semiprivate booth in the back of the restaurant.

Wanting to cut back on the quantity of food they had been consuming lately, Chenoa ordered soup and salad. Martha and Little Feather followed suit. Being less worried about their figures Ben, Glenn, and Jerry ordered filet mignon with loaded baked potatoes. An oft repeated axiom of Glenn was "Never pass up a watering hole." Jackpot was certainly a watering hole worth exploiting.

The conversation for the first few minutes centered on their hotel accommodations; Cactus Petes verses the Horseshu Club. Then it turned to the casinos. Everyone had resisted the urge to gamble, so there was nothing much to talk about on that subject.

What no one was willing to talk about was what they had been doing; it cost less and was a lot more fun than gambling. When one of the guys got close to the subject, Aunt Martha quickly changed it. She was old school when it came to talking about sex. It just wasn't something you talked about in public.

A few other subjects were probed a bit, but planning for their future was the topic which finally caught fire. What were they going to do post honeymoon? Uncle Glenn assured Jerry he could continue to work for him. Ben wasn't sure how much he could afford to pay them but offered to employ both Jerry and Chenoa. Doing so would double the number of people his ranch would need to support. Jerry and Chenoa finally brought up the subject of helping Ben market his horses. If they could attend horse shows, and find buyers like Susie and Doctor Dean, Jerry and Chenoa expressed their confidence they could add value to Ben's horses sufficient to pay for their services. Among other things, Jerry and Chenoa felt they could break Ben's horses to ride and train them to do other things to add value. A well-trained horse would potentially sell for twice or three times what a raw horse would. They could help build Ben's reputation for fine, well-trained horses. Jerry was new to the horse world, but Chenoa had been involved since she was a little girl. She knew if she could train a horse to be a cutting horse, its value could triple or quadruple.

What really caught Glenn and Ben's attention, was when Chenoa brought up the possibility of buying the Crooked Creek Ranch from Gerald and Merna Marchant. It would provide Jerry and Chenoa a base of operation on the highway system, a source of hay for wintering horses, a cash crop to pay the mortgage, a house in which to live, and an operation with a proven history of success. Jerry was new to farming and ranching, but they would be close enough to Uncle Glenn, Ben and others so they could help him learn the ropes. Chenoa added, "The best feature is, it would be a great place to raise a family."

"Do you know how much they are asking for it?" asked Uncle Glenn.

"No, not yet," answered Jerry.

"Do you have enough money for a down payment," asked Ben.

"We can help them with that," said Aunt Martha. "Then be a silent partner until they pay us off."

"If they raise hay, I could buy what they don't need," chimed in Uncle Glenn, "I am always looking for good quality hay to help get my cattle through the winter."

Chenoa hugged Jerry's arm tightly, looked into his eyes, and exclaimed happily, "It sounds like it should work. I'll have to pray about it and ask God. Maybe he will send my mom again to advise us."

"What we really need first is the appraisal," opined Jerry. "In the meantime, I am going to start looking into what loan programs may be available through the Small Business Administration, U.S. Department Of Agriculture (USDA), or Farm Service Agency (FSA). With any luck, we may be able to swing the purchase without family help.

"I agree, whole heartedly," piped in Uncle Glenn. "The government sets aside a ton of money to help newcomers to agriculture get their operations off the ground. We may as well get our share for the newest Mr. and Mrs. Briggs. Heaven knows you will need help to get going."

The conversation took a new turn when the waitress reappeared with the first tray of their order. The aroma of the steaks was so heavenly, Chenoa decided to abandon her soup and salad decision, and invite herself to share Jerry's filet mignon. The precedence was sent. Martha and Little Feather followed suit. Ben and Glenn were soon cutting their meat in half to share with their sweethearts, as well.

All said and done, everyone enjoyed their meal immensely. Everyone enjoyed themselves so much, they agreed to meet again tomorrow night, same time, different station; next time at Cactus Petes. This might be their only chance to check out the competition.

Jerry and Chenoa were ready to return to their suite in the Horseshu Club, when Little Feather asked to be excused to visit the restroom. Suddenly all three women were off to the same destination.

"Women!" exclaimed Glenn, "I'm on the far side of eighty, and I still don't understand why when you get two or more women together, one can't go to the bathroom alone."

"Not much of a problem where I come from," declared Ben. "I suppose it is some sort of herd instinct."

"I have no clue. I am till looking at women as a wonderful mystery," confessed Jerry.

"Jerry, I'm intrigued by the possibilities of buying the Crooked Creek Ranch," said Uncle Glenn. "I think it is a great idea if you and Chenoa want to live in this area. I think it would be a greater culture shock for Chenoa to follow you to Philadelphia, than for you to stay here in the west. After having spent the summer here, you should have a pretty good idea of what ranch life is like. By marrying her, I think you are more or less obligated to merge your life with Chenoa's rather than the other way around. What's more, you are right, Jerry, we really need the appraisal."

The girls returned, and the group worked their way to the exit. Uncle Glenn ask Jerry to give him the contact information for the Marchants. He advised Jerry he would call tomorrow to find out who their appraiser is, and see if he could contact him.

Jerry and Chenoa saw the others off, then did a little wandering through the Horseshu Casino before returning to their suite. Chenoa had no idea what the various games were as they strolled from one game to another. Jerry had to tell her what she was looking at when they walked past a Roulette Wheel, and a Big Six Wheel. Jerry started to explain how one played them, but Chenoa walked on. They looked too complicated to interest her.

She stopped and stared when they reached a Blackjack table.

"What is this?" Chenoa quietly asked Jerry.

"21 or Blackjack," answered Jerry.

Chenoa was standing behind the players, so they didn't notice her at first. But she was in plain view of the young male dealer. He was so distracted by Chenoa's looks that he started making dealer errors right and left. The pit boss noticed the commotion when several players made big wins, then noticed Chenoa. He, too, was blown away by the stunning beauty who was watching the game of 21 but had the presence of mind to send a female dealer to take over for the rattled young man.

The pit boss reviewed the security tapes later, and figured Chenoa's brief pause at the Blackjack table had cost the casino about three thousand dollars.

Later, while walking around the slot machines, they heard the whistles, bells, and clanging sounds of a slot machine paying off. They were a bit shocked to see for whom the "one-armed bandit" had paid off. It was a little old lady playing the nickel slots. They recognized and remembered her because among other things she was very animated and wearing a flowered bonnet. She was also playing two machines at the same time. It would have been hard not to remember her. She was a character. She gave her part of the casino a Mardi Gras atmosphere. It was easy to see how she inspired a party mood in those around her. She apparently had been playing the whole time while Jerry's party of six had been eating. Jerry would have liked to stop and talk to her to find out if she was ahead of the game, but the new Mrs. Briggs hustled him on.

"The best way to avoid temptation, my dear, is to not go near it," counseled Chenoa. "We are as close already as we should ever get!"

"Kill joy!" whispered Jerry.

"Don't be a party pooper," retorted Chenoa. "Let's get back to some serious honeymooning."

"Well, if you are going to frame it that way," replied Jerry, "I think I'm up to it, no pun intended. Here's to getting to know you!" He pantomimed clicking glasses and making a toast.

Chenoa rubbed up against Jerry, and in her most sultry voice said, "Now you are singing my tune, cowboy!"

They headed to the elevates, and never looked back.

CHAPTER—21 MARRIED LIFE

The knock on the honeymoon suite door came precisely at 9 AM, as requested. Jerry answered the door in his hotel supplied terry cloth bath robe. Chenoa had the bed covers pulled up over her head. It was difficult to detect whether someone were actually in the bed or not. The porter, server, waiter, bellman, or whatever you want to call him, wheeled the food cart into the room, and set up breakfast for Mr. and Mrs. Jerry Briggs.

The what-ever-you-call-him nearly dropped the pitcher of orange juice when Chenoa startled him by suddenly throwing back the covers, which were now covering her shoulders.

"Oh, that smells good!" exclaimed Chenoa. The next assault on the poor, young guys nerves was when Chenoa continued, "I'm hungry; this honeymooning is exhausting!" The statement plus the unbelievable, surprising beauty of the girl who had just come, albeit only partially, out from under the covers so shocked the server, he choked on, then swallowed a big wad of chewing gum. Jerry felt so sorry for the poor guy, he gave him an extra-large tip.

"Sweetheart, if you had thrown those covers down a little further, I probably would have had to put my CPR skills to use," surmised Jerry.

Chenoa peeked under the covers, and ask, "You think so?"

"Yes I think so," affirmed Jerry.

"Haven't these guys ever seen a girl?" ask Chenoa.

Jerry brought Chenoa a crescent roll. He extended it to her right hand with, which she was holding the covers. When she released the

covers to grab the roll, Jerry seized the opportunity and snatched the covers down to her ankles. "Not anyone like this girl," boasted Jerry.

Rather than trying to cover herself, Chenoa sat up, did as much of a curtsy as sitting in bed would allow, and teasingly said to Jerry, "Aren't you the lucky one!"

"Baby, luckier than I ever thought possible," said Jerry as he shed his robe. Breakfast was room temperature again by the time the young lovers got around to eating it.

"Why didn't we just ask for an 11:00am breakfast delivery?" asked Chenoa. "It would be nice to eat warm bacon and eggs one time."

Jerry responded, "I can eat a warm breakfast any time any place I want. Breakfast can wait; I have been waiting for you for a lifetime. Priorities my precious; priorities!"

Chenoa quietly, softly said to Jerry as she hugged him tightly, "Honey, we are married now. You don't need to eat cold meals anymore. You can have me anytime you want. Breakfast, lunch, or dinner; I can be on your menu!"

"Well, if you put it that way, I may be an old worn-out man by the time I reach thirty," kidded Jerry.

Chenoa responded in kind, "Yes, my dear, but you won't be out of shape, if you keep up with me!"

Jerry reflected on the evening he had tried to keep up with Chenoa when they were swimming laps.

"We may both be right; I'll either be in magnificent shape or worn out!" speculated Jerry.

"I'm banking on the former," said Chenoa. Pulling Jerry towards her, "Come, time to get to know each other better."

By the time the server had reached the kitchen, he had recovered pretty much from his visit to Room 624. His supervisor took note of his noticeable discombobulation, though, and ask if he were ok.

"Boss have you seen the bride in 624?" ask Romano, the room service waiter.

"No, why?" ask Roberto, the supervisor.

"She is amazing, to say the least! I've never seen a girl so unbelievably gorgeous. She redefines the word beautiful. I have never seen anyone like her. Have you ever watched the Miss America or Universe

pageants? Even without makeup, she makes any of those girls look plain. I kid you not, this girl is off the 1 to 10 scale. She has hair and eyes black as obsidian, olive complexion, dimpled cheeks, perfect teeth, and a cheerful voice. I tell you, it is like Mother Nature put together one girl whose every aspect was perfect; I think she is absolutely flawless!" reported Romano.

"This I have to see for myself," said Roberto "I just got an order from Room 624 for breakfast for two at 11am. I need to practice my serving skills; I will take this one!"

"Be prepared for the eye-candy treat of your life, Sir. You won't be disappointed," promised Romano.

"I am counting on it," declared Roberto. "The girls around here aren't what they used to be."

Chenoa and Jerry, both enjoyed each other and their accommodations for the second night, but they were uneasy about something. They were having difficulty identifying what was bothering them, until in early morning they decided to say a prayer together. A feeling of peace settled over them, and within minutes they fell asleep with Chenoa spooned in Jerry's arms.

It was the right time of the month for Chenoa. She told Jerry when they awoke, "Unless you are shooting blanks, I don't see how you don't "know me" by now!", continuing the metaphor.

"I agree," said Jerry. "I have been thinking, why don't we forego a little love making this morning, cut down the risk of you getting cystitis, and go visit the Merchants?"

"Cystitis, what's that?" ask Chenoa.

"Honeymooner's urinary infection," said Jerry. "Brides can get it from their husbands "getting to know them" too much! Another example of the wisdom of "all things in moderation.""

"Oh, then I could be in big trouble, I suspect," speculated Chenoa. "Maybe we should slow it down and go visit the Marchants."

"Why don't you call room service, and change our order to sack lunches," suggested Jerry. "I'll call the Marchants and see if and when we can drop by."

Jerry and Chenoa were ready to leave their room by 7:00. Jerry called Cactus Petes, however, to coordinate with Uncle Glenn and Aunt Martha.

Uncle Glenn expressed an interest in going along to meet the Marchants. Chenoa suggested inviting her dad and mom to go along, too.

Jerry made a call back to the Marchants, who were delighted to have the others come, too. Chenoa called her parents, who accepted the invitation to tag along. The whole group loaded into Lily and was on the road by 8:30.

It was a beautiful early fall morning. Calm wind, scatter clouds, mild temperature, low humidity, and sparse traffic on US 93. Since they were driving south into brilliant sunshine, everyone in the front seat dawned sunglasses. Uncle Glenn drove with Aunt Martha at his side, Ben rode shotgun, and Chenoa sat between Jerry and Little Feather in the back seat. Chenoa and Little Feather had lots to chat about. It was a pleasant morning for a ride in the old Chevrolet. It was as though they had all been transported back to their high school days and were out for a joy ride.

The old Chevy was a good cruiser. The miles clicked by quickly. The car was filled with chatter. Everyone was in good spirits. They passed through Delaplaine first, then San Jacinto.

The irrigated areas were lush and green this time of year in this section of Nevada. Those areas, which had to rely on normal rainfall, were dry and dusty. Some areas benefited from passing thunderstorms, but they were few in number.

Next was Contact, followed a few minutes later by Henry, Nevada. Uncle Glenn saw the "For sale" sign and turned off Hwy 93. When they arrived at the Crooked Creek ranch, the Marchants were on the porch to welcome them.

After a few minutes of introduction, the gathering drifted into three groups. Merna, Martha, and Little Feather went in the house engaged in big girl talk. Gerald, Glenn, and Ben went to the barn talking shop from the perspective of men who knew the ranching business from years of experience. Jerry and Chenoa walked around the premises, holding hands, and trying to take in every detail as prospective buyers.

Uncle Glenn was particularly interested in finding out from Gerald about the status of the appraisal, and who was conducting it.

Gerald shared the following information. The appraiser he retained is a man named Vince Coan. He came highly recommended by several ranchers for whom Vince had worked. He was born and raised in Nevada, got his education for the most part there, and had appraised properties from Las Vegas to Jackpot. He arguably knew the state better than any man alive.

What had been said about Mr. Coan which most impressed Gerald was his reputation for being a straight shooter. He did his research, and when he gave his opinion of what a property was worth, his word was the gold standard in Nevada.

"Have you talked to him lately to check on the status of his report?" asked Uncle Glenn.

"When I learned you all were coming, I put a call in to his office," reported Gerald. His secretary said he was doing some research for the project today, as a matter of fact.

"Tell me, Gerald, what do you think your ranch is worth in today's market? What price were you hoping to get? How much would you take for it, if I were to write a check for it today?" asked Glenn

"Could you do that?" ask Gerald somewhat shocked by the question.

"Well, probably not today," admitted Glenn. "But I'm no tire kicker, either! You tell me a reasonable price, and I will tell you if it is in my price range."

"Well, I would have to think on that a bit, and talk to the Mrs., before I could give you an answer we could shake on," said Gerald.

"Would you be willing to carry some of the paper to facilitate a sale," inquired Glenn, "or do you want to be cashed out at the time of sale?"

"Well, my papa always maintained in a sales agreement there is the price, and then there are the terms. I'll come up with the price and see if you can live with it. You come up the terms, and I'll see if I can live with them," suggested Gerald.

"Sounds pretty much like what I was taught," said Glenn.

"Do you have a legal description for the property?" asked Uncle Glenn.

"Sure thing," said Gerald. "It is in the house. Follow me there, and I'll show you my whole file on the subject.

Gerald led the way, and the three men walked to the house. They entered through the back entrance or "mud room". This is a feature of

most country homes, where during inclement weather, folks can remove their muddy shoes before entering the rest of the house.

While Glenn and Gerald were talking business, Merna and Martha
were engaged in some serious girl talk.

"Oh, good, you are here!" exclaimed Merna as the men walked
into the kitchen. "I was just about to call you."

"Something smells great!" declared Ben as the aroma of lunch hit
their noses.

"Gerald, would you ring the dinner bell, please? By the time those
young ones get back here, lunch should be ready to eat," estimated Merna.

Gerald stepped back through the mud room to the back porch.
There, hanging at about eye level was a classic triangular chime, or
what the Marchants called "the dinner bell". Its metallic ring could be
heard for miles in still air. When their boys were young, Merna would
ring it when their lunch was ready. Seldom did anyone miss lunch,
because they couldn't hear it.

Chenoa and Jerry were honeymooning again in a small patch of
Quakes when they heard Gerald's enthusiastic ringing. No-one had to
tell them what it meant. In a few moments they were presentable, and
off to quell their growing hunger pains. They had not thought to take
water with them, so they were even more thirsty than hungry.

Jerry and Chenoa were in a playful mood. The trek back to the
ranch house soon evolved into a foot race. Jerry discovered yet another quality of Chenoa; she could run. By the time she reach the house,
Jerry was 50 yards behind her. He had intended to beat her. Though
running as fast as he could, he was no match. Apparently, Jerry had
married a female Jim Thorpe in yet another way.

The ranch house had a dining room large enough to accommodate all eight people. After washing up, Jerry was the last to be seated.
He was still breathing heavily from the foot race. Chenoa's breathing
was back to normal. Still playful, Chenoa ask Jerry if he were feeling
ok or needed oxygen.

Looking at all the garden-fresh vegetables covering the table, Jerry
said, "I think everything I need is right here, thank you."

Grace was offered by Merna at Gerald's invitation. She offered
thanks to God for the bounty of which they were about to partake,

expressed thanks to God for their new friends, and ask God to bless them with safe travel, and the food that it might nourish and strengthen all those present.

"Amen!" said everyone in unison.

Uncle Glenn was impressed at how many different items were on the table when Gerald noted it had all come from Merna's garden.

Jerry wasted no time digging in. Corn-on-the-cob was one of his favorite foods. Aunt Martha helped herself to fresh garden peas, then paused to note which direction the food was being passed. Little Feather took some baby carrots, and then passed them to Ben who had just dished up some sliced "Fat-boy" tomatoes. Merna started off with baked squash. Gerald took a big helping of mashed potatoes. Glenn took some fried zucchini; Chenoa started off with some green onions. They tasted different from the sego lilies she found in the mountains, but she liked them anyway. Ben was the first to get some of Merna's fried chicken.

"This came from your garden, too?" asked Ben.

"Well, technically, yes," replied Merna. "That's where the chicken was when I finally caught up to it." Everybody laughed whose mouth wasn't full of food.

String beans, lettuce, radishes, and cucumbers were also served; all garden fresh. Merna apologized that the butter was store bought but explained that their milk cow had dried up three weeks ago. There was no cream left to churn.

When lunch was over, Chenoa helped the other women clear the table and wash the dishes

Ben and Glenn accompanied Gerald to his office to look at his file of legal papers for the property. They appeared to be in good order.

At length Glenn asked Gerald if he might lend him his office to confer with the newlyweds? Ben went looking for the couple and invited them to conference with Glenn and himself. Aunt Martha and Little Feather invited themselves to the meeting.

When the door closed and everyone was comfortable, Uncle Glenn brought the meeting to order with one question. "Well, Jerry, what are you two thinking? Is this the place where you want to plant your flag?"

The question didn't get an immediate response. Jerry and Chenoa looked into each other's eyes, and considered the idea. After a long moment, Chenoa spoke first.

"Yes, this is the place where I want to live and devote my every waking moment to making a life with my husband and family, to being Mrs. Jerry Briggs. We need, as you say, to plant our flag somewhere. I can't imagine a better place than right here on Crooked Creek. I don't think there could be a more perfect place to raise our family and horses."

Looking at Jerry, she continued, "The decision, though, is yours, my darling! I will go wherever you go, live the life you choose, suffer the consequences, whatever they may be, and thank God for every day we have together for as long as I am permitted to live on this earth. I am your woman; you are my man for as long as we draw breath."

Tears were rolling down Chenoa's cheeks by the time she finished. Jerry stood, faced Uncle Glenn and Ben, and cleared his throat. "I'm not used to swimming in the deep end of the pool. For me life has been free of almost any serious responsibilities. Then lightning struck me and changed my life forever. I awoke in the tender loving care of an angel whose life is now joined with mine, and with whom I have made sacred vows. I swear before God that I will honor those vows to my dying day, God as my witness. I see a bright future for us in a place such as this. You all know I am not wealthy in terms of money. I agree with Chenoa, Crooked Creek feels like a good place to plant our flag. If we can figure a way to do it, Chenoa and I are ready to make it happen."

An afternoon thunderstorm had quietly moved over the ranch while they had been talking. As everyone joined in a hardy "Let's do it!", a clap of thunder hit so close, it rattled the house.

Jerry turned to Chenoa and said, "I'll bet that's your mother again!"

"Probably!" said Chenoa innocently.

Chapter 22—Forging a Deal

It was Merna and Aunt Martha who really sealed the decision to sell the Crooked Creek Ranch to Jerry and Chenoa. After the lunch dishes and items had been cleared away, they took a stroll out to look at the garden from whence such a bountiful meal had come, and then just kept on going.

They walked and talked about family and ranch life until they had left the ranch house far behind. Merna had a favorite spot where she liked to go when something was troubling her. She called it her "Prayer Spot". It was where she went when she needed to chill and meditate on the situation.

There she could talk to whomever she wished. She really didn't pray to them. She had been taught that you only pray to God in the name of Jesus Christ. But she didn't see anything wrong in at least talking to them and explaining her problems to them. It helped her organize her thoughts.

It was a quiet place, where no one ever came and bothered her. No phone ever rang. No one ever came there searching for a lost item. There she seemed to be able to think clearer. She could remember more clearly the long-ago advice of her parents. There she was able to forget her troubles and remember the things about the good times that made them good. It was above all else, where she could come when she needed to feel the love of her Heavenly Father, and talk to Him.

Merna and Martha talked for hours. They found a natural friendship springing from common experience. Both had weathered the frequent lean years, and been the pillars their husbands could turn to when the hard years had beaten them into near submission. They had both nursed sick children all night, then spent the following day on a tractor to help husbands get in a crop so poor as to make meeting the mortgage

payment, come fall, look impossible. They both had had to stretch nickels into dollars to keep their children from going hungry. They had both had to mend worn out clothes to make them last another school year. They both had husbands for whom they had devoted their lives for more than a half century and raised their children to be upstanding people.

Now it was time to consider what they would leave behind as they rode into the sunset of their lives. Merna and Gerald had worked hard to make the Crooked Creek ranch into the success story it represented.

Martha asked Merna a simple question, "What would you most like to have the future of your ranch be?"

Merna sat quietly for a few minutes considering the question, then answered softly, "I'd like it to continue as much like it is today as possible!"

"Well, in Jerry and Chenoa you have a young couple who I think would like to give that vision of the future an honest try!" said Martha. With Ben and Glenn's help, not to mention Little Feather and me, I think they have an outstanding chance to succeed.

Merna was excited at the prospect of coming back to visit the ranch in a few years and seeing what they had worked so hard to create still there, and even better.

Martha asked Merna, "Do you have any idea what the market value of the ranch is, or for what amount you were hoping to sell it?

"I remember hearing Gerald mentioning the amount $200,000 one time. But I don't know, if he thought that was what it was worth, or how much he was hoping to get when we sold it."

Have you thought about where you will go, and what you will do when you sell out?" inquired Aunt Martha.

"Well, yes. We have a daughter in North Dakota. Her husband is in the Oil business. They have done quite well. They live on a small spread just outside Bismarck. Though her husband does well in Oil, he does not know the difference between a hoe and a shovel, when it comes to farming. They have a guest house on the property, and have invited us to come, and live with them.

They have asked if Gerald would take on the responsibility of caring for their "farm"; the whole 5 acres. We would have our own house. We would be around family. Gerald loves working with our grandchildren. We could travel and visit family and friends. Gerald would be able to keep a horse and a few other animals. My daughter and I get along great. I think it is a good idea!" concluded Merna.

"How much do you think you will need to live on?" asked Aunt Martha.

"Living rent free in our daughter's guest house, probably not a lot," spectated Merna.

"Do you think you could make ends meet on say $10,000 a year in addition to your Social Security and your other investment income?" asked Martha.

"I think so," said Merna.

"For a moment, let's use that $200,000 figure. Let's say the kids agreed to pay you $10,000 each year for 20 years. You would have the money you need to live on, and they would have a ranch. But in lieu of interest, let's say they agreed to keep paying the $10,000 each year for as long you live, so you don't have to worry about running out of money in your old age," explained Martha.

"Running out of money is something we have been concerned about," admitted Merna.

"It is something we all worry about as we get older," agreed Martha. "This plan helps alleviate that concern."

"I think it is a wonderful plan!" said Merna excitedly.

"I wish I could take credit for the idea, but it really was my father who used the life annuity concept first when he came back from the war and went into business with his brother-in-law. He agreed to pay $2000 a year for 20 years for his first farm and keep paying it for as long as the folks lived from whom he bought it. It turned out to be what is commonly called now-a-days a "Win-Win" situation. It didn't require any bank loan, with their approval process, high interest rates, and threats of foreclosure, if you have a bad year. It gave the sellers a sense of security that they wouldn't outlive their resources, and they still have the farm as security.

The husband died shortly before the twenty years were up, but his widow lived several years longer. True to his word, my dad continued his payments for as long as she lived. My dad was an honest, smart, hardworking man. He experienced some good years, some better years, and a few hard years, but every year he went personally to hand them their check for $2000. I was very young back then, but I remember going with my dad several times to the modest little house in town where the couple lived to make the payment," concluded Martha.

"If we needed it, I know anyone of a number of our children could and would step up and help us,. But this type of agreement would give us such a sense of security," said Merna. "I really like it, and I'm sure Gerald will, too. $10,000 per year for life. Let's go tell the boys what we have decided"

With that Merna, Martha knelt by the log upon which they had been sitting and offered a short prayer of thanks for the inspiration which had guided them in formulating their proposal. They ask God for help in seeing it through the discussions which would be needed to see its implementation. Lastly, they prayed for Jerry and Chenoa that their union might prosper and bring them great joy and happiness.

As they concluded their prayer, they both had the strongest impression that they were not alone. Then a dove landed on a tree close to them and started cooing.

"Hi little one," said Aunt Martha as she held out her arm toward the pure-white bird. Martha had had more than a few parakeets and other birds in her home over the years. She was never-the-less surprised when the dove flew over and landed on her outstretched arm, then transferred smoothly to the index finger of her opposite hand. The dove cooed softly for a few moments then flew over and landed on Merna's shoulder where it sat as Merna and Martha started the hike back to the ranch house.

"My goodness," exclaimed Merna. "In all my life, I have never had this happen."

The dove rode on Merna's shoulder for about fifty yards, then fluttered over to Martha where it rode for another fifty yards. Finally, the dove took flight, circled twice, then flew away.

"I think we have just been visited," declared Merna in stunned amazement.

A no less surprised Martha agreed, "Well there was no burning bush, but I would have to say you are right!"

A calm assurance settled over the two conferees that their idea was approved by those beyond the veil. They met Jerry and Chenoa about

500 yards from the house walking arm in arm and talking about the prospect of buying the Crook Creek Ranch, and what they would like to do with it.

"I figure we could sell about half of the hay as a cash crop and keep the other half to feed our own livestock," proposed Jerry.

"I would like to bring my father's horses here he is preparing to sell," said Chenoa, "and add value to them by breaking and training them. Why, do you know that a good cutting horse can sell for as high as thirty or forty thousand dollars? Even just a well-trained saddle horse is worth double an unbroken one. With this ranch as our home base, Jerry and I could take our stock to horse shows and rodeos all over the west."

"I don't know much about farming and ranching," admitted Jerry, "but with Ben and Uncle Glenn to advise me, I can learn fast. And another thing, do you suppose you and Gerald would be willing to spend a couple of summers out here, to teach me some of the things I need to know?"

"I think that is a good possibility," said Merna. "Let's bring up the idea when we get together to talk."

When they got back to the ranch house, they found Ben, Glenn, and Gerald discussing the details of the property: total acres, irrigated farmland, acres leased from the Bureau of Land Management (BLM), deeded land, AUM's, average frost free days during the growing season; lots of factors Vince would be analyzing to formulate his appraisal.

The discussion was interrupted when Merna and Martha drew their husbands aside for some private talks. They weren't gone too long before they returned with their minds focused on the purchase plan Merna and Martha were proposing.

"I find the idea totally acceptable," conceded Gerald. I particularly like the life annuity idea. Eliminates the need to try to sell for as high of a price as possible."

"I think the concept is absolutely genius," said Ben when it was explained to him. "I'll have to remember it when the time comes for me to retire."

"How much of a down payment were you wanting to have?" Glenn asked Gerald when the proposal had been explained to everyone.

Chenoa and Jerry listened to the chatter in stunned silence as they realized that their future was being discussed. Were they really ready for this? Were they ready to settle down and make this sort of commitment? It was one thing to work on a ranch, but this was owning and operating a ranch. This was making sure the bills got paid. This was hoping that some act of God beyond your control didn't wipe you out. This was real life.

Chenoa saw the "deer-in-the-headlights" look on Jerry's face, and knew it was her move to do as all good ranch wives have had to do before her; support your man. She gently squeezed Jerry's hand and looked him in the eyes. It was just the message that Jerry needed. When he turned, and gazed into Chenoa's eyes, a feeling of peace swept over him. Suddenly, he had a confidence with her at his side, no challenge would be too great, no problem beyond solution. After all, wasn't she the most beautiful women in the world, and great at everything she put her mind to. If she had consented to marry him, undoubtedly, she would be a great wife, too. His doubts faded like a morning dew. Chenoa could see the difference immediately. Her man was rising to the occasion. Her man was a man and would cower no more.

Jerry joined in the discussion. He surprised everyone, except Chenoa, with his intensity. He was now engaged. He was the one leading the direction of the conversation. He and Chenoa were the ones buying, or not buying a ranch. Chenoa sat at his side, pleased with herself for recognizing a moment when her man needed her, and she was there. It wasn't anything she had said, only quietly conveying the message, "I am yours, I am with you!"

A deal was struck, the details carefully outlined in a handwritten contract, drafted largely by Uncle Glenn. It was a good opportunity to put his experience and knowledge of contracts to work.

Gerald had agreed to the $200,000 sale price for the ranch, but not the inventory. The cattle would be sold at auction in Elko, and the inventory of hay to a large dairy in Jerome, Idaho. All else: equipment, tools, house, barn, and irrigation equipment would be part of the sale price. The contents of the house would remain the property of the Marchant's, along with their personal vehicle.

The Marchants (Gerald) had wanted 10% down, but agreed to take 5% down after Merna and Gerald took a time out to discuss the issue.

Uncle Glenn explained to everyone present that if the down payment were 5%, he could write a check on the spot; at 10% he couldn't. The closing date was set for September 21st. Gerald said he had an attorney with whom he would like to work. Gerald would have him arrange all the closing papers. All agreed; Uncle Glenn wrote a check, and the meeting was adjourned.

As Lily carried the group back to Jackpot, no one spoke. They all seemed to be pondering the import of this special day. No one seemed especially hungry, so they all just went to bed, except the occupants of room 624 at the HorseShu Casino. They were celebrating their new life, and working hard to create yet another, till long after the others had fallen asleep.

Surprisingly, Chenoa and Jerry were the first ones up the next morning. They hadn't gotten a lot of sleep, so it had to have been the adrenaline rush of buying the Crooked Creek ranch which energized them. As they ate their room service breakfast, they excitedly shared their ideas about how they might profitably run their new ranch. They could barely stand the thought of having to wait till September 21st for the closing.

In the meantime what were they to do? Jerry half-jokingly suggested they might take up residence in the sheep camp where they had met. Chenoa, remembering her embarrassment of that morning said, "This time I will let you get up and stoke the fire!"

Realizing they had both abandoned full-time jobs to get married, the thought struck them that they had obligations back home to which they needed to be attend.

Jerry had planned to stay only for the summer, after which he would return to his studies in Philadelphia. So Uncle Glenn wasn't depending on him. But with Ben it was a different story. Chenoa had been his only helper. True, he was married now, but could Little Feather fill the role played by Chenoa? Good question. Chenoa would need to consult with Ben and Little Feather?

Although Chenoa thought Little Feather capable of riding the range, perhaps it was time for a role reversal. Maybe it was time for Little Feather to tend the home fires, and have Ben look after the stock.

After all, if he were going to pick out horses for Chenoa and Jerry to train, didn't he need to be the one getting to know his horses by working with them on a daily basis.

By checkout time Chenoa knew what she needed to discuss with her father. He had been contemplating the same problems but had not as yet drawn the same conclusions. He had been thinking of hiring a brave from the Duck Valley Reservation, Johnny Eagle Eyes, a good horseman, but without his glasses practically blind beyond 10 feet. He was a cousin of Little Feather.

After they had all checked out, they met at the HorseShu Club for lunch. Jerry and Chenoa were the first to arrive. They were noticeably excited and ate heartily.

Uncle Glenn and Aunt Martha questioned of how they were all going to get home. Chenoa and Jerry had arrived driving Lilly; Ben and Little Feather had hitched a ride with Orrie. Now they needed a way home. Chenoa needed to pick a up a few personal items from home. It was decided the best strategy would be for Ben and Little Feather to ride with Jerry and Chenoa back to Ben's ranch.

At 1pm sharp the new Mr. and Mrs. Jerry Briggs left Jackpot, Nevada with Lily's the top down, and Ben and Little Feather as company. Hard on their heels were Uncle Glenn and Aunt Martha driving the Dually. In a matter of minutes, they were passing through Rogerson where the two vehicles parted.

The pickup continued north to Holster; the Chevy turned west. As long as they were on paved road, the drive was very enjoyable. When they left the pavement behind, the dust was insufferable. They stopped, and put the top up, then drove the rest of the way home.

Upon arriving at the ranch, Chenoa packed her bag, tossed it in the car, then went to visit Sky Walker. There was no way to explain her absence. Ben came close with a bucket of oats. Sky Walker seemed to sense that things had changed. Chenoa stroked Sky Walker in all the usual places, planted a kiss on his forehead, then slowly walked to the car.

She sobbed uncontrollably for the first 10 miles. Jerry didn't know what to do for her. He finally just held her close and let her cry it out. By the time they reached the pavement, Chenoa was getting control of her emotions. By the time they reached Rogerson, she had dried her eyes and was starting to act like Mrs. Jerry Briggs again.

CHAPTER 23—POST HONEYMOON

When the vehicle reached home, it was well past dark. Jerry and Chenoa could hardly believe that in less than 60 hours, they had morphed into Mr. and Mrs. Jerry Briggs. It was simply unreal. Ole George was waiting for them.

"I know this is nothing like Cactus Pete's or the Horseshu Club, but there are a couple of bottles of Sparkling Cider and Cheese sandwiches in your room if you are hungry," offered George.

"Thanks, George," expressed Jerry, "but do you think you could set that up by the pool for us? Chenoa and I thought we would like to take a swim?"

"Sure thing!" agreed Ole George.

Chenoa suddenly nudged Jerry, and whispered in his ear, "I still don't have a swimsuit!"

"Oh, it wasn't a big problem 72 hours ago; I don't think it will be now!" answered Jerry. "If you have clean underwear."

Chenoa was first in the pool. She again outpaced Jerry. He was no match for her speed. What's more, she made it look easy. Jerry could only stare in disbelief.

When they took a break to enjoy their snack, Jerry asked, "What is the Shoshone word for fish?"

"Oh, there are lots of names depending on what you mean. 'painkwi' is the word we used around the Duck Valley Reservation, but it can be different for different kinds of fish, for whether you are talking about a fishhook, fish trap, fish net, fish line, or a host of other things. What you got in mind?"

"A girl like you who can swim like a fish," admitted Jerry.

"Umh, I'm not sure. You thinking of trying to hook another one? I think there is a bag limit of one in possession."

"No, I'm happy with what I've already got. I think I've already got the finest fish in the sea, wouldn't you agree?" asked Jerry.

There was no knock on the door the next morning. Ole George decided to let the honeymooners be. Nor was there any need for Chenoa to sneak back to the guest room. Actually, there was no need to wake them at all. Uncle Glenn was a bit surprised to find them up, dressed, and waiting in his office when he walked in.

"What do you have on your mind?" asked Uncle Glenn, surprised to see them in his office instead of being under the covers getting to know each other better. "How may I help you?"

"We were thinking we ought to help the Merchants wrap up their affairs," explained Jerry. "We don't have a lot of time before they will be gone along with our chance to learn anything from them."

"Good point," agreed Glenn. "What is your proposed solution?"

"We are here to pick your brain," offered Chenoa. "What suggestion might you have to offer?"

"Well, let's look at the facts. You are here, in Holister. The ranch is in Nevada. You don't own a vehicle. Chenoa, have you ever learned to drive?" asked Glenn. We need to finish up some paperwork. I think it would be a good idea to spend some time with the Marchants. What you lack in vehicular horsepower you can make up in actual horsepower. There are a number of ways we could skin this cat, but the simplest would be to use the horses you already have.

What if you were to go back out to your dad's place and have him pick out the 10 best horses he would like to sell during this next year. Then you two trail them to Nevada and start working with them. You'll need two horses you can ride, and two you can pack. That will give you a minimum of six horses you can start breaking.

I can have Martha come down once a month and bring supplies. Sell some horse flesh, and you can work on getting your own pickup. You already know where there is a stock trailer, if you need it.

Uncle Glenn and Aunt Martha had enough wealth that they could easily afford to help Jerry procure a motor vehicle to travel back and forth to the Crooked Creek ranch, of which they were now the proud owners. But there was something in Uncle Glenn's proposal that they liked; really liked.

What was the challenge in having something handed to you? Uncle Glenn had already helped them arrange the purchase. He had not bought it outright. They were going to have to work hard to make the payments. But the collective wisdom of everyone involved had been employed to work out the deal whereby they would have the opportunity to make it work. In retrospect, it was sheer genius because it worked for everyone.

It worked for Ben and Little Feather by helping them improve the marketing of their horses. They didn't use a lot of hay, but what they did need, they could get from Crooked Creek.

It worked for Uncle Glenn and Aunt Martha because they now had a hay supplier upon whom they could rely. Also it gave them access to more summer pasture.

Most importantly it worked for Jerry and Chenoa because now they had work and a home of their own. Here they could live, raise a family, and experience the pride of ownership. Glenn's idea had appeal because it let them really start on the ground floor. They would be able to tell their posterity how they got their start at Crooked Creek leading in a string of Grandpa Ben's Appaloosa horses some 80 or so miles on horseback. It would be their version of the ole story from an earlier generation of having to "walk 5 miles to school; up hill, both ways".

Jerry and Chenoa talked the idea over while they ate breakfast. Ben didn't have a telephone. They needed to talk with him to implement the plan. Lack of communication had always been a problem for Ben. But over the years, Ben's main objective had been to grow his herd. To do so he didn't want or need to sell too many animals, as long as he kept the overhead low; thus, he had never gotten a telephone. If he really needed to make a phone call, he could use Orie's. Chenoa agreed to call Orie's place and try to get in touch with her dad. Jerry had a second discussion with Uncle Glenn, and asked him if he had thought it through any further?

I have one idea I think will help you implement the plan. I know Ben has plenty of horses, but Martha and I would like to give you Fleet and Gypsie as a wedding present. That way you will have two seasoned animals you can count on as you get started with this venture.

Gee, Uncle Glenn, that would be awesome. Chenoa is going to need a good horse now that Sky Walker will need to stay with Ben to continue their great Appaloosa bloodline.

"Wait, there is more!" injected Uncle Glenn, sounding a bit like a game show host. "If you are going to pack in all of your personal possessions to Crooked Creek, we want you to take you Frank and Fred, our experienced pack mules. The two of them could probably carry about as much as a small U-Haul truck."

Chenoa was able to get a message to Ben to start rounding up the horses he wanted to sell. Jerry hadn't brought much with him from Philadelphia, so loading up his stuff didn't take long. Aunt Martha washed all his clothes so he could start out with clean ones.

Chenoa still had most of her things at her dad's home. What she had with her didn't take long to clean and pack, either. They were going to ride horse back and lead the pack mules all the way to Ben's place. They decided to leave at dawn.

Aunt Martha suggested she and Ole George would prepare some food for the journey, if Jerry and Chenoa wanted to go for one last swim.

Uncle Glenn offered to let them borrow a tent, a Coleman stove, and some camping gear. Chenoa gladly accepted the offer. Ole George set about rounding it up, along with the pack saddles for Frank and Fred.

Chenoa didn't feel good about leaving their work to others. She suggested to Jerry they pitch in, and help get things ready; then swim later. Jerry didn't quite have as refined work ethic as Chenoa, but he never-the-less agreed with her.

Frank, Fred, Gypsie, and Fleet were moved to the stable beneath the east side of the house and groomed in preparation for the early morning departure. Ole George showed Jerry how to load the pack saddles. Then the saddles were unloaded.

Ole George and Jerry went next to help Aunt Martha and Chenoa make sandwiches and other food for the trip to Crooked Creek. When all was ready, Jerry and Chenoa went swimming. Aunt Martha found Chenoa

an old, one-piece swimsuit. She felt that with as many guys around the house as there were, wet panties and a bra were just a bit too revealing.

When Chenoa got through to the Dimond Bar ranch, the cook promised to get a message to Ben. Late that evening Ben and Little Feather called. Chenoa explained Uncle Glenn's idea, now their plan, to Ben and Little Feather. Chenoa asked her father how long he thought it would take to get 10 horses corralled at the ranch headquarters. Chenoa further explained they were leaving Holister at daybreak and planned to be home by nightfall. Ben said he thought he could have the job done by then.

Jerry set his alarm for two hours before daybreak. He wanted to be ready to leave at first light. He went to the stable only to find Ole George had been there first. Fleet and Gypsie had been saddled, and were eating lazily. Fred and Frank were wearing their loaded pack saddles, polishing off a ration of oats, and starting on some fresh hay in their manager.

With nothing left to do but eat, Jerry followed the scent of bacon to find Ole George talking with Chenoa as he cooked their breakfast. Chenoa was hungry. Upon leaving their room, she had skipped the detour to the stable and gone straight to the kitchen. This was a rare luxury; Ole George was a good cook. Normally, she had to cook for herself. Once they hit the trail, they would be on their own.

Uncle Glenn and Aunt Martha were there to see them off, when the first light of dawn appeared. There were hugs, kisses, and well wishes. Ole George got an especially big kiss and hug from Chenoa for his part in seeing them off. With each of them leading a pack mule, Jerry and Chenoa stared down the road at a trot. They would travel at this pace for most of the day.

Their path was roughly the same as that of the cow drive earlier in the spring. Then, Jerry had been an inexperienced tenderfoot. Now he was married to possibly the most beautiful girl ever. They were setting out on an adventure in love and marriage unlike anything he could have imagined, when he stepped off the bus at Henstock's just a few short months ago.

Jerry held back, and let Chenoa and Gypsie take the lead. It was not light enough to see clearly. But Jerry sat in awe of how beautiful Chenoa was. She sat a horse particularly well. There was just no way to describe how fortunate Jerry felt. You could say he had found "the pot of Gold at the end of the rainbow" or any number of descriptions of good fortune. They all seemed to be understatements for what he was feeling.

Jerry started thinking of a prayer as they rode south toward the Salmon Falls Dam. As day light burst upon them, he thought about how some folks start out marriage in love, but soon lose the magic. He didn't want to have that that happen to them. Chenoa deserved better than that. Didn't a girl who possessed the superlative attributes of Chenoa, also deserve the best in marriage.

Jerry's thoughts morphed into a sort of a prayer, "Please, God, help me to be the man she deserves; help me to be and remain the man of her dream!"

After an hour of riding, Chenoa slowed their pace to a walk, and then complete stop. They dismounted and checked the pack saddles. Things were still well tied down, but Jerry helped Chenoa tighten the bindings a bit never-the-less. After a drink of water from their canteens and walking for a few minutes, Chenoa and Jerry re-mounted and continued their trek.

Chenoa, too, was in deep thought as the honeymooners rode in silence. She was reflecting on her mother's intervention on her behalf. Just a few short months ago she was single, working with her dad, and unsure about her future. Now she was married, planning her future with her husband, and well on her way to securing her future.

She wondered, if Jerry and she were on their own now, or if, her mother were going to continue to guide them on their path to "happily ever after". There was just something comforting about having a guardian angel looking after you, even if, they were only heard from occasionally.

By maintaining a steady pace Chenoa and Jerry covered the miles quickly. By lunch time they had reached the ridge where for them, it had all started.

"You thinking what I am thinking?" Chenoa asked Jerry.

"If you are wondering, why we are in such a hurry, we might be reading off the same page." answered Jerry.

"I know this little place nearby, where we could relax and have lunch," said Chenoa suggestively.

"Why not," asked Jerry. "I think that is a great idea!

Maybe I could pick a wildflower, while we are at it."

"Think you can get past the thorns this time?" said Chenoa with a sly wink.

With that thought they simultaneously turned Fleet and Gypsie toward Clarke's Crossing. Both were remembering their first encounter at said location; neither was too concerned about food.

Their horses and mules were well rested by the time Jerry and Chenoa returned to the trail. The Flower of China Mountain was in full bloom. Chenoa had held nothing back.

Jerry had never pondered much about heaven or paradise, but he was sure he had experienced it at least once, that afternoon at a humble old sheep camp at Clarke's Crossing. Could life possibly get better?

It was time to make tracks! Chenoa led the way; she knew the lay of the land better. Besides, it made looking at her easier for Jerry. There was an urgency in the pace at which Chenoa rode. She had ridden these hills all of her life. She road with the ease of one, who literally knew every rock and reel between the camp and home.

The sun had slipped below the horizon by the time they reached the ridge overlooking Ben's ranch headquarters. Jerry was getting saddle sore, but for Chenoa it was just another day in the saddle. Smoke was coming from the chimney as they surveyed the scene below.

Chenoa counted 10 horses waiting for them in the pasture next to the barn. She directed Gypsie down the well-worn trail to the barn.

They had unloaded the bulk of the pack items at the Clarke's Crossing camp; no use having Fred and Frank haul the heavy packs all the way home, only to re-trace their trail when they head to Crooked Creek.

With the critters safely bedded down for the evening, Chenoa and Jerry headed to the house. The scent of beef stew greeted their nostrils before they got there. The smell of fresh baked bread was noted as they entered the home. A partially eaten apple pie sat on the counter next to the stove.

Greetings were exchanged, and Little Feather apologized for not waiting for them. Jerry and Chenoa assured them no apology was necessary; they were a bit late because they had stopped to rest and smell the wildflowers.

"Didn't know there was anything still in bloom," admitted Ben. Little Feather smiled knowingly, and let it pass.

She dished some stew for Jerry and Chenoa, cut some bread, and applied a thick layer of butter.

Ben asked about the events of the day, and how the horses had held up?

"Are you going to rest them a day before you head south?" asked Ben.

"We will need a little time to gather up my things," said Chenoa.

"Some of those horses, I rounded up for you haven't been taught to lead, yet," said Ben. "They are pretty raw, to say the least!"

"We will need to deal with that first thing," said Chenoa. "The basis of our whole plan is to trail them to Crooked Creek. They will lead well by the time we get there, for sure."

"How do you teach a horse to lead?" asked Jerry. "All I know about it is the old expression, 'You can lead a horse to water, but you can't make him drink!' It doesn't explain anything about how you get the horse to lead."

"There are different ways," offered Ben. "There are rough ways; and there are gentle ways."

"We have always sought to be gentle with our horses," added Chenoa. "The simplest way is to first start out leading them somewhere they already want to go."

"Works the same with men," teased Little Feather.

"I'll have to remember that," said Chenoa, agreeably.

"Sort of work both ways!" said Ben just loud enough to be heard.

"Pa, do we have enough tack to accommodate all 10 horses?" asked Chenoa.

"No, I'll need to get to work in the morning, and make a few more halters," conceded Ben. "Some of our old stuff just isn't good enough anymore. If one of those young horses fought being restrained, he could probably break away, easily."

"We are in the horse marketing business now. Everything needs to show well!" said Jerry speaking to his marketing contribution to their new business plan.

After enjoying the savory beef stew and bread, everyone decided to call it a day. Not even the idea of more intimacy won out over the idea of getting some much-needed rest. Everyone was asleep within minutes.

Ben's old rooster announced the dawn of a new day. Ben had an old Timex, but who needed it when you had the elements of nature calling cadence during the day. Up at dawn, work till dusk, with lunch at high noon. If the weather is overcast, judge it from the amount of daylight. If you are off by a few minutes, who cares. You are working for yourself!

No one is going to be checking your timecard. No one pays any attention to whether you are 10 minutes early or 20 minutes late. If you need to meet an outsider at a specific time, well then you may need to dig the ole Timex out of your pocket and see if it is still running.

Jerry was still in awe of Chenoa. She had gotten out of bed first to start packing her things. Jerry propped his head up on his arm and watched her as she worked. Again and again, he asked himself, "How could I be so lucky? Why me?"

It had to be more than luck, like winning the lottery. It wasn't just that he was now married to perhaps the prettiest girl who ever lived; she loved him. How could that be? How could his life get any better?

Suddenly Chenoa pounced on him. Jerry had not recognized her getting within striking distance, so innocently had she made her move.

"I've got you; you are mine. If I were a mountain lion, you would the dead or slashed to pieces! I would eat my fill of you, then drag what was left back to my lair," Chenoa declared dramatically. With that she started roughly kissing his face, and neck pretending her cougar attack.

Jerry had never realized it before, but he was actually quite ticklish. He started to laugh, and Chenoa "attacked" even more "viciously". Soon they both toppled right out of bed.

As they hit the floor, they heard Little Feather calling out, "Breakfast!"

"Saved by the bell," exclaimed Chenoa.

"Unfair, sneak attack," responded Jerry.

"Well, that's what you get when you lie in bed daydreaming while I am up working," said Chenoa.

"Even if I am thinking of you?" asked Jerry plaintively.

"How am I supposed to know whether you are thinking of me, or not?" asked Chenoa.

"Because you are all I think about!" asserted Jerry.

"What about food?" asked Chenoa.

"Good question," replied Jerry. "But when you are around, I don't think much about food."

"I am going to put you to the test," declared Chenoa. "What are you thinking of right now, me or breakfast?"

"Dressed like that," asked Jerry. Chenoa had already packed her night gown. "Want a hint?"

"Ok, point made. We better not keep the cook waiting," concluded Chenoa. "let's get dressed and eat!"

Little Feather had a large stack of sourdough pancakes waiting for them when Jerry and Chenoa sat down to breakfast.

"How many more do you want?" asked Little Feather. "I've got more batter, if you have the appetite."

"What about you and pa?" inquired Chenoa. "Have you eaten already?"

"Ben wanted to get an early start on making those halters, so we ate earlier," explained Little Feather, then asked, "Who wants eggs, and how many?"

"One, sunny side up," responded Chenoa.

"Three, over easy!" requested Jerry. "I need something that will stick to my ribs!"

"Be careful or 'that something' will be sticking to your butt," quipped Chenoa.

"I've got a few years before I'll need to worry on that score," asserted Jerry.

"Especially, if you keep riding as many miles as you did yesterday," said Little Feather.

When breakfast was finished, Jerry offered to help Little Feather clean up while Chenoa finished packing.

"Sweetheart, when you are finished, would bring in the pack saddle that was on Frank?" asked Chenoa "I will use that one to haul my belongs to Crooked Creek."

By mid-morning Chenoa was packed, and it was time to find out which of the 10 horses was willing to be led to Crooked Creek. The 10 were corralled, and a brand-new halter was put on each of them.

Chenoa saddled up Sky Walker. She led him around amongst the 10 to show them what it was like to be lead around the corral. The

magnificent stallion had a calming effect on the 10, who were all his progeny from the last 3 or 4 years. Each of the 10 had a lead rope attached to his halter and was tied alongside of Sky Walker.

Chenoa led Sky Walker around the corral. There was some reluctance on the part of the 10 to follow at first, but soon each was walking along side Sky Walker, offering little resistance.

Ben, Little Feather, and Jerry sat on the corral fence watching Chenoa and Sky Walker work their magic with the 10. Not one of them put up a stink of any significant degree. Jerry was some taken aback when he saw Chenoa tying a lead rope to the tail of the horse in front of it instead of to the horn of the saddle on Sky Walker.

Jerry turned to Ben in search of an explanation.

"Just watch!" counseled Ben.

First two horses were lined up, then three, and finally four. Chenoa walked around the corral leading Sky Walker with his string of young followers. Eventually she mounted up and rode Sky Walker leading this procession.

With a few hours more work, it was working beautifully.

"I've been thinking, Ben confided to Chenoa. For this first trip to Crook-ed Creek, don't you think you ought to take Sky Walker. It is obvious, he is a good influence on the youngsters. You'll be going through Jackpot and right down US93; lots of people are going to see what we have to offer.

"Could be an advertising bonanza," commented Jerry who had been listening in on their conversation. Having Sky Walker on display would be a singular opportunity. Right now, the way it is, he is sort of our little secret. Few people know we have him and what an amazing horse he is. These 10 are a good sample of his progeny. If we have him lead these horses through Jackpot and for some fifty miles down Highway 93, all that changes. Our horses will quickly be known far and wide."

"We can get him back here to resume his stud services in a couple weeks," postulated Chenoa.

"I think we are all in agreement," said Ben

Chenoa, Little Feather, and Jerry nodded in agreement.

Chenoa spent the rest of the afternoon working with the rest of the 10. They were responding wonderfully.

Ben rode over to the Dimond Bar ranch late in the afternoon with Little Feather to ask if they could borrow their pack saddle. When everyone saw how much stuff Chenoa had to take, it was obvious even to a tenderfoot such as Jerry, that two pack saddles wouldn't handle it all. You just wouldn't be able to load Fred and Frank up with all the items that she needed to move. Since it had been decided to have Chenoa ride Sky Walker, Gypsie would to able and available to pack additional stuff.

By the end of the day Jerry and Chenoa were ready for the trail. They planned on getting an early start in the morning. Morning found them riding into the rising sun. Ben was proud of his "little girl". Here she was, married, headed with" her man" to their new home.

Ben knew that she wasn't going all that far away. He knew he would see her again, soon. But he cried never-the-less as the horses crested the ridge above the ranch house and disappeared from sight.

Chenoa's eyes, too, were full of tears. So much so that she couldn't see the trail. Consequently, she let Sky Walker choose his path. He had come this way hundreds of times before. It was not hard to trust the big fellow.

Jerry led Fred; Chenoa led Frank. Each mule had a string of 5 freshly broke-to-lead Appaloosa horses tied to their tail. Chenoa on Sky Walker was in the lead. They kept up a steady pace. It was like speed walking. Jerry was surprised when Chenoa turned Gypsie loose. She followed along like a dog off lease. She never once fell behind or went off on her own. She kept behind the last Appaloosa, her head down, her gate smooth and steady.

Jerry and Chenoa decided they would set a pace to reach Clarke's Crossing at about sunset, spend the night there, and then plan to make Jackpot by evening the next day. The 10 were trailing well. Not one of them was a problem. This promised to be "a piece of cake!" Just to demonstrate the point, Chenoa decided to circle around a big boulder which lie in their path. Much to Chenoa's satisfaction, the string of horses paraded around the big rock without breaking stride. Jerry followed suit, a little puzzled at first, why she was doing it.

Chenoa was curious what would happen, if she quickened the pace? After hours of just walking, Chenoa urged Sky Walker into a trot. The string of horses seemed a bit confused at first, but quickly adjusted to the change of pace. A few minutes more, and Chenoa slowed back to a walk.

The sun was low in the western sky, when they reached Peter's Ridge. It was dusk, when they reached camp. They took the packs off Gypsie, Fred, and Frank. There was an enclosure into which the horses and mules were released.

Sky Walker and Fleet were fed hay and oats but confined to a sort of stable. Jerry and Chenoa retired to the camp but were too tired to worry about cooking a meal. They satisfied themselves by eating a couple old George's now nearly three-day old sandwiches. They kidded each other, the first one to complain had to cook breakfast. Other than a bit dry, Ole George's sandwiches weren't bad.

As Jerry and Chenoa got ready for bed, memories of their first encounter here inevitably became the topic of conversation. They both expressed their amazement at the miraculous way their lives had been brought together. Jerry wondered out loud, why of all the people in the world God should care about them?

"I remember my mother telling me one time, 'where much is given, much is expected'. What do you suppose God wants from us? He sure seems to have gone out of his way to bring us together!" opined Jerry.

"I wonder what part my mother played in all of this?" asked Chenoa. "I had a thought come to me one day; it didn't seem like I was daydreaming, just a whole complete idea burst upon my mind. God was talking to my mother, holding her in his arms. He asked her what he could do for her; what she was most concerned about? My mom said, Chenoa, her little girl had been left without a mother. She wanted permission to watch over her daughter more closely than is usually allowed. The thought concluded with God asking my mother, "What? You think I, God the Almighty, am too busy to do my job properly? Ok, ok, if you want to help, permission granted!""

Chenoa snuggled close to Jerry who hugged her tightly, and asked, "Hey, you think your mother is getting a bit worn guarding you, and put in a requisition for a husband to take over some of the workload?"

"Could be; you never know!" whispered Chenoa.

The call of nature substituted for an alarm clock come morning. Jerry dressed quickly and headed out into the woods. Chenoa made use of an old coffee can she kept under the wood stove. Jerry returned from his morning stroll with disturbing news: the 10 were gone. Not a single one of them was in the enclosure; Fred and Frank, ditto. All thoughts of breakfast were forgotten.

Jerry and Chenoa quickly saddled Sky Walker and Fleet. Clarke's Crossing took its name from a location where it was particularly easy to cross Cedar Creek due to a rather flat rock formation that kept the water from eroding its course into a gully with steep sides. A nearby meadow had lush, exceptionally tempting vegetation; all the more so because an early rancher had sown some non-native variety of clover midst the native grasses.

On a hunch Chenoa grabbed a bucket of oats and headed for the meadow. She told Jerry to gather up the lead ropes and follow.

Sure, enough Fred, Frank, and all 10 Appaloosas were there munching on the lush grass. With a sigh of relief Chenoa dismounted. Shaking the bucket so the grain could be heard sloshing around, she headed first to Fred and Frank. They eagerly came for the oats as Chenoa approached. Jerry handed Chenoa two lead ropes, and the capture was executed at the cost of two mouthfuls of grain, each.

"That was easy," said Jerry.

"Easy for you to say," whispered Chenoa. "Here's where it gets tricky."

Shaking the bucket vigorously, Chenoa slowly moved toward the closest of the 10. She had purposely not tried to capture Gypsie, yet. She wanted her to be trying to get at the bucket; Chenoa wanted the 10 to see that there was something really desirable in the bucket. Chenoa took note of the direction of a slight breeze. She wanted the horses to smell the desirable treat in the bucket.

One by one the 10 succumbed to their curiosity about what was so good in the bucket. As they would stick their nose in the bucket to take their turn, Chenoa would clip on their lead rope. When the last one was caught, Chenoa had no trouble gathering all 10 ropes as the 10 crowded around hoping to enjoy another bite of this most delicious food.

Jerry began tying the escapees head to tail in preparation for their late departure. Two hours late Chenoa and Jerry finally hit the trail, with reaching Jackpot by the end of the day their goal.

Sky Walker and Chenoa took the lead, again. They started off walking, but after a while tried kicking it up a notch. Sky Walker began a slow easy trot at the urging of Chenoa. The thing she was concerned most about was the shaking of the pack saddles. With a little experimenting Chenoa found a speed at which the packs appeared to be jostled the least. They held that speed for many miles.

They rested for a few minutes at the entrance to North Fork. Uncle Glenn would soon be rounding up his stock and selling the calves. Then the cows would make the trek back to the winter pasture at Hollister.

The older cows, who had experienced a few cycles of the seasons, were always the ones out front. They anticipated the stop Uncle Glenn routinely arranged in his neighbor's hay fields to dine on the regrowth which took place between the last hay cutting, and the onset of winter.

After gleaning the alfalfa fields, they would move on eventually to the dry crested wheat fields to spend the winter. Crested wheat worked as a winter feed because it was a medium height stiff grass that didn't get matted down under the snow, but rather stood erect where the cows could eat it.

Going off China mountain, down the trail which would lead them to Cedar Creek road, was easy going. When they reached the road, they headed east, eventually crossing the Salmon Falls Canyon Dam.

Reaching US 93, they turned south. Now they were in unfamiliar territory, having been here only once when they traveled to Elko to get their marriage license. Except for the highway, neither Chenoa, nor Jerry had ever traveled this way. They decided the KISS (Keep It Simple Stupid) Method of solving problems would require them to simply follow the highway. So, they did. For a change, Jerry took the lead.

Not wanting to chance Gypsie getting hurt, they decided to tie her into the string behind Fred. Jerry thought he detected a look in Gypsie's eye like she was saying, "Ah, boss! All this way, and now you don't trust me?"

As they traveled along the side of highway towards Jackpot, they became a noticeable tourist attraction. Cars and trucks would slow, and cameras start clicking as people realized what they were seeing. When people started getting ahead of them, getting out of their vehicles, and lining up alongside of the road to take pictures, Jerry called to Chenoa, " I told you this would be a great advertising opportunity!"

"Looks like you could not have been more right, our marketing genius," answered Chenoa.

When they came to where one particularly large group had gathered, Jerry pulled up and gave the crowd a chance to get some still pictures. Chenoa did him one better, and rode Sky Walker up to the edge of the highway.

Sky Walker came to a halt with his nose so close to the nearest person, he could reach out, and pet him, Chenoa called out in a clear, soft voice, "Hello, folks, my name is Chenoa." As Jerry and Fleet came close, Chenoa continued, "This is my husband, Jerry. We recently got married."

One quick witted old man quipped, "Ah shucks, you mean I'm too late?"

In a voice that portrayed she was equally quick witted and playing along, Chenoa replied, "Not necessarily; stick around. Maybe it won't work out."

The crowd roared with laughter.

"Where are you going?" ask a teen girl as she took numerous pictures.

"To our new home on a ranch about forty miles south of Jackpot," answered Chenoa.

"That's a beautiful horse you're riding," exclaimed another person whose attire screamed tourist.

"Yes," said another lady with an expensive looking camera. "What breed is he?"

Pretty good thought Jerry. She at least knows enough to recognize she is asking about a stallion and not a mare.

"He is an Appaloosa, a North American breed of horses raised early on primarily by the Nez Perce Indians on the Columbia River Plateau," explained Jerry. "My wife is of Shoshone Indian descent. She and her father raise Appaloosas west of here in the Jarbidge mountains. We have purchased a ranch south of here where we hope to share these magnificent horses with the outside world.

"May I pet him, please?" asked a girl with long braids who emerged from the crowd. Chenoa dismounted from Sky Walker fast to keep him from inadvertently head butting anyone.

"Sure, he is usually quite gentle," advised Chenoa. "Just let him smell your hand, first.

The young girl expressed her delight at being able to pet the big stallion. She was followed by several more children who lined up behind her and made the same request. Chenoa and Sky Walker satisfied all comers.

After standing back and watching from a distance, a man from the back of the crowd called out, "Are any of these horses for Sale?"

"Did you need a pack animal?" asked Chenoa teasingly. Then seriously she continued, "Yes most certainly! All of the Appaloosas, except Sky Walker. He is our main stud. We will be stopping tonight in Jackpot. If you are interested, you can see us there. We shouldn't be hard to find. It's not a very big place."

"How much do they cost?" ask someone from the crowd.

"That's negotiable!" responded Jerry.

The crowd started to dissolve, its curiosity seeming to have been satisfied for now. There were a few people left standing on the roadside as Jerry and Chenoa continued towards Jackpot.

Jerry was glad to see the sign announcing the state line: "Welcome to Nevada." He was tired. He was ready for a rest. Jerry was getting saddle sore again; all the hair had been rubbed off his inner thighs. He would be happy to walk awhile, as soon as they found a place to camp.

Jerry felt as if he were becoming bowlegged like one of the Ox Brothers. The Ox Brothers were a popular local singing group who got their name from their appearance on stage. One brother was bowlegged; the other knock-kneed. They used the phenomena in a self-deprecating way to good effect. Their routine was nothing short of hilarious.

Jerry found a small cluster of brush behind the Horseshu Club Casino. After watering their animals at the near-by Sinclair gas station, they made camp. They set up a picket line to which they tethered the horses, then pitched their tent.

When they were settled, they thought about having their evening meal in the restaurant. But their presence had not gone unnoticed. They were concerned about the safety of the horses. Like happened along the highway, the Appaloosas were attracting onlookers, so many they discussed the idea of moving their camp away from Jackpot. In the end, they figured people would eventually get tired and fade away.

In the meantime, they were getting hungry. Chenoa suggested one of them go for food, the other stand guard, and answer questions. Jerry liked the idea. He volunteered to let Chenoa go eat first. Chenoa appreciated the kind offer, and graciously accepted.

A man in a cowboy hat had been standing back, listening to the questions, but not saying anything. After Chenoa petted Sky Walker affectionately, and left the camp for some chow, the man worked his way forward to the front of the throng. He introduced him as Joe Carter, and explained he was in the business of buying and selling horses in California.

"How much are you asking for these horses?" asked Joe.

"Before or after we train them?" asked Jerry. 'You see my wife and I are on our way to a ranch just a ways south of here, where we plan to break, train, and sell the Appaloosa horses my father-in-law raises. This is our first string with which we are starting."

"You haven't answered my question, though" prodded Joe.

"Well, what they are worth right now isn't near what they'll be worth after we spend the winter working with them," speculated Jerry. "There is some good blood and fine potential in this string of mountain raised ponies! If these were just any old string of stock, I'd be embarrassed to ask more than $2,000 a head for them. But these were hand-picked by Ben Walker, my wife's father. By-the-way the Stallion is not for sale. I figure of these 10 horses ought to be worth no less than $10,000 a head after we have had a chance to work with them a bit. By next spring, double that."

Jerry was doing his best sales job with Joe; straight out of marketing 301. But he couldn't believe his ears when Joe spoke.

"Sold! I'll take all 10." said Joe matter-of-factly. "Where can I pick them up in a week?"

"At the Crooked Creek ranch about 50 miles south of here. By next week, we will have a big sign installed. You'll not be able to miss it!" promised Jerry. As an afterthought Jerry continued. "So that will be 10 Appaloosa horses at $10,000 a head, right?"

"Yes, it's a deal!" exclaimed Joe.

"Do you need more?" ask Jerry as smoothly as any veteran salesman.

"No, that should do. I've got a client who is a stock contractor for a movie studio." claimed Joe. "They just issued a casting call for 10 Indian ponies. This couldn't have come at a more perfect time. These horses will be perfect. I would have paid double to get them!"

"That will be 10 x $10,000; Joe, you just bought yourself some horses. How would you like to take care of that?" asked Jerry.

"Do you accept cash, check, or credit card?" asked Joe.

"Cash, check, or chickens!" quipped Jerry with a broad grin.

"How about I give you a check for half down; balance upon delivery?" ask Joe.

"Sounds acceptable," stated Jerry. "Movie, huh? Will have to go see it."

Jerry couldn't believe his good luck. He couldn't wait to tell Chenoa. The number of on-lookers was dwindling by the time Chenoa returned. She had gotten Jerry some take-out.

"A man came by and tried to take all 10 of your dad's horses!" Jerry told Chenoa trying to set her up for a big whopper story.

"Oh, no! Did you stop him?" asked Chenoa.

"We still have the horses, but he got away," claimed Jerry. "He will probably come to Crooked Creek, and try to take the horses, if he gets a chance."

Chenoa was talking about different ways she could hide the horses, when Jerry pulled out the check to show her.

Chenoa was stunned.

"I sold them," said Jerry with a big grin on his face.

"All 10?" asked Chenoa in stunned amazement.

"Yes, and I got half down," said Jerry proudly. "We can make this year's mortgage payment before it is even due!"

"My dad can even buy a pickup truck; we can buy a pickup, too," said Chenoa excitedly. "We can pay a big portion of what we owe Uncle Glenn and Aunt Martha. My dad and Little Feather will be so pleased!"

"Wonder what he'll say when we show up and ask for more horses. How many does he have?" questioned Jerry. "We need to know what our inventory is so we will know how many horses we can sell each year."

"I really don't know, if dad has an exact count," admitted Chenoa.

Chenoa was pleased that Jerry had been so successful in selling the 10 horses. She knew that he had a lot to learn about ranching, but he had other skills which Ben and she lacked. They could help each other.

Next morning Chenoa decided to wear her buckskins, and really put on a show for the tourists. Sky Walker was his usual magnificent self. Gambling came to a near stop as people poured out of the casinos to gaze in awe at the sight of Chenoa and Sky Walker parading through town.

Joe had spent the night in Jackpot. He decided as soon as he got back to Hollywood, he was going to arrange for a talent scout he knew to accompany him when he picked up his purchase. He would bet every dollar he had the studio would be interested in this beautiful girl and her magnificent horse.

Jerry led the pack animals, and Chenoa all but three of the Appaloosas. In her buckskins Chenoa looked amazing. They followed the railroad right-of-way from which the rails had been salvaged years ago. It paralleled the highway so closely that people had no trouble seeing them from the roadway. By now the 10 Appaloosas were well broke to lead.

The caravan headed south at a quick trot. They wanted to make Crooked Creek by night fall. Chenoa took the lead riding Sky Walker. She had a string of seven Appaloosas trailing behind.

Jerry was riding Fleet followed by Fred, Frank, and Gypsie carrying pack saddles. Three more Appaloosas were tied nose to tail behind Gypsie. They we're making good time towards Crooked Creek.

Joe was among the tourists/onlookers who stopped along the side of the road, camera at the ready. He was concerned that no one would believe him when he told them how beautiful this girl riding a remarkable stallion was. He wanted proof. He was going to get pictures to prove his point. He had leap frogged ahead twice already to stake out a good spot from which to shoot some pictures.

Chenoa had noticed Joe several times among the onlookers. She surprised him when she suddenly turned off the trail and rode right up to him. As if to say 'Hello, stranger', Sky Walker pawed the ground several times. Jerry followed Chenoa off the trail, and immediately recognized Joe.

It was Chenoa's turn now to be surprised, when Joe and Jerry started talking like old friends. Jerry introduced Joe to Chenoa as the man who had agreed to buy their whole string of Appaloosas. Chenoa was delighted to make his acquaintance.

"Are you trying to get some pictures of your purchase?" inquired Chenoa.

Not wanting to reveal his real interest, Joe said, "Yes, they are beautiful horses! A real credit to their breed! Did Jerry tell you what our plans for them are? You know, there might be a role for you and your stallion in the picture.

Joe was fishing for Chenoa's reaction to the idea of being in a movie.

"Oh, we are going to have our hands full running the ranch we just purchased. I don't see how we could spare the time for anything else," opined Chenoa. "But you could always try to change my mind."

"If the price were right, we might be interested," agreed Jerry.

"Where is this ranch you bought?" asked Joe.

"It is where we are headed now; just down the ole railroad a piece," said Jerry trying to talk more western than was normal.

"We would be honored if you were to drop in for a visit. You could be our first guest!" said Chenoa welcomely.

"I would love to some other time, but I got to be in Reno by this evening," said Joe by way of explanation for turning down the invitation.

Chenoa posed for a few pictures for some other people who had stopped to see what was happening. One young boy was especially interested in these spotted horse.

"Gee, I have never seen spotted horses. If you give them a bath, do the spots wash off?" The question got a few chuckles from the crowd.

After some more small talk with the assembled tourists, and a lot of pictures, Jerry and Chenoa excused themselves explaining they had a long way to go to get these horses to their new home. Riding side-by-side on the old, abandoned railroad grade, Jerry and Chenoa were able to talk with one another.

"Well, that was a surprise," stated Jerry matter-of-factly. "I didn't expect to see Joe again so soon. What was your reason for stopping, when we have such a long way to go?

"Its hard to explain," confessed Chenoa. "He just stood out from the rest. I spotted him the first time just a few miles from Jackpot. He didn't act like just a tourist or curious onlooker. There was a serious-ness or intensity, the others didn't have. Then he didn't go away. When

I noticed him for about the fourth time in about two hours, I decided to go see what he was all about. If he is the buyer, I can see why he might be more intensely interested than the others. He has 100,000 reasons to be interested. I guess he wanted to get a better look at the merchandise. Maybe he wanted some daytime action pictures."

"I don't know. He is a professional buyer. Guys like him can size up a purchase without so much as a second glance. You may be right about wanting to get some day light pictures. But he would have had what he needed the first time you saw him. No, I think there is some other reason for his following us for two hours," concluded Jerry.

"I'll bet you're right," agreed Chenoa. "I wonder what it could be?"

At noontime the procession took time for lunch. They rode a few hundred yards up a side draw to a grassy area where the horses could graze and drink from a small stream. Chenoa retrieved some of the food Ole George had fixed. There is nothing that tastes quite like a jelly sandwich which has been tenderized by bounce around in a saddle bag, or in this case, a pack saddle for a couple days. The jelly and butter, or peanut butter, soaks into the bread. It simple tastes different than a fresh made sandwich. It tastes great! Well, maybe it is an acquired taste.

After satisfying their hunger, Chenoa and Jerry stretched out in the warm afternoon sunshine and took a brief nap. They awoke when a wandering cumulonimbus cloud blocked the sunshine. They chilled quickly, so decided to forge on.

Chenoa noticed one of the horses lead by Jerry limping slightly. She called a halt to the caravan and discovered he had picked up a sharp rock in his right hind hoof. She always carried a pair of pliers with one handle sharpened into a screwdriver. This was Ben's invention predating the multi-tool known as a Leather Man Super Tool. One flick of the wrist, and the offending stone was sent flying. In less than three minutes they were back on the trail again. Chenoa noticed the horse was no longer limping.

The sun had set below the western horizon by the time Jerry and Chenoa reached the highway turn off leading to Crooked Creek. It was dusk, fast approaching dark when they reached the ranch house.

Hearing the commotion outside, Gerald came out and helped the new arrivals unpack Fred, Frank, and Gypsy When Fleet and Sky

Walker were unsaddled, given some oats, and turned out with the others, they both lay down in the dusty corral and rolled in the dirt. Dust bath over, they shook themselves like a pair of dogs emerging from a water tank, then joined the others at the hay manger.

Merna and Gerald were excited to see Jerry and Chenoa. They asked how the trip had gone. Uncle Glenn and Aunt Martha had telephoned to tell them they were coming, but they hadn't been able to tell them when Jerry and Chenoa would arrive.

Merna quickly set about fixing them a bite to eat. On a ranch, the custom is to eat your big meal of the day at noon. Supper, or the evening meal, is usually a much lighter meal.

In keeping with this tradition, Merna set out some bread and milk. Jerry and Chenoa poured their bowl full of milk, then broke up the bread into the bowl in small pieces. Alongside the bowl of bread and milk is placed a small saucer of jam and peanut butter, or something similar.

One takes a bit of jam and peanut butter with his spoon, spoons out a chunk of bread soaked in milk, and enjoys what might otherwise be termed a glass of milk and a piece of bread, and jam.

Gerald and Merna were anxious to hear how the trip had gone. They chatted for about half an hour after supper, discussing the events of the last several days, then Merna showed them to a spare bedroom so they could get some much-needed rest. A squeaky bed suggested to Gerald and Merna that Jerry and Chenoa were not as tired as they professed.

Jerry whispered to Chenoa, "When we cash our check, this bed has got to go!"

"Agreed," whispered Chenoa.

"Give you any ideas?" Merna asked Gerald.

"Go to sleep, dear!" retorted Gerald.

"Party pooper!" teased Merna.

"Don't start anything you are not willing to finish," warned Gerald with a bit of an evil chuckle.

When Gerald and Merna drifted off to sleep with memories of their younger days, the doomed bed was still squeaking.

Chapter 24—Ranch life

Jerry and Chenoa were first up next morning. They needed to make sure the 10 were ready for Joe when he took delivery. They worked with each horse individually to make sure they responded well to being lead with a halter and lead rope.

Being led gently by hand was very different from following a string of horse; you either followed willingly or got drug. To Chenoa's great pleasure, every one of the 10 responded to the slightest pull on the lead rope.

Chenoa changed direction frequently, changed speed, and challenged the horses in every way she could think. They proved themselves worthy of all the praise Chenoa heaped upon them. Chenoa decided to start breaking them to ride.

Merna interrupted the effort by ringing the dinner bell, although in this case it was the breakfast bell. Without delay they ran for the house.

Even before they reached the house, the aroma of fresh bread and bacon greeted them. Everyone ate heartily. Merna's cooking was every bit the equal of Ole George. Chenoa thought the breakfast rolls were in fact, better.

The two couples chatted after breakfast about matters attendant to the Marchants moving out, and the Jerry Briggs's moving in. Chenoa pointed out that they had moved all or most of their things in the pack saddles which were now lying in the barn. They were ready to move in as soon as the ranch house was vacated. The closing date wasn't until September 28th, so Gerald and Merna could take their time.

Gerald was somewhat surprised to learn that the 10 Appaloosas were sold.

When Gerald learned how Jerry had pulled off the sale, he was impressed. Now Jerry and Chenoa needed to go back for more horses. Chenoa asked, if she might use the telephone to contact Ben. He would need some time to gather up a new batch of horses. Jerry wanted to call Uncle Glenn to inform him of recent developments. Jerry felt they ought to return Fred, Frank, Gypsy, and Fleet. Uncle Glenn would let him keep them, if they were needed, but the facts were, they weren't.

Jerry wanted to be off on their own as soon as possible. His marketing strategy called for putting their horses on display as much as possible. Ben had the horses, why not use them.

Chenoa needed to return Sky Walker, too. He couldn't do his job, if he were toting Chenoa around in Nevada. Bringing him on this first trip had proved invaluable in forging the deal with Joe, but now Sky Walker was needed at home.

Their available inventory had all been promised to Joe. They could get replacements, when they returned Sky Walker to Ben. Chenoa had spent her life tending her father's horses. She thought she knew a couple of especially good replacements. She told Jerry about them. He was excited to go back and see for himself.

Jerry wanted to see the look on Uncle Glenn's face when he returned Fred, Frank, Gypsy, and Fleet; then told him they had sold their first 10 horses for $100,000.

Knowing that Ben would need time to round up the next group of horses, Chenoa and Jerry decided to focus on breaking as many of the 10 Appaloosas as time would permit. They ask Gerald to borrow as much tack as he could spare, so they could use it to get the ten accustomed to it.

For a rancher, he had surprising little. Gerald explained. His kids had each taken their personal gear with them, when they left the ranch. The saddles, blankets, and bridles were of more sentimental than practical value, but it was a bit of home that they could touch, feel, and smell. It was priceless, and so they took it with them. Gerald had seen no need to replace it, so he didn't.

Using their own tack, plus what little Gerald could offer, Chenoa and Jerry commenced. First thing was to select which horses they wanted to train. Second, was to choose names for them. Names are often chosen based on some physical characteristic. The first name Jerry picked was, of all things, "Spot". Chenoa teased him gently saying, "How clever!"

Chenoa got the next pick. Let's call this one, "Blue".

"I like it," confessed Jerry.

"Let's pick the next one together," suggested Chenoa. "What do you think?"

"How about something classical?" offered Jerry. "What do you think of Galahad?"

"I love it. He was the noblest on King Arthur's Knights," said Chenoa, surprising Jerry with her knowledge. "Ok, we have Spot, Blue, and Galahad. One more for now."

"I like those names," said Gerald, who had happened upon the scene. "Mind if I choose one?"

"Be our guest," replied Jerry and Chenoa in unison.

"How about 'Spunky,'" suggested Gerald. "He seems to be a real fireball. It was my pony's name, when I was a kid."

With the names chosen, Jerry and Chenoa started the next phase in the process of breaking a horse to ride. They needed to get the horses used to being saddled. They started by petting them all over. They stroked their necks, their noses, their backs, and finally their legs. They did this until Spot, Blue, Galahad, and Spunky were no longer afraid of being toughed anywhere.

Next, they rubbed the horses with a saddle blanket in all the same places. When they heard the dinner bell, they left the four horses tied to the corral fence with a saddle blanket on their back. When they finished lunch, they added a saddle to the items with which the four needed to become familiar.

As slowly as possible, the horses were allowed to smell the saddles, before they were strapped on. Again, they were allowed time to get used to the strange gear.

Jerry took Spot and Spunky, and Chenoa took the lead ropes of Blue and Galahad to go for a walk.

Getting familiar with wearing a saddle is sometimes a very big hurdle in training a horse, especially a horse raised in the wild like these four. Wearing a saddle on a long walk will hopefully familiarize a horse to the feel of a saddle. The horses responded well to the gradual introduction of this riding apparel.

Chenoa had one more technique to employ prior to trying to ride the horses. She asked Gerald, if she might borrow four sacks of grain. Four sacks was about all the grain on the ranch. In fact, Gerald needed to substitute a sack of alfalfa seed in order to come up with a sack for Spunky.

With the horses carrying a weigh approximating that of a rider, they went for another walk. Only difference was this one was longer. This time the walk lasted most of the afternoon.

When they got back Chenoa thought the time was right. Tired horses are less likely to buck a rider off. She removed the sack of grain from Blue's saddle.

Chenoa had Jerry hold the halter while she climbed aboard. Blue followed Jerry willingly with Chenoa astride.

"Piece of cake," said Chenoa softly.

"What will he do tomorrow when he is not so tired?" asked Jerry. "He could go to bucking and eat your cake!"

"Possible; let's try Galahad," said Chenoa confidently. Galahad was a "piece of cake," also.

"Do you want to try Spot or Spunky," Chenoa asked Jerry.

"I'll give Spot a go," ventured Jerry. "If he doesn't murder me, maybe I'll give Spunky a try"

Chenoa helped Jerry to get on Spot. He was having none of it. All of a sudden, he bolted, went to bucking, and left Jerry in a dusty heap.

"Well, that didn't go well!" said Chenoa stating the obvious. "I guess we will have to resort to plan B."

"What is plan B?" ask Jerry dusting himself off.

"Help me saddle Sky Walker," requested Chenoa. "Take my saddle off Blue, please."

When Sky Walker was ready, Chenoa climbed aboard. She took hold of Spot's lead rope near the halter. She wrapped the halter rope around her saddle horn a couple of times. The effect was to draw Spot's head up high.

"Try again, cowboy," Chenoa told Jerry. "Let's see if you are going to make a rancher or an astronaut."

With Spot tethered to Sky Walker, Spot was unable to put his head down in order to buck. Sky Walker, being much bigger, was able to pull Spot along with him when he started walking. Jerry was able to stay on Spot, until they had travelled about a mile down the trail. Spot quit resisting being ridden. Thereafter, Chenoa loosened the lead rope.

"Spot is a good boy. See Jerry ride Spot!" said Chenoa, paraphrasing the old primary school book with which she had learned to read.

Taking no chances with Spunky, Jerry ask if they could employ Plan B from the git-go. Jerry didn't want to be asked for his pilot's license. Chenoa and Sky Walker were glad to oblige.

Merna made an evening meal this time that was a little more elaborate than bread and milk. Gerald reported that he had arranged for a rental track to be delivered day after tomorrow. He and Merna could start packing. Gerald figured Merna and he could be ready to hit the road in a week. Chenoa asked Merna, if they had anyone to help?

"Not really. Most of our kids live too far away, and we don't have many available close neighbors," said Merna.

"Why don't we simplify this for you?" suggested Chenoa. "We are newlyweds. We don't have a lot of the things that will be needed to survive and thrive here in this remote area.

Let's 'kill two birds with one stone'. If we were to buy all the things you will no longer need, then we will have them, and you won't have to pack them.

"It is a win-win," said Jerry, remembering a popular concept from a business class. Chenoa and I don't need to be back for a few days. We have two strong backs and the time to help you get packed."

"We would be honored to give you a hand!" added Chenoa. "We will have you ready to roll by the closing date!"

Jerry wanted to talk to Uncle Glenn. He felt it was important to advise him of recent developments. Chenoa and he wouldn't need as much help in order to buy Crooked Creek from the Marchants since they had sold the entire first lot of Appaloosas.

Jerry wanted to find out if things were going well with the lawyers; would they be ready for closing by September 28?

Merna and Chenoa decided they would get to work on the house. For everything there would be a mark indicating either to go or stay.

When the time came to load the van, the decisions of what to leave and what to take would have already been made.

Chenoa and Jerry decided Jerry should be the one to work with the Appaloosas while Chenoa helped Merna with the house. Jerry needed the experience if they were to succeed at ranching. They had gotten lucky with the big sale to Joe.

Future sales might be dependent on how well the horses were trained, rather than on how much they looked like Indians ponies. Their reputation would be benefited, if your average actor could get on them and ride, first thing out of the box.

Jerry had seen how Chenoa approached the challenge of breaking their horses to lead and ride. He needed to see if he could do it.

Chenoa and Merna went to work on the contents of the house; Jerry on the horses. When Merna found some multi-colored tape, they decided red would signify stay; green, pack it!

As Merna and Chenoa moved through the contents of the house, they discovered taping every single item was time consuming and in-efficient. This led to merely putting a patch of red tape on the items which Chenoa wanted to purchase. Additionally, they started marking the tape with a price.

Merna would name a price at which she was willing part with an item; Chenoa would say "ok" or counteroffer. Once they settled on a price, the red tape would be applied, and the price noted.

Meanwhile, back at the corral, Jerry was re-learning that people who are really good at something make it look easy.

Jerry decided he would try his luck first with Spot. He went through the same process as the day before: petting the horse all over, letting him smell the saddle blanket, putting the blanket on him, and then the saddle.

All went as before, until it came to the saddle. Before Jerry was able to cinch the saddle on Spot, he was able to unburden himself with an easy, quick move. Jerry realized too late; he was moving too fast. Picking the saddle off the ground, this time, Jerry let Spot smell the saddle for as long as he wanted.

Next, Jerry re-tied Spot with his head high. Then he took the sad-dle and put the cinch straps on top. This way he was able to set the saddle on Spot without the loose straps spooking him. As slow and gently as possible, Jerry lowered the straps and tightened them. As they had done yesterday, Jerry placed some extra weight in the saddle in the form of a sack of grain.

Jerry took Spot for a walk again to get him used to the feel of a weighted saddle. After about an hour of walking, Jerry returned Spot to the corral and tied him with his head high. He spent some time petting Spot to get him used the feel of being touched all over. When Jerry was able to do so without Spot flinching, he was ready to see if Spot would let him get on.

Jerry had not noticed Chenoa, who had taken a break from helping Merna, come out of the house. She was watching him from his blind side of the corral. She watched as Jerry was able to mount Spot. For about 5 minutes he just sat still. Then Jerry started shifting his weight in the saddle. Spot exhibited some nervousness, but didn't try to unload him. Jerry was all the while talking softly to Spot.

Jerry decided to try getting on and off repeatedly. Spot appeared to dislike this exercise but tolerated it. At length Jerry decided to take a chance. He untied Spot and got on. Not wanting to provoke Spot, Jerry just sat quietly on Spot for about 10 minutes.

So motionless were they, you could have mistaken them for the statue of Stonewall Jackson. It appeared Spot was going to behave without a fuss. Jerry urged him forward to walk around the corral. Halfway around Jerry spotted Chenoa watching him with an approving smile.

"And that my Dear is the way it is done." said Jerry, proud of himself.

"Congratulations, do you want me to open the corral gate so you two can go for a long ride?" inquired Chenoa.

"Sure, but if he comes back without me, change his name to Widow Maker," jested Jerry.

"The first thing you need to learn, now, is how to take a fall," coached Chenoa.

"I fell in love with you, does that count?" retorted Jerry.

"It just means there will more likely be someone around to scrap you up," said Chenoa.

Jerry exited the corral and started down the dirt road. Chenoa went back to the house to help Merna. By evening they were pretty well finished. They started making an inventory list of the items Chenoa had selected, so they could add up the cost.

Jerry and Spot returned. They had been gone for hours. Spot was obviously tired. Chenoa noticed he was reining very well and said as much.

"He was fighting me at first, when we left the corral. So, I just let him go wherever he want," recounted Jerry. "After about an hour, he started responding to gentle attempts to guide him. The further we went and the more tired he became, the more willing he became to let me guide him. This last while, he was actually reining quite well."

Chenoa was impressed with Jerry's intuitive ability to work with Spot. Jerry told Chenoa, he thought he should work with Spot again tomorrow before moving on with Spunky. Chenoa thought it was a good idea.

With the house assessment completed Chenoa was ready to go back to helping Jerry with the breaking of the horses. By the end of the third day, Spot, Spunky, Blue, and Galahad were being ridden easily. They were ready for Joe and the movies. Jerry was gaining confidence as a horse trainer. Chenoa was becoming a very proud wife.

There were six more horses to break before Joe took delivery, if they were to reach Jerry's marketing goal of selling only horses which one could get on and ride.

Not that it really mattered, but Chenoa and Jerry decided to finish naming the remaining horses.

At supper Chenoa mentioned they were going be choosing six more names. She asked Merna, if she would care to choose one.

Without hesitation Merna suggested, "Why don't you go with the story of Goldie Locks? You would have: Mama Bear, Papa Bear, Baby Bear, and Goldie Locks."

"I like the idea," said Jerry. "But that is only four names."

"Well, then you could have 'Too hard' and 'Just Right', if you like," explained Merna.

"What a fabulous idea," exclaimed Chenoa. "I love it, and they are easy to remember!"

"Remember, these are supposed to be Indian ponies," said Jerry.

"You want me to translate?" asked Chenoa.

After breakfast the next morning, Jerry and Chenoa set about assigning names. They picked Mama Bear and Papa Bear to be the next two to break.

Looking like bona fide tourists, everyone was surprised about 10:30 AM., when Uncle Glenn and Aunt Martha showed up driving Lilly. Everyone was pleased to see them. Merna invited them to stay for lunch.

Uncle Glenn, Gerald, and Jerry met for a few minutes to discuss the appraisal report. It contained nothing that was at odds with the deal which had been struck. Jerry showed Uncle Glenn the check from Joe.

"You may be a tender foot when it comes to ranching," said Uncle Glenn of Jerry. "But you could certainly show us a thing or two when it comes to marketing."

Jerry gave the check to Uncle Glenn, so a joint account could be opened in the name of Jerry, Chenoa, and Ben. Uncle Glenn asked if Jerry and Ben had an agreement about how things were going to work? Uncle Glenn advised Jerry an agreement ought to be settled upon as quickly as possible.

Jerry asked Uncle Glenn which of two optional ways of doing business he would recommend: 1) Have Ben sell the horses to Jerry and Chenoa at a set price, or 2) Operate as a partnership, and just divide up the final sale price according to some agreed upon formula?

Without hesitation Uncle Glenn advised Chenoa and Jerry to go with the first option. "No one has ever be able to make communism work, nor do I think it would work for you," advised Glenn. "When you remove the incentive for individual initiative, you can expect a lessor out come," further commented Uncle Glenn.

"The pilgrims tried it, the Mormons tried it, the Russians tried it, the east Germans tried it, the Cubans, the Cambodians, the Chinese, and the North Koreans have tried it; it just doesn't work.

Merna fixed a fine lunch. Uncle Glen and Aunt Martha started back to Holister in Lilly, top down, sun shining, and their hair blowing in the wind. Jerry and Chenoa headed to the corral to work on their goal. Gerald and Merna returned to preparing for their move.

By evening Mama Bear and Papa Bear were cooperating nicely.

"Six down, four to go," counted Jerry and Chenoa as they retired for the evening.

Chenoa had declined Merna's gracious offer to give the squeaky bed to the newly-weds. In a few days it would betray them no longer. In the meantime, they abandoned the bed, and slept on the floor; well, some of the time.

After breakfast the next day, Jerry and Chenoa saddled up Spunky and Blue and went for a ride to find out if the horses were retaining what they had been taught.

Spot and Galahad were next. Chenoa was very pleased after Mama Bear and Papa Bear, too, passed the check ride.

Now, it was Baby Bear and Goldie Lock's turn to experience the feel of a saddle. Chenoa and Jerry spent the remainder of the day with them. They proved to be quick learners, also.

Too Hard and Just Right proved to be more of a challenge than the others had been. In the end they succumb to Chenoa's training technique.

Jerry continued the check rides, while Chenoa went back to helping Merna pack the house. Gerald spent some time, too, with Jerry showing him what he needed to know about the farming operation.

Joe showed up as scheduled to take delivery of the 10 Appaloosas. Jerry introduced him to each one. Joe liked the names, so he took a marker, and wrote the name of each horse on its halter.

To everyone's surprise, Joe had brought along a professional photographer. He took still pictures of each horse as well. Joe asked Chenoa, if she would be willing to put on the buckskins she was wearing when they had met on trail. Chenoa agreed to be photographed with each horse, if they could have copies? Joe and the photographer agreed.

Jerry informed Joe that all 10 Appaloosas were now broke to ride.

"But I thought you said, they weren't broke when we spoke in Jackpot," recalled Joe.

"They weren't, then," said Jerry. "But they are now; we have been busy this past week!"

"I was going to have to pay a trainer a $1000 a head to do that job!" said Joe. "But you are telling me, I can pick anyone of the 10, get on I'm and ride?"

"Let me demonstrate," said Chenoa, who had just returned dressed in her beautiful buckskins with their intricate beadwork. "Choose anyone of the 10, and I'll save you the trouble."

Joe motioned to the photographer, and mouthed the words," Get this!"

Joe picked Blue. Jerry smiled. With Blue this was going to be "a piece of cake", quoting Chenoa.

No saddle needed; Chenoa grabbed a hunk of main, and swung onto Blue. Having become accustomed to the saddle, Blue was hesitant at first, but quickly adjusted to the new circumstance.

Chenoa started out slow, demonstrating Blue's grasp of neck reining. She turned him right and left, then brought him to a full stop. Blue responded to the command to back up. Chenoa was able to get Blue to walk, trot, canter, and gallop.

Joe was impressed. Blue was everything he needed to fulfill his contract. If the others were as good, he was set. But Chenoa was magnificent. Boy, oh boy, if he could only get her under contract. He assumed the photographer had been able to get some good pictures of her. He wanted more.

"Let's see what a different horse can do," said Joe not caring a whit about the horse. "Let's take a look at this one," pointing to Too Hard.

Jerry was worried. They had worked the least with Too Hard. If there were one horse which might give them trouble, it was him.

Chenoa thought her chances were better with a saddle, so she told Joe she wanted to demonstrate the horses were saddle broke as well. She gently saddled Too Hard and led him through a series of maneuvers to show Joe how well he was halter broke. Too Hard responded nicely.

The photographer, whose name was Pierre, asked Chenoa to pose for him so he could get some still shots of her and Too Hard. Chenoa asked Pierre if he would be so kind as to take some pictures of her, Jerry, and Too Hard. Joe joined them. Then Merna and Gerald. The photo fest ended after Joe had Pierre take a group photo of Chenoa standing in front on all ten Appaloosas.

Chenoa asked Joe if he would mind if Pierre took a picture of her aboard Sky Walker? After years riding the range together, their time together was about to come to an end. Chenoa envisioned having the picture framed and hung over their mantel.

"Sure!" answered Joe. Then added, "If I can have a copy."

Merna invited Joe and Pierre to join them for lunch. Afterward Joe said jokingly, "I have some good news and some bad news. First the bad news; there is a bunch of paperwork, releases, that you needed to read and sign, so we will be able to use the pictures Pierre has taken. The good news is I have some money for you, more than you think."

"Why is that?" asked Jerry.

"Well, you are due the $10,000 for breaking the horses, the $50,000 balance for the 10 horses, and I am offering Chenoa $20,000 for the right to use her imagine in the pictures Pierre has taken today, if you agree.

That is our standard modeling fee for a Class A model. I know Chenoa has no modeling experience, but I never-the-less think she qualifies. I am willing to double that amount for the exclusive right to act as her agent.

Chenoa was shocked. $20,000 was more money than see had ever seen. It could be the means of paying for Crooked Creek early. She expressed her appreciation to Joe for this generous, unexpected sum. Chenoa had no problem agreeing to the use of today's pictures. Something told her no more than that.

She suddenly had a flashback to being chased by men on the Jarbidge mountains, how Sky Walker had nearly run himself to death to saved her. In her mind she heard her mother's voice warning her not to make any long-term agreement. Chenoa heard herself saying "Thanks, but no thanks!" to Joe's agency offer.

Jerry asked to speak with Chenoa alone. Joe was hopeful Jerry would intercede on his behalf. Jerry and Chenoa retired to their bed-room and sat upon the squeaky bed.

"What are you thinking, sweetheart?" asked Jerry. "Are you sure about this?"

"I was blessed many times as a young girl riding all alone in a big dangerous wilderness. I don't know in hindsight, if it were my mother, a guardian angel, or just a loving God, but I was warned. I lived un-harmed because I heeded the warnings. What am I thinking? Time to get on Sky Walker and run! Don't know why but run fast; run now!"

"That is good enough for me," said Jerry. "No squeaky bed tonight."

Chenoa and Jerry returned to the meeting which had migrated to the parlor. Jerry thanked Joe for the opportunity to do business with him, offered to help get the Appaloosas loaded, but explained that Chenoa wasn't ready to sign any long-term contract for representation.

Joe delivered the money as agreed, loaded his horses in a large horse van, and departed Crooked Creek in a cloud of dust. He hadn't gotten everything he wanted, but he had the important things. He was happy.

Jerry and Chenoa thanked Merna and Gerald for their hospitality, but explained they felt a need to get started back north. They promised to send help for the move, saddled up Fleet and Sky Walker, then placed the now almost empty pack saddles on Frank, Fred, and Gypsy. Thirty minutes behind Joe, Jerry and Chenoa departed Crooked Creek at a run.

Gerald turned to Merna, who was still waving as the Briggs disappeared from sight, "What do you suppose lit a fire under them?"

"I don't exactly know, what did it, but I saw fear, genuine fear in Chenoa's eye's. I think she was fine till Joe offered her another $20,000 to sign with him as her agent. I thought it was a good offer." said Merna

"She has the looks to be a Super Model. They could make a fortune. Maybe she knows something we don't. Maybe $20,000 is chump-change in the modeling world," surmised Gerald.

"But why would she be so frightened," asked Merna. "I don't understand!"

Jerry led Fred and Frank: Chenoa led Gypsy. They rode all afternoon and into the evening. There were a few tourists who stopped alongside of the highway to take pictures. Chenoa paid them no attention.

It is 62 miles from Wells to Jackpot, Nevada. Jerry estimated Crooked Creek was about 20 miles north of Wells, so they needed to travel roughly 42 miles to reach Jackpot. At 8mph they would need 5 hours. Jerry and Chenoa saw no need to push faster than 8 mph.

At 7 PM they crossed into Jackpot and set up their camp. Jerry found a phone and called Uncle Glenn. At approximately 8:15 PM, Uncle Glenn, Aunt Martha, and Old George rolled into Jackpot. Old George volunteered to watch the critters while the rest went to dinner at the HorseShu Club.

Uncle Glenn and Aunt Martha were quite fascinated to hear Jerry and Chenoa recount their experiences of the last week. They were especially surprised to hear of the $20,000 Chenoa had earned modeling for Joe.

Aunt Martha was vaguely aware of the world of Super Models. That someone would offer a country girl from the Jarbidge mountains that kind of money was amazing, although Chenoa certainly had the beauty to command big money.

As Jerry and Chenoa ate their medium rare prime rib, they couldn't help but think of their dining on bread and milk a few nights ago. Uncle Glenn reminisced about the lean years, he and Martha had had.

Uncle Glenn and Aunt Martha suggested Jerry and Chenoa ought to celebrate their good fortune of the last week by getting a room for the night. They offered to tend the stock, and see that Old George got fed. Without asking Chenoa, Jerry blurted out, "We accept!"

Uncle Glenn laughed, "You sure you don't want to think about it?"

This time it was Chenoa who spoke first, "If they can find a room for us where the bed doesn't squeak, I'm all for it!"

"We tried out the honeymoon suite, when we were here a few weeks ago. It was fine," stated Aunt Martha. She blushed a bit when she realized what her statement was implying.

Forgoing the temptation to sleep in, Jerry and Chenoa were on the trail by sun rise the next morning. They hadn't bothered to eat breakfast; they wanted to surprise someone. They were able to reach Rogerson by the time the diner opened. They tied their horses and pack animals to a fence out back. When they walked in Kim was the only waitress on duty. Joe was cooking.

Jerry opened the conversation by asking, "Say, we were wondering if you could tell us who won the contest you had running a while back?"

"I did," said Kim proudly. Then recognizing Jerry, she started screaming, "Oh my gosh, oh my gosh; it's you, it's you!"

A trucker, who was just coming through the door heard all the screaming, and was ready to do battle, "It's who Miss; It's who?"

"Have you heard of the Flower of China Mountain?" asked Kim

"Who hasn't heard of her in these parts?" asked the trucker. "Have they ever figured if she is myth or for real?

"Oh she is for real," said Kim half screaming still. "And she is right there! Oh my gosh!"

"Yup, that's her," witnessed Joe the cook.

"Well by golly, I just thought she was a figment of somebody's imagination," said the trucker.

Kim, Chenoa, and Jerry caught up on the latest as Kim served the breakfast. And then they were gone, but not before Kim took a few more photos, just for the record.

By mid-morning Chenoa and Jerry had reached the ranch at Hollister. Jerry was getting less saddle sore now-a-days. They put Fleet, Gypsy, Frank, and Fred in the barn. They also returned the two pack saddles, they had borrowed. Now it was time to go shopping.

Uncle Glenn said he thought he knew where they could get a good deal on a pickup truck and horse trailer. First stop, though, was the bank. They needed to set up a checking account with the $130,000 they had gotten from Joe. Chenoa reminded Jerry that that figure was not quite accurate. $20,000 was hers. Jerry said $10,000 was from breaking the horses. Chenoa said, "Good point, $5,000 for you; $5,000 for me. Ok?"

"Works for me," said Jerry. "Apparently, they teach you more than berry picking, and basket weaving in squaw school."

"Yes," said Chenoa. "We spend a lot of time learning how to count, too!"

Everybody had a good laugh.

Jerry made sure Chenoa got her own account. Uncle Glenn found a great deal on a pickup and horse trailer. The seller actually had another truck for sale as well.

Chenoa thought they should probably let Ben make his own vehicle purchase. The dealer promised Uncle Glenn, he would make Ben the same great offer, if he wanted to buy a pickup in the next 30 days.

"Have you or your dad ever learned how to drive," asked Jerry. "Have you ever driven anything but a wagon?"

"No," admitted Chenoa. "But how hard could it be, you do it?"

"Oh, I think you just got verbally body slammed!" said Uncle Glenn.

After registering the vehicles, Jerry and Chenoa returned to Uncle Glenn's ranch for Sky Walker, then started for Ben's ranch. Sky Walker had never before been in a horse trailer. It was obvious, he didn't like it. With his trust in Chenoa, though, they were able to get him loaded. Jerry was certain, if Chenoa had not been there, Sky Walker would have refused to load in the trailer. Chenoa might have had to ride him home.

Ben watched from the ridge as a cloud of dust came closer to the ranch. A strange pickup pulling a two-horse trailer stopped next to the barn. As quickly as he could, he descended the trail to the barn. He arrived in time to see Chenoa unloading Sky Walker.

"Picked up these hitchhikers, down the road a piece," said Jerry. "The big guy hasn't said much, but the pretty one said you might feed us if we stopped in here. That true?"

Ben chuckled, "I'm sure that could be arranged. Nice looking rig you got there. You strike it lucky in Jackpot or something?"

"Well, you might say that," said Jerry. "Met a fellow from Hollywood; he bought all 10 of your horses. Paid top dollar to boot. Picked up the rig here from a dealer in Twin Falls. Says he has another just like it, if you are interested."

Chenoa gave Ben a big hug and a kiss.

"Hi dad! How's Little Feather? inquired Chenoa.

"Oh, she's doing just fine. Say, what's this about you hitch-hiking? Didn't I teach you better? You never know what could happen to you; you might fall in love with some tall, dark stranger from a faraway place like Philadelphia," jested Ben in an usual attempt at humor.

"I see your point," said Chenoa in mock contrition. "Won't happen again, I promise."

Chenoa, Ben, and Jerry headed to the house where they were greeted warmly by Little Feather. This time, instead of bread and milk, they had elk stew and some of Little Feather's homemade bread.

"Where did you get the elk, dad?" ask Chenoa. No answer was offered.

Next morning Chenoa wasn't feeling too well. Jerry thought perhaps something about the stew hadn't agreed with her. Little Feather suspected a different diagnosis after Chenoa threw up her breakfast.

She took Chenoa aside and asked her a few girl questions. It was a happy day in the Jarbidge mountains when Little Feather gave her opinion of what was ailing Chenoa. The Flower of China was going to bloom in the Spring.

EPILOGUE

Chenoa wasn't feeling well on her first wedding anniversary. Instead of having Jerry take her to one of the finer area restaurants, she was eating no less expensive hospital food. She had been in labor for 12 hours by the time she gave birth to a 7-pound, 8-ounce girl. The baby had a full head of jet-black hair and black eyes, just like her mom.

Jerry and Chenoa had been staying with Uncle Glenn and Aunt Martha for the last week in case Chenoa's false labor turned into the real thing. It did just that the day before their anniversary.

With the sale of the horses, Ben and Little Feather had been able to get their own truck, telephone, and a few other modern conveniences. When Chenoa's water broke, she called her stepmom to update her. Jerry had driven her to the hospital in Twin Falls.

Ben and Little Feather had arrived at the hospital only 10 minutes before the stork. Jerry and Chenoa ask Ben if he would like the honor of naming his granddaughter.

Ben took Chenoa's hand and asked so quietly, no one else could hear him, "Sweetheart, would you like a daughter, or a sister named Abby, after your mother?"

At first, Chenoa didn't understand the cryptic announcement in her dad's question. When she understood, Chenoa let out a squeal that shocked everyone in the room, if not everyone in the maternity ward.

She was still squealing excitedly, when Little Feather opened her coat just enough to reveal a small but definite baby bump. Aunt Martha was one of the first to understand what Ben had just disclosed. She hugged Little Feather, and congratulated her, then Ben.

After giving it a few moments thought, Chenoa whispered to her dad, "You're sure it's a girl?"

"Got the ultrasound picture right here in my pocket," said Ben. "Got it from the doctor himself."

"In that case, how about a sister, Dad?" said Chenoa. "Jerry, it appears it is up to us!"

"Well, we could do Sacagawea, if you want to name her after a famous native American woman. Chenoa, if you want her to have a nick name to avoid confusion. How about a cheery name of her own, like Krystal?" suggested Jerry.

"I like Krystal," said Chenoa. "Short, clear, happy name. I think it will do fine!"

The choice of Krystal for the baby's name was whispered from person to person until everyone heard and understood the decision. Everyone expressed their approval.

Chenoa was discharged after two days in the hospital. She and Jerry stayed again with Aunt Martha, Uncle Glenn, and Old George for a couple days. Krystal had no time to cry before one or more of their hosts were picking her up. There had not been a baby in this home for forty years.

Ben took Little Feather home to get her clothes and cook a few meals for him. She returned the second day, and went with Jerry and Chenoa to Nevada to help take care of the new mom for a few weeks.

Chenoa was returning to Crooked Creek with a mountain of supplies, complements of the generous merchants of Twin Falls county, baby #267 for the year.

Gerald and Merna returned as planned to help Jerry harvest the hay for two seasons. After two years, Jerry had a pretty good understanding of how to do it.

Merna was also able to help Chenoa learn how to grow a garden, bottle fruit, sew, and a lot of the other aspects of being a rancher's wife she had not learned growing up without a mom.

Jerry and Chenoa bought a few head of black Angus, and got their feet wet in the cattle business. They made friends with a horse trainer at a horse show in Reno, Nevada who agreed to show them how to train a cutting horse.

Joe stopped occasionally and updated Jerry and Chenoa on what he knew of the fate of their 10 initial Appaloosas. After appearing in the movie for which they had been purchased, they went on to appear in other movies. Last he knew, they had been purchased by a high-end riding school.

Joe made several attempts to sign Chenoa to a movie contract. She politely declined the offer saying she had a family to raise.

Krystal was turning out to be a chip off the old block; she not only had her mom's good looks, but she was turning out to be a superb horse trainer. She traveled with her parents to the various horse shows. Krystal could train a horse to do tricks in a few weeks. Nothing cemented a sale quite like having a young beautiful girl get the horse to perform a few tricks.

Grandpa Ben, as Krystal called him, was selling all the horses he could raise because of the training that Chenoa and Krystal were able to provide. Jerry became very good at breaking the horses to ride, Chenoa at teaching barrel racing and cutting, and Krystal tricks.

The fewer horses the Jerry Briggs family had to sell, the more time they got to work with them; the more highly trained they became.

Chenoa was particularly happy to have a sister. It was an odd relationship having a sister younger than your own daughter, but she never-the-less loved her deeply. Abby became very close to Krystal.

Abby took to riding the range for Ben when he developed arthritis in his knees. Like her mother, her sister, and her niece, she too became extremely beautiful.

Sky Walker was eventually retired and put out to pasture at Crooked Creek where he could be with Chenoa. Sky Walker became bonded to Krystal as well as Chenoa. Ben was able to buy another registered stud for his herd, a big fellow named Chenook.

Abby and Chenook became more than good friends. Like Sky Walker before him, he seemed to understand that he was Abby's protector. Like Chenoa before her, the stories grew of the beautiful girl on the Appaloosa stallion, who rode the Jarbidge Mountains, and avoided strangers, especially white men. As the stories spread, old timers were heard to claim, "The Flower of China Mountain" rides again!